Pan was founded in 1944 by Alan Bott, then owner of The Book Society. Over the next eight years he was joined by a consortium of four leading publishers – William Collins, Macmillan, Hodder & Stoughton and William Heinemann – and together they launched an imprint that is an international leader in popular paperback publishing to this day.

Pan's first mass-market paperback was *Ten Stories* by Rudyard Kipling. Published in 1947, and priced at one shilling and sixpence, it had a distinctive logo based on a design by artist and novelist Mervyn Peake. Paper was scarce in post-war Britain, but happily the Board of Trade agreed that Pan could print its books abroad and import them into Britain provided that they exported half the total number of books printed. The first batch of 250,000 books were dispatched from Paris to Pan's warehouse in Esher on an ex-Royal Navy launch named *Laloun*. The vessel's first mate, Gordon Young, was to become the first export manager for Pan.

Around fifty titles appeared in the first year, each with average print runs of 25,000 copies. Success came quickly, largely due to the choice of vibrant, descriptive book covers that distinguished Pan books from the uniformity of Penguin paperbacks, which were the only real competitors at the time.

Pan's expertise lay in its ability to popularize its authors, and a combination of arresting design coupled with energetic marketing and sales helped turn the likes of Leslie Charteris, Eric Ambler, Nevil Shute, Ian Fleming and John Buchan into bestsellers. The first book to sell a million copies was *The Dam Busters* by Paul Brickhill, first published in 1951. Brickhill was among the first to receive a Golden Pan award, for sales of one million copies. His fellow prize winners in 1964 were Alan Sillitoe for *Saturday Night and Sunday Morning* and Ian Fleming, who won it seven times over. It was also given posthumously to Grace Metalious for *Peyton Place*.

In the Sixties and Seventies authors such as Dick Francis, Wilbur Smith and Jack Higgins joined the fold, and 1972 saw the founding of the ground-breaking literary paperback imprint, Picador. Then-Editorial Director Clarence Paget signed up the third novel by the relatively unknown John le Carré, and transformed the author's career. Pan also secured paperback rights in James Herriot's memoirs of a Yorkshire vet in 1973, and a year later fought off tough competition to publish *Jaws* by Peter Benchley. Inspector Morse made his first appearance in Colin Dexter's *Last Bus to Woodstock* in 1974.

By 1976 Pan had sold over 30 million copies of its books and was outperforming all its rivals. Over the ensuing decades they published some of the biggest names in popular fiction, such as Jackie Collins, Dick Francis, Martin Cruz Smith and Colin Forbes.

By the late Eighties, publishers had stopped buying and selling paperback licences and in 1987 Pan, now wholly owned by Macmillan, became its paperback imprint. This was a turbulent time of readjustment for Pan, but with characteristic energy and zeal Pan Macmillan soon established itself as one of the largest book publishers in the UK. By 2010, the advent of ebooks allowed the audience for popular fiction to grow dramatically, and Pan's bestselling authors, such as Peter James, Jeffrey Archer, Ken Follett and Kate Morton – not to mention bestselling saga writers Margaret Dickinson and Annie Murray – now reach an even wider readership.

Personally, my years working at Pan were incredibly exciting and a time of countless opportunities. The paperback market was exploding, and Pan was at the forefront. Sales were incredible – I remember selling close to a million copies of a Colin Dexter novella alone. I'm proud that today, Pan retains the same energy and vibrancy.

In the year that Pan celebrates its 70th anniversary its mission remains the same – to publish the best popular fiction and non-fiction for the widest audience.

David Macmillan

TEN STORIES

RUDYARD KIPLING was born in India in 1865. After intermittently moving between India and England during his early life, he settled in the latter in 1889, published his novel *The Light That Failed* in 1891 and married Caroline Balestier the following year. They returned to her home in Brattleboro, Vermont, where Kipling wrote the two *Jungle Books* and *Captains Courageous*. He continued to write prolifically and was the first Englishman to receive the Nobel Prize for Literature in 1907, but his later years were darkened by the death of his son John at the Battle of Loos in 1915. He died in 1936.

RUDYARD KIPLING

TEN STORIES

P A N 7 O

These stories are selected from volumes originally published by Macmillan & Co. Ltd

This edition first published 1947 by Pan Books Ltd

This paperback edition published 2017 by Pan Books
an imprint of Pan Macmillan
20 New Wharf Road, London N1 9RR
Associated companies throughout the world
www.panmacmillan.com

ISBN 978-1-5098-5840-8

135798642

A CIP catalogue record for this book is available from the British Library.

Typeset by Palimpsest Book Production Limited, Falkirk, Stirlingshire
Printed and bound by CPI Group (UK) Ltd, Croydon, CR0 4YY

Visit **www.panmacmillan.com** to read more about all our books
and to buy them. You will also find features, author interviews and
news of any author events, and you can sign up for e-newsletters
so that you're always first to hear about our new releases.

Contents

THE MAN WHO WOULD BE KING

> Brother to a Prince and fellow to a beggar if he
> be found worthy.

The Law, as quoted, lays down a fair conduct of life, and one not easy to follow. I have been fellow to a beggar again and again under circumstances which prevented either of us finding out whether the other was worthy. I have still to be brother to a Prince, though I once came near to kinship with what might have been a veritable King, and was promised the reversion of a Kingdom—army, law-courts, revenue, and policy all complete. But, to-day, I greatly fear that my King is dead, and if I want a crown I must go hunt it for myself.

The beginning of everything was in a railway train upon the road to Mhow from Ajmir. There had been a Deficit in the Budget, which necessitated travelling, not Second-class, which is only half as dear as First-class, but by Intermediate, which is very awful indeed. There are no cushions in the Intermediate class, and the population are either Intermediate, which is Eurasian, or native, which for a long night journey is nasty, or Loafer, which is amusing though intoxicated. Intermediates do not buy from refreshment-rooms. They carry their food in bundles and pots, and buy sweets from the native sweet-meat-sellers, and drink the roadside water. That is why in the hot weather Intermediates are taken out of the carriages dead, and in all weathers are most properly looked down upon.

My particular Intermediate happened to be empty till I reached Nasirabad, when a big black-browed gentleman in shirt-sleeves entered, and, following the custom of Intermediates, passed the time of day. He was a wanderer and a vagabond like myself, but with an educated taste for whisky. He told tales of things he had seen and done, of out-of-the-way corners of the Empire into which he had penetrated, and of adventures in which he risked his life for a few days' food.

'If India was filled with men like you and me, not knowing more than the crows where they'd get their next day's rations, it isn't seventy millions of revenue the land would be paying—it's seven hundred millions,' said he; and as I looked at his mouth and chin I was disposed to agree with him.

We talked politics—the politics of Loaferdom, that sees things from the underside where the lath and plaster is not smoothed off—and we talked postal arrangements because my friend wanted to send a telegram back from the next station to Ajmir, the turning-off place from the Bombay to the Mhow line as you travel westward. My friend had no money beyond eight annas, which he wanted for dinner, and I had no money at all, owing to the hitch in the Budget before mentioned. Further, I was going into a wilderness where, though I should resume touch with the Treasury, there were no telegraph offices. I was, therefore, unable to help him in any way.

'We might threaten a Station-master, and make him send a wire on tick,' said my friend, 'but that'd mean inquiries for you and for me, and *I*'ve got my hands full these days. Did you say you are travelling back along this line within any days?'

'Within ten,' I said.

'Can't you make it eight?' said he. 'Mine is rather urgent business.'

'I can send your telegram within ten days if that will serve you,' I said.

'I couldn't trust the wire to fetch him now I think of it. It's this way. He leaves Delhi on the 23rd for Bombay. That means he'll be running through Ajmir about the night of the 23rd.'

'But I'm going into the Indian Desert,' I explained.

'Well *and* good,' said he. 'You'll be changing at Marwar Junction to get into Jodhpore territory—you must do that—and he'll be coming through Marwar Junction in the early morning of the 24th by the Bombay Mail. Can you be at Marwar Junction on that time? 'Twon't be inconveniencing you because I know that there's precious few pickings to be got out of these Central India States—even though you pretend to be correspondent of the *Backwoodsman*.'

'Have you ever tried that trick?' I asked.

'Again and again, but the Residents find you out, and then you get escorted to the Border before you've time to get your knife into them. But about my friend here. I *must* give him a word o' mouth to tell him what's come to me or else he won't know where to go. I would take it more than kind of you if you was to come out of Central India in time to catch him at Marwar Junction, and say to him: "He has gone South for the week." He'll know what that means. He's a big man with a red beard, and a great swell he is. You'll find him sleeping like a gentleman with all his luggage round him in a Second-class compartment. But don't you be afraid. Slip down the window, and say: "He has gone South for the week," and he'll tumble. It's only cutting your time of stay in those parts by two days. I ask you as a stranger—going to the West,' he said with emphasis.

'Where have *you* come from?' said I.

'From the East,' said he, 'and I am hoping that you will give him the message on the Square—for the sake of my Mother as well as your own.'

Englishmen are not usually softened by appeals to the memory of their mothers, but for certain reasons, which will be fully apparent, I saw fit to agree.

'It's more than a little matter,' said he, 'and that's why I asked you to do it—and now I know that I can depend on you doing it. A Second-class carriage at Marwar Junction, and a red-haired man asleep in it. You'll be sure to remember. I get out at the next station, and I must hold on there till he comes or sends me what I want.'

'I'll give the message if I catch him,' I said, 'and for the sake of your Mother as well as mine I'll give you a word of advice. Don't try to run the Central India States just now as the correspondent of the *Backwoodsman*. There's a real one knocking about here, and it might lead to trouble.'

'Thank you,' said he simply, 'and when will the swine be gone? I can't starve because he's ruining my work. I wanted to get hold of the Degumber Rajah down here about his father's widow, and give him a jump.'

'What did he do to his father's widow, then?'

'Filled her up with red pepper and slippered her to

death as she hung from a beam. I found that out myself, and I'm the only man that would dare going into the State to get hush-money for it. They'll try to poison me, same as they did in Chortumna when I went on the loot there. But you'll give the man at Marwar Junction my message?'

He got out at a little roadside station, and I reflected. I had heard, more than once, of men personating correspondents of newspapers and bleeding small Native States with threats of exposure, but I had never met any of the caste before. They lead a hard life, and generally die with great suddenness. The Native States have a wholesome horror of English newspapers which may throw light on their peculiar methods of government, and do their best to choke correspondents with champagne, or drive them out of their mind with four-in-hand barouches. They do not understand that nobody cares a straw for the internal administration of Native States so long as oppression and crime are kept within decent limits, and the ruler is not drugged, drunk, or diseased from one end of the year to the other. They are the dark places of the earth, full of unimaginable cruelty, touching the Railway and the Telegraph on one side, and, on the other, the days of Harun-al-Raschid. When I left the train I did business with divers Kings, and in eight days passed through many changes of life. Sometimes I wore dress-clothes and consorted with Princes and Politicals, drinking from crystal and eating from silver. Sometimes I lay out upon the ground and devoured what I could get, from a plate made of leaves, and drank the running water, and slept under the same rug as my servant. It was all in the day's work.

Then I headed for the Great Indian Desert upon the proper date, as I had promised, and the night Mail set me down at Marwar Junction, where a funny little happy-go-lucky, native-managed railway runs to Jodhpore. The Bombay Mail from Delhi makes a short halt at Marwar. She arrived as I got in, and I had just time to hurry to her platform and go down the carriages. There was only one Second-class on the train. I slipped the window and looked down upon a flaming red beard, half covered by a railway rug. That was my man, fast asleep, and I dug him gently in the ribs. He woke with a grunt, and I saw his face in the light of the lamps. It was a great and shining face.

'Tickets again?' said he.

'No,' said I. 'I am to tell you that he is gone South for the week. He has gone South for the week!'

The train had begun to move out. The red man rubbed his eyes. 'He has gone South for the week,' he repeated. 'Now that's just like his impidence. Did he say that I was to give you anything? 'Cause I won't.'

'He didn't,' I said, and dropped away, and watched the red lights die out in the dark. It was horribly cold because the wind was blowing off the sands. I climbed into my own train—not an Intermediate Carriage this time—and went to sleep.

If the man with the beard had given me a rupee I should have kept it as a memento of a rather curious affair. But the consciousness of having done my duty was my only reward.

Later on I reflected that two gentlemen like my friends could not do any good if they forgathered and personated correspondents of newspapers, and might, if they blackmailed one of the little rat-trap states of Central India or Southern Rajputana, get themselves into serious difficulties. I therefore took some trouble to describe them as accurately as I could remember to people who would be interested in deporting them; and succeeded, so I was later informed, in having them headed back from the Degumber borders.

Then I became respectable, and returned to an Office where there were no Kings and no incidents outside the daily manufacture of a newspaper. A newspaper office seems to attract every conceivable sort of person, to the prejudice of discipline. Zenana-mission ladies arrive, and beg that the Editor will instantly abandon all his duties to describe a Christian prize-giving in a back-slum of a perfectly inaccessible village; Colonels who have been overpassed for command sit down and sketch the outline of a series of ten, twelve, or twenty-four leading articles on Seniority *versus* Selection; Missionaries wish to know why they have not been permitted to escape from their regular vehicles of abuse and swear at a brother-missionary under special patronage of the editorial We; stranded theatrical companies troop up to explain that they cannot pay for their advertisements, but on their return from New Zealand or Tahiti will do so with interest; inventors of patent punkah-pulling machines, carriage couplings, and unbreakable swords and axle-trees, call with specifications in their pockets and hours at their disposal; tea-companies enter and elaborate their prospectuses with the office pens; secretaries of ball-committees clamour to have the glories of their last dance more fully described; strange ladies rustle in and say, 'I want a hundred lady's cards printed *at once*, please,' which is manifestly part of an Editor's duty; and every dissolute ruffian that ever tramped the Grand Trunk Road makes it his business to ask for employment as a proof-reader. And, all the time, the telephone-bell is ringing madly, and Kings are being killed on the Continent, and Empires are saying, 'You're another,' and Mister Gladstone is calling down brimstone upon the British Dominions, and the little black copy-boys are whining, '*kaa-pi chay-ha-yeh*' (copy wanted) like tired bees, and most of the paper is as blank as Modred's shield.

But that is the amusing part of the year. There are six other months when no one ever comes to call, and the thermometer walks inch by inch up to the top of the glass, and the office is darkened to just above reading-light, and the press-machines are red-hot of touch, and nobody writes anything but accounts of amusements in the Hill-stations or obituary notices. Then the telephone becomes a tinkling terror, because it tells you of the sudden deaths of men and women that you knew intimately, and the prickly-heat covers you with a garment, and you sit down and write: 'A slight increase of sickness is reported from the Khuda Janta Khan District. The outbreak is purely sporadic in its nature, and, thanks to the energetic efforts of the District authorities, is now almost at an end. It is, however, with deep regret we record the death, etc.'

Then the sickness really breaks out, and the less recording and reporting the better for the peace of the subscribers. But the Empires and the Kings continue to divert themselves as selfishly as before, and the Foreman thinks that a daily paper really ought to come out once in twenty-four hours, and all the people at the Hill-stations in the middle of their amusements say: 'Good gracious! Why can't the paper be sparkling? I'm sure there's plenty going on up here.'

That is the dark half of the moon, and, as the advertisements say, 'must be experienced to be appreciated.'

It was in that season, and a remarkably evil season, that the paper began running the last issue of the week on Saturday night, which is to say Sunday morning, after the custom of a London paper. This was a great convenience, for immediately after the paper was put to bed, the dawn would lower the thermometer from 96° to almost 84° for half an hour, and in that chill—you have no idea how cold is 84° on the grass until you begin to pray for it—a very tired man could get off to sleep ere the heat roused him.

One Saturday night it was my pleasant duty to put the paper to bed alone. A King or courtier or a courtesan or a Community was going to die or get a new Constitution, or do something that was important on the other side of the world, and the paper was to be held open till the latest possible minute in order to catch the telegram.

It was a pitchy black night, as stifling as a June night can be, and the *loo*, the red-hot wind from the westward, was booming among the tinder-dry trees and pretending that the rain was on its heels. Now and again a spot of almost boiling water would fall on the dust with the flop of a frog, but all our weary world knew that was only pretence. It was a shade cooler in the press-room than the office, so I sat there, while the type ticked and clicked, and the night-jars hooted at the windows, and the all but naked compositors wiped the sweat from their foreheads, and called for water. The thing that was keeping us back, whatever it was, would not come off, though the *loo* dropped and the last type was set, and the whole round earth stood still in the choking heat, with its finger on its lip, to wait the event. I drowsed, and wondered whether the telegraph was a blessing, and whether this dying man, or struggling people, might be aware of the inconvenience the delay was causing. There was no special reason beyond the heat and worry to make tension, but, as the clock-hands crept up to three o'clock, and the machines span their fly-wheels two or three times to see that all was in order before I said the word that would set them off, I could have shrieked aloud.

Then the roar and rattle of the wheels shivered the quiet into little bits. I rose to go away, but two men in white clothes stood in front of me. The first one said: 'It's him!' The second said: 'So it is!' And they both laughed almost as loudly as the machinery roared, and mopped their foreheads. 'We seed there was a light burning across the road, and we were sleeping in that ditch there for coolness, and I said to my friend here, "The office is open. Let's come along and speak to him as turned us back from the Degumber State,"' said the smaller of the two. He was the man I had met in the Mhow train, and his fellow was the red-bearded man of Marwar Junction. There was no mistaking the eyebrows of the one or the beard of the other.

I was not pleased, because I wished to go to sleep, not to squabble with loafers. 'What do you want?' I asked.

'Half an hour's talk with you, cool and comfortable, in the office,' said the red-bearded man. 'We'd *like* some drink—the Contrack doesn't begin yet, Peachey, so you needn't look—but what we really want is advice. We don't want money. We ask you as a favour, because we found out you did us a bad turn about Degumber State.'

I led from the press-room to the stifling office with the maps on the walls, and the red-haired man rubbed his hands. 'That's something like,' said he. 'This was the proper shop to come to. Now, sir, let me introduce to you Brother Peachey Carnehan, that's him, and Brother Daniel Dravot, that is *me*, and the less said about our professions the better, for we have been most things in our time. Soldier, sailor, compositor, photographer, proof-reader, street-preacher, and correspondents of the *Backwoodsman* when we thought the paper wanted one. Carnehan is sober, and so am I. Look at us first, and see that's sure. It will save you cutting into my talk. We'll take one of your cigars apiece, and you shall see us light up.'

I watched the test. The men were absolutely sober, so I gave them each a tepid whisky and soda.

'Well *and* good,' said Carnehan of the eyebrows, wiping the froth from his moustache. 'Let me talk now, Dan. We have been all over India, mostly on foot. We have been boiler-fitters, engine-drivers, petty contractors, and all that, and we have decided that India isn't big enough for such as us.'

They certainly were too big for the office. Dravot's beard seemed to fill half the room and Carnehan's shoulders the other half, as they sat on the big table. Carnehan continued: 'The country isn't half worked out because they that governs it won't let you touch it. They spend all their blessed time in governing it, and you can't lift a spade, nor chip a rock, nor look for oil, nor anything like that, without all the Government saying, "Leave it alone, and let us govern." Therefore, such *as* it is, we will let it alone, and go away to some other place where a man isn't crowded and can come to his own. We are not little men, and there is nothing that we are afraid of except Drink, and we have signed a Contrack on that. *Therefore*, we are going away to be Kings.'

'Kings in our own right,' muttered Dravot.

'Yes, of course,' I said. 'You've been tramping in the sun, and it's a very warm night, and hadn't you better sleep over the notion? Come to-morrow.'

'Neither drunk nor sunstruck,' said Dravot. 'We have slept over the notion half a year, and require to see Books and Atlases, and we have decided that there is only one place now in the world that two strong men can Sar-a-*whack*. They call it Kafiristan. By my reckoning it's the top right-hand corner of Afghanistan, not more than three hundred miles from Peshawar. They have two-and-thirty heathen idols there, and we'll be the thirty-third and fourth. It's a mountaineous country, and the women of those parts are very beautiful.'

'But that is provided against in the Contrack,' said Carnehan. 'Neither Woman nor Liqu-or, Daniel.'

'And that's all we know, except that no one has gone there, and they fight, and in any place where they fight a man who knows how to drill men can always be a King. We shall go to those parts and say to any King we find—"D'you want to vanquish your foes?" and we will show him how to drill men; for that we know better than any-thing else. Then we will subvert that King and seize his Throne and establish a Dy-nasty.'

'You'll be cut to pieces before you're fifty miles across the Border,' I said. 'You have to travel through Afghanistan to get to that country. It's one mass of mountains and peaks and glaciers, and no Englishman has been through it. The people are utter brutes, and even if you reached them you couldn't do anything.'

'That's more like,' said Carnehan. 'If you could think us a little more mad we would be more pleased. We have come to you to know about this country, to read a book about it, and to be shown maps. We want you to tell us that we are fools and to show us your books.' He turned to the bookcases.

'Are you at all in earnest?' I said.

'A little,' said Dravot sweetly. 'As big a map as you have got, even if it's all blank where Kafiristan is, and any books you've got. We can read, though we aren't very educated.'

I uncased the big thirty-two-miles-to-the-inch map of India, and two smaller Frontier maps, hauled down volume INF-KAN of the *Encyclopædia Britannica*, and the men consulted them.

'See here!' said Dravot, his thumb on the map. 'Up to Jagdallak, Peachey and me know the road. We was there with Roberts' Army. We'll have to turn off to the right at Jagdallak through Laghmann territory. Then we get among the hills—fourteen thousand feet—fifteen thousand—it will be cold work there, but it don't look very far on the map.'

I handed him Wood on the *Sources of the Oxus*. Carnehan was deep in the *Encyclopædia*.

'They're a mixed lot,' said Dravot reflectively; 'and it

won't help us to know the names of their tribes. The more tribes the more they'll fight, and the better for us. From Jagdallak to Ashang—h'mm!'

'But all the information about the country is as sketchy and inaccurate as can be,' I protested. 'No one knows anything about it really. Here's the file of the *United Services' Institute*. Read what Bellew says.'

'Blow Bellew!' said Carnehan. 'Dan, they're a stinkin' lot of heathens, but this book here says they think they're related to us English.'

I smoked while the men pored over Raverty, Wood, the maps, and the *Encyclopædia*.

'There is no use your waiting,' said Dravot politely. 'It's about four o'clock now. We'll go before six o'clock if you want to sleep, and we won't steal any of the papers. Don't you sit up. We're two harmless lunatics, and if you come to-morrow evening down to the Serai we'll say good-bye to you.'

'You *are* two fools,' I answered. 'You'll be turned back at the Frontier or cut up the minute you set foot in Afghanistan. Do you want any money or a recommendation down-country? I can help you to the chance of work next week.'

'Next week we shall be hard at work ourselves, thank you,' said Dravot. 'It isn't so easy being a King as it looks. When we've got our Kingdom in going order we'll let you know, and you can come up and help us to govern it.'

'Would two lunatics make a contrack like that?' said Carnehan, with subdued pride, showing me a greasy half-sheet of notepaper on which was written the following. I copied it, then and there, as a curiosity—

*This Contract between me and you persuing witnesseth
in the name of God—Amen and so forth.*

(One) That me and you will settle this matter together;
i.e. *to be Kings of Kafiristan.*

*(Two) That you and me will not, while this matter is
being settled, look at any Liquor, nor any Woman black,
white, or brown, so as to get mixed up with one or the
other harmful.*

*(Three) That we conduct ourselves with Dignity and
Discretion, and if one of us gets into trouble the other
will stay by him.*

Signed by you and me this day.

    Peachey Taliaferro Carnehan.

    Daniel Dravot.

    Both Gentlemen at Large.

'There was no need for the last article,' said Carnehan,
blushing modestly; 'but it looks regular. Now you know
the sort of men that loafers are—we *are* loafers, Dan, until
we get out of India—and *do* you think that we would
sign a Contrack like that unless we was in earnest? We
have kept away from the two things that make life worth
having.'

'You won't enjoy your lives much longer if you are
going to try this idiotic adventure. Don't set the office on
fire,' I said, 'and go away before nine o'clock.'

I left them still poring over the maps and making notes
on the back of the 'Contrack.' 'Be sure to come down to
the Serai to-morrow,' were their parting words.

The Kumharsen Serai is the great four-square sink of humanity where the strings of camels and horses from the North load and unload. All the nationalities of Central Asia may be found there, and most of the folk of India proper. Balkh and Bokhara there meet Bengal and Bombay, and try to draw eye-teeth. You can buy ponies, turquoises, Persian pussy-cats, saddle-bags, fat-tailed sheep and musk in the Kumharsen Serai, and get many strange things for nothing. In the afternoon I went down to see whether my friends intended to keep their word or were lying there drunk.

A priest attired in fragments of ribbons and rags stalked up to me, gravely twisting a child's paper whirli-gig. Behind him was his servant bending under the load of a crate of mud toys. The two were loading up two camels, and the inhabitants of the Serai watched them with shrieks of laughter.

'The priest is mad,' said a horse-dealer to me. 'He is going up to Kabul to sell toys to the Amir. He will either be raised to honour or have his head cut off. He came in here this morning and has been behaving madly ever since.'

'The witless are under the protection of God,' stammered a flat-cheeked Usbeg in broken Hindi. 'They foretell future events.'

'Would they could have foretold that my caravan would have been cut up by the Shinwaris almost within shadow of the Pass!' grunted the Eusufzai agent of a Rajputana trading-house whose goods had been diverted into the hands of other robbers just across the Border, and whose misfortunes were the laughing-stock of the bazaar. 'Ohé, priest, whence come you and whither do you go?'

'From Roum have I come,' shouted the priest, waving his whirligig; 'from Roum, blown by the breath of a hundred devils across the sea! O thieves, robbers, liars, the blessing of Pir Khan on pigs, dogs, and perjurers! Who will take the Protected of God to the North to sell charms that are never still to the Amir? The camels shall not gall, the sons shall not fall sick, and the wives shall remain faithful while they are away, of the men who give me place in their caravan. Who will assist me to slipper the King of the Roos with a golden slipper with a silver heel? The protection of Pir Khan be upon his labours!' He spread out the skirts of his gaberdine and pirouetted between the lines of tethered horses.

'There starts a caravan from Peshawar to Kabul in twenty days, *Huzrut*,' said the Eusufzai trader. 'My camels go therewith. Do thou also go and bring us good luck.'

'I will go even now!' shouted the priest. 'I will depart upon my winged camels, and be at Peshawar in a day! Ho! Hazar Mir Khan,' he yelled to his servant, 'drive out the camels, but let me first mount my own.'

He leaped on the back of his beast as it knelt, and, turning round to me, cried: 'Come thou also, Sahib, a little along the road, and I will sell thee a charm—an amulet that shall make thee King of Kafiristan.'

Then the light broke upon me, and I followed the two camels out of the Serai till we reached open road and the priest halted.

'What d'you think o' that?' said he in English. 'Carnehan can't talk their patter, so I've made him my servant. He makes a handsome servant. 'Tisn't for nothing that I've been knocking about the country for fourteen years.

Didn't I do that talk neat? We'll hitch on to a caravan at Peshawar till we get to Jagdallak, and then we'll see if we can get donkeys for our camels, and strike into Kafiristan. Whirligigs for the Amir, O Lor'! Put your hand under the camel-bags and tell me what you feel.'

I felt the butt of a Martini, and another and another.

'Twenty of 'em,' said Dravot placidly. 'Twenty of 'em and ammunition to correspond, under the whirligigs and the mud dolls.'

'Heaven help you if you are caught with those things!' I said. 'A Martini is worth her weight in silver among the Pathans.'

'Fifteen hundred rupees of capital—every rupee we could beg, borrow, or steal—are invested on these two camels,' said Dravot. 'We won't get caught. We're going through the Khyber with a regular caravan. Who'd touch a poor mad priest?'

'Have you got everything you want?' I asked, over-come with astonishment.

'Not yet, but we shall soon. Give us a memento of your kindness, *Brother*. You did me a service, yesterday, and that time in Marwar. Half my Kingdom shall you have, as the saying is.' I slipped a small charm compass from my watch-chain and handed it up to the priest.

'Good-bye,' said Dravot, giving me a hand cautiously. 'It's the last time we'll shake hands with an Englishman these many days. Shake hands with him, Carnehan,' he cried, as the second camel passed me.

Carnehan leaned down and shook hands. Then the camels passed away along the dusty road, and I was left alone to wonder. My eye could detect no failure in the disguises. The scene in the Serai proved that they were complete to the native mind. There was just the chance, therefore, that Carnehan and Dravot would be able to wander through Afghanistan without detection. But, beyond, they would find death—certain and awful death.

Ten days later a native correspondent, giving me the news of the day from Peshawar, wound up his letter with: 'There has been much laughter here on account of a certain mad priest who is going in his estimation to sell petty gauds and insignificant trinkets which he ascribes as great charms to H.H. the Amir of Bokhara. He passed through Peshawar and associated himself to the Second Summer caravan that goes to Kabul. The merchants are pleased because through superstition they imagine that such mad fellows bring good fortune.'

The two, then, were beyond the Border. I would have prayed for them, but, that night, a real King died in Europe, and demanded an obituary notice.

The wheel of the world swings through the same phases again and again. Summer passed and winter thereafter, and came and passed again. The daily paper continued and I with it, and upon the third summer there fell a hot night, a night-issue, and a strained waiting for something to be telegraphed from the other side of the world, exactly as had happened before. A few great men had died in the past two years, the machines worked with more clatter, and some of the trees in the office garden were a few feet taller. But that was all the difference.

I passed over to the press-room, and went through just such a scene as I have already described. The nervous tension was stronger than it had been two years before, and I felt the heat more acutely. At three o'clock I cried,

'Print off,' and turned to go, when there crept to my chair what was left of a man. He was bent into a circle, his head was sunk between his shoulders, and he moved his feet one over the other like a bear. I could hardly see whether he walked or crawled—this rag-wrapped, whining cripple who addressed me by name, crying that he was come back. 'Can you give me a drink?' he whimpered. 'For the Lord's sake give me a drink!'

I went back to the office, the man following with groans of pain, and I turned up the lamp.

'Don't you know me?' he gasped, dropping into a chair, and he turned his drawn face, surmounted by a shock of grey hair, to the light.

I looked at him intently. Once before had I seen eyebrows that met over the nose in an inch-broad black band, but for the life of me I could not tell where.

'I don't know you,' I said, handing him the whisky. 'What can I do for you?'

He took a gulp of the spirit raw, and shivered in spite of the suffocating heat.

'I've come back,' he repeated; 'and I was the King of Kafiristan—me and Dravot—crowned Kings we was! In this office we settled it—you setting there and giving us the books. I am Peachey—Peachey Taliaferro Carnehan, and you've been setting here ever since—O Lord!'

I was more than a little astonished, and expressed my feelings accordingly.

'It's true,' said Carnehan, with a dry cackle, nursing his feet, which were wrapped in rags. 'True as gospel. Kings we were, with crowns upon our heads—me and Dravot—poor Dan—oh, poor, poor Dan, that would never take advice, not though I begged of him!'

mules. Dravot up and dances in front of them, sing-ing—"Sell me four mules." Says the first man—"If you are rich enough to buy, you are rich enough to rob"; but before ever he could put his hand to his knife, Dravot breaks his neck over his knee, and the other party runs away. So Carnehan loaded the mules with the rifles that was taken off the camels, and together we starts forward into those bitter cold mountaineous parts, and never a road broader than the back of your hand.'

He paused for a moment, while I asked him if he could remember the nature of the country through which he had journeyed.

'I am telling you as straight as I can, but my head isn't as good as it might be. They drove nails through it to make me hear better how Dravot died. The country was mountaineous and the mules were most contrary, and the inhabitants was dispersed and solitary. They went up and up, and down and down, and that other party, Carnehan, was imploring of Dravot not to sing and whistle so loud, for fear of bringing down the tremenjus avalanches. But Dravot says that if a King couldn't sing it wasn't worth being King, and whacked the mules over the rump, and never took no heed for ten cold days. We came to a big level valley all among the mountains, and the mules were near dead, so we killed them, not having anything in special for them or us to eat. We sat upon the boxes, and played odd and even with the cartridges that was jolted out.

'Then ten men with bows and arrows ran down that valley, chasing twenty men with bows and arrows, and the row was tremenjus. They was fair men—fairer than you or me—with yellow hair and remarkable well built.

Says Dravot, unpacking the guns—"This is the beginning of the business. We'll fight for the ten men," and with that he fires two rifles at the twenty men, and drops one of them at two hundred yards from the rock where he was sitting. The other men began to run, but Carnehan and Dravot sits on the boxes picking them off at all ranges, up and down the valley. Then we goes up to the ten men that had run across the snow too, and they fires a footy little arrow at us. Dravot he shoots above their heads and they all falls down flat. Then he walks over them and kicks them, and then he lifts them up and shakes hands all round to make them friendly like. He calls them and gives them the boxes to carry, and waves his hand for all the world as though he was King already. They takes the boxes and him across the valley and up the hill into a pine wood on the top, where there was half a dozen big stone idols. Dravot he goes to the biggest—a fellow they call Imbra—and lays a rifle and a cartridge at his feet, rubbing his nose respectful with his own nose, patting him on the head, and saluting in front of it. He turns round to the men and nods his head, and says—"That's all right. I'm in the know too, and all these old jim-jams are my friends." Then he opens his mouth and points down it, and when the first man brings him food, he says—"No"; and when the second man brings him food he says— "No"; but when one of the old priests and the boss of the village brings him food, he says—"Yes," very haughty, and eats it slow. That was how we came to our first village, without any trouble, just as though we had tumbled from the skies. But we tumbled from one of those damned rope-bridges, you see, and—you couldn't expect a man to laugh much after that.'

'Take some more whisky and go on,' I said. 'That was the first village you came into. How did you get to be King?'

'I wasn't King,' said Carnehan. 'Dravot he was the King, and a handsome man he looked with the gold crown on his head and all. Him and the other party stayed in that village, and every morning Dravot sat by the side of old Imbra, and the people came and worshipped. That was Dravot's order. Then a lot of men came into the valley, and Carnehan and Dravot picks them off with the rifles before they knew where they was, and runs down into the valley and up again the other side and finds another village, same as the first one, and the people all falls down flat on their faces, and Dravot says—"Now what is the trouble between you two villages?" and the people points to a woman, as fair as you or me, that was carried off, and Dravot takes her back to the first village and counts up the dead—eight there was. For each dead man Dravot pours a little milk on the ground and waves his arms like a whirligig, and "That's all right," says he. Then he and Carnehan takes the big boss of each village by the arm and walks them down into the valley, and shows them how to scratch a line with a spear right down the valley, and gives each a sod of turf from both sides of the line. Then all the people comes down and shouts like the devil and all, and Dravot says—"Go and dig the land, and be fruitful and multiply," which they did, though they didn't understand. Then we asks the names of things in their lingo—bread and water and fire and idols and such, and Dravot leads the priest of each village up to the idol, and says he must sit there and judge the people, and if anything goes wrong he is to be shot.

'Next week they was all turning up the land in the valley as quiet as bees and much prettier, and the priests heard all the complaints and told Dravot in dumb show what it was about. "That's just the beginning," says Dravot. "They think we're Gods." He and Carnehan picks out twenty good men and shows them how to click off a rifle, and form fours, and advance in line, and they was very pleased to do so, and clever to see the hang of it. Then he takes out his pipe and his baccy-pouch and leaves one at one village, and one at the other, and off we two goes to see what was to be done in the next valley. That was all rock, and there was a little village there, and Carnehan says—"Send 'em to the old valley to plant," and takes 'em there, and gives 'em some land that wasn't took before. They were a poor lot, and we blooded 'em with a kid before letting 'em into the new Kingdom. That was to impress the people, and then they settled down quiet, and Carnehan went back to Dravot who had got into another valley, all snow and ice and most mountaineous. There was no people there and the Army got afraid, so Dravot shoots one of them, and goes on till he finds some people in a village, and the Army explains that unless the people wants to be killed they had better not shoot their little matchlocks; for they had matchlocks. We makes friends with the priest, and I stays there alone with two of the Army, teaching the men how to drill, and a thundering big Chief comes across the snow with kettle-drums and horns twanging, because he heard there was a new God kicking about. Carnehan sights for the brown of the men half a mile across the snow and wings one of them. Then he sends a message to the Chief that, unless he wished to be killed, he must come and shake hands with me and leave his arms behind. The Chief comes alone first, and Carnehan shakes hands with him and whirls his arms about, same as Dravot used, and very much surprised that Chief was, and strokes my eyebrows. Then Carnehan goes alone to the Chief, and asks him in dumb show if he had an enemy he hated. "I have," says the Chief. So Carnehan weeds out the pick of his men, and sets the two of the Army to show them drill, and at the end of two weeks the men can manœuvre about as well as Volunteers. So he marches with the Chief to a great big plain on the top of a mountain, and the Chief's men rushes into a village and takes it; we three Martinis firing into the brown of the enemy. So we took that village too, and I gives the Chief a rag from my coat and says, "Occupy till I come"; which was scriptural. By way of a reminder, when me and the Army was eighteen hundred yards away, I drops a bullet near him standing on the snow, and all the people falls flat on their faces. Then I sends a letter to Dravot wherever he be by land or by sea.'

At the risk of throwing the creature out of train I interrupted—'How could you write a letter up yonder?'

'The letter?—Oh!—The letter! Keep looking at me between the eyes, please. It was a string-talk letter, that we'd learned the way of it from a blind beggar in the Punjab.'

I remember that there had once come to the office a blind man with a knotted twig and a piece of string which he wound round the twig according to some cipher of his own. He could, after the lapse of days or hours, repeat the sentence which he had reeled up. He had reduced the alphabet to eleven primitive sounds, and tried to teach me his method, but I could not understand.

'I sent that letter to Dravot,' said Carnehan; 'and told him to come back because this Kingdom was growing too big for me to handle, and then I struck for the first valley, to see how the priests were working. They called the village we took along with the Chief, Bashkai, and the first village we took, Er-Heb. The priests at Er-Heb was doing all right, but they had a lot of pending cases about land to show me, and some men from another village had been firing arrows at night. I went out and looked for that village, and fired four rounds at it from a thousand yards. That used all the cartridges I cared to spend, and I waited for Dravot, who had been away two or three months, and I kept my people quiet.

'One morning I heard the devil's own noise of drums and horns, and Dan Dravot marches down the hill with his Army and a tail of hundreds of men, and, which was the most amazing, a great gold crown on his head. "My Gord, Carnehan," says Daniel, "this is a tremenjus business, and we've got the whole country as far as it's worth having. I am the son of Alexander by Queen Semiramis, and you're my younger brother and a God too! It's the biggest thing we've ever seen. I've been marching and fighting for six weeks with the Army, and every footy little village for fifty miles has come in rejoiceful; and more than that, I've got the key of the whole show, as you'll see, and I've got a crown for you! I told 'em to make two of 'em at a place called Shu, where the gold lies in the rock like suet in mutton. Gold I've seen, and turquoise I've kicked out of the cliffs, and there's garnets in the sands of the river, and here's a chunk of amber that a man brought me. Call up all the priests and, here, take your crown."

'One of the men opens a black hair bag, and I slips the crown on. It was too small and too heavy, but I wore it for the glory. Hammered gold it was—five pound weight, like a hoop of a barrel.

'"Peachey," says Dravot, "we don't want to fight no more. The Craft's the trick, so help me!" and he brings forward that same Chief that I left at Bashkai—Billy Fish we called him afterwards, because he was so like Billy Fish that drove the big tank-engine at Mach on the Bolan in the old days. "Shake hands with him," says Dravot, and I shook hands and nearly dropped, for Billy Fish gave me the Grip. I said nothing, but tried him with the Fellow Craft Grip. He answers all right, and I tried the Master's Grip, but that was a slip. "A Fellow Craft he is!" I says to Dan. "Does he know the word?"—"He does," says Dan, "and all the priests know. It's a miracle! The Chiefs and the priests can work a Fellow Craft Lodge in a way that's very like ours, and they've cut the marks on the rocks, but they don't know the Third Degree, and they've come to find out. It's Gord's Truth. I've known these long years that the Afghans knew up to the Fellow Craft Degree, but this is a miracle. A God and a Grand-Master of the Craft am I, and a Lodge in the Third Degree I will open, and we'll raise the head priests and the Chiefs of the villages."

'"It's against all the law," I says, "holding a Lodge without warrant from any one; and you know we never held office in any Lodge."

'"It's a master-stroke o' policy," says Dravot. "It

means running the country as easy as a four-wheeled bogie on a down grade. We can't stop to inquire now, or they'll turn against us. I've forty Chiefs at my heel, and passed and raised according to their merit they shall be. Billet these men on the villages, and see that we run up a Lodge of some kind. The temple of Imbra will do for the Lodge-room. The women must make aprons as you show them. I'll hold a levee of Chiefs to-night and Lodge to-morrow."

'I was fair run off my legs, but I wasn't such a fool as not to see what a pull this Craft business gave us. I showed the priests' families how to make aprons of the degrees, but for Dravot's apron the blue border and marks was made of turquoise lumps on white hide, not cloth. We took a great square stone in the temple for the Master's chair, and little stones for the officers' chairs, and painted the black pavement with white squares, and did what we could to make things regular.

'At the levee which was held that night on the hillside with big bonfires, Dravot gives out that him and me were Gods and sons of Alexander, and Past Grand-Masters in the Craft, and was come to make Kafiristan a country where every man should eat in peace and drink in quiet, and specially obey us. Then the Chiefs come round to shake hands, and they were so hairy and white and fair it was just shaking hands with old friends. We gave them names according as they was like men we had known in Indian—Billy Fish, Holly Dilworth, Pikky Kergan, that was Bazar-master when I was at Mhow, and so on, and so on.

'*The* most amazing miracles was at Lodge next night. One of the old priests was watching us continuous, and

I felt uneasy, for I knew we'd have to fudge the Ritual, and I didn't know what the men knew. The old priest was a stranger come in from beyond the village of Bash-kai. The minute Dravot puts on the Master's apron that the girls had made for him, the priest fetches a whoop and a howl, and tries to overturn the stone that Dravot was sitting on. "It's all up now," I says. "That comes of meddling with the Craft without warrant!" Dravot never winked an eye, not when ten priests took and tilted over the Grand-Master's chair—which was to say the stone of Imbra. The priest begins rubbing the bottom end of it to clear away the black dirt, and presently he shows all the other priests the Master's Mark, same as was on Dravot's apron, cut into the stone. Not even the priests of the temple of Imbra knew it was there. The old chap falls flat on his face at Dravot's feet and kisses 'em. "Luck again," says Dravot, across the Lodge to me; "they say it's the missing Mark that no one could understand the why of. We're more than safe now." Then he bangs the butt of his gun for a gavel and says: "By virtue of the authority vested in me by my own right hand and the help of Peachey, I declare myself Grand-Master of all Freemasonry in Kafiristan in this the Mother Lodge o' the country, and King of Kafiristan equally with Peachey!" At that he puts on his crown and I puts on mine—I was doing Senior Warden—and we opens the Lodge in most ample form. It was an amazing miracle! The priests moved in Lodge through the first two degrees almost without telling, as if the memory was coming back to them. After that, Peachey and Dravot raised such as was worthy—high priests and Chiefs of far-off villages. Billy Fish was the first, and I can tell you we scared the soul out of him. It was not in any way according to Ritual, but it served our turn. We didn't raise more than ten of the biggest men, because we didn't want to make the Degree common. And they was clamouring to be raised.

'"In another six months," says Dravot, "we'll hold another Communication, and see how you are working." Then he asks them about their villages, and learns that they was fighting one against the other, and were sick and tired of it. And when they wasn't doing that they was fighting with the Mohammedans. "You can fight those when they come into our country," says Dravot. "Tell off every tenth man of your tribes for a Frontier guard, and send two hundred at a time to this valley to be drilled. Nobody is going to be shot or speared any more so long as he does well, and I know that you won't cheat me. You are *my* people, and by God," says he, running off into English at the end—"I'll make a damned fine Nation of you, or I'll die in the making!"

'I can't tell all we did for the next six months, because Dravot did a lot I couldn't see the hang of, and he learned their lingo in a way I never could. My work was to help the people plough, and now and again go out with some of the Army and see what the other villages were doing, and make 'em throw rope-bridges across the ravines which cut up the country horrid. Dravot was very kind to me, but when he walked up and down in the pine wood pulling that bloody red beard of his with both fists I knew he was thinking plans I could not advise about, and I just waited for orders.

'But Dravot never showed me disrespect before the people. They were afraid of me and the Army, but they loved Dan. He was the best of friends with the priests and the Chiefs; but any one could come across the hills with a complaint, and Dravot would hear him out fair, and call four priests together and say what was to be done. He used to call in Billy Fish from Bashkai, and Pikky Kergan from Shu, and an old Chief we called Kafuzelum—it was like enough to his real name—and hold councils with 'em when there was any fighting to be done in small villages. That was his Council of War, and the four priests of Bashkai, Shu, Khawak, and Madora was his Privy Council. Between the lot of 'em they sent me, with forty men and twenty rifles and sixty men carrying turquoises, into the Ghorband country to buy those hand-made Martini rifles, that come out of the Amir's workshops at Kabul, from one of the Amir's Herati regiments that would have sold the very teeth out of their mouths for turquoises.

'I stayed in Ghorband a month, and gave the Governor there the pick of my baskets for hush-money, and bribed the Colonel of the regiment some more, and, between the two and the tribes-people, we got more than a hundred hand-made Martinis, a hundred good Kohat Jezails that'll throw to six hundred yards, and forty man-loads of very bad ammunition for the rifles. I came back with what I had, and distributed 'em among the men that the Chiefs sent in to me to drill. Dravot was too busy to attend to those things, but the old Army that we first made helped me, and we turned out five hundred men that could drill, and two hundred that knew how to hold arms pretty straight. Even those cork-screwed, hand-made guns was a miracle to them. Dravot talked big about powder-shops and factories, walking up and down in the pine wood when the winter was coming on.

"'I won't make a Nation,' says he. 'I'll make an Empire! These men are English! Look at their eyes—look at their mouths. Look at the way they stand up. They sit on chairs in their own houses. They're the Lost Tribes, or something like it, and they've grown to be English. I'll take a census in the spring if the priests don't get frightened. There must be a fair two million of 'em in these hills. The villages are full o' little children. Two million people—two hundred and fifty thousand fighting men—and all English! They only want the rifles and a little drilling. Two hundred and fifty thousand men, ready to cut in on Russia's right flank when she tries for India! Peachey, man,' he says, chewing his beard in great hunks, 'we shall be Emperors—Emperors of the Earth! Rajah Brooke will be a suckling to us. I'll treat with the Viceroy on equal terms. I'll ask him to send me twelve picked English—twelve that I know of—to help us govern a bit. There's Mackray, Sergeant-pensioner at Segowli—many's the good dinner he's given me, and his wife a pair of trousers. There's Donkin, the Warder of Tounghoo Jail; there's hundreds that I could lay my hand on if I was in India. The Viceroy shall do it for me. I'll send a man through in the spring for these men, and I'll write for a dispensation from the Grand Lodge for what I've done as Grand-Master. That—and all the Sniders that'll be thrown out when the native troops in India take up the Martini. They'll be worn smooth, but they'll do for fighting in these hills. Twelve English, a hundred thousand Sniders run through the Amir's country in driblets—I'd be content with twenty thousand in one year—and we'd be an Empire. When everything was shipshape, I'd hand over the crown—this crown I'm wearing now—to Queen Victoria on my knees, and she'd say: 'Rise up, Sir Daniel Dravot.' Oh, it's big! It's big, I tell you! But there's so much to be done in every place—Bashkai, Khawak, Shu, and everywhere else."

"'What is it?' I says. "There are no more men coming in to be drilled this autumn. Look at those fat, black clouds. They're bringing the snow."

"'It isn't that,' says Daniel, putting his hand very hard on my shoulder; "and I don't wish to say anything that's against you, for no other living man would have followed me and made me what I am as you have done. You're a first-class Commander-in-Chief, and the people know you; but—it's a big country, and somehow you can't help me, Peachey, in the way I want to be helped."

"'Go to your blasted priests, then!' I said, and I was sorry when I made that remark, but it did hurt me sore to find Daniel talking so superior when I'd drilled all the men, and done all he told me.

"'Don't let's quarrel, Peachey,' says Daniel without cursing. "You're a King too, and the half of this Kingdom is yours; but can't you see, Peachey, we want cleverer men than us now—three or four of 'em, that we can scatter about for our Deputies. It's a hugeous great State, and I can't always tell the right thing to do, and I haven't time for all I want to do, and here's the winter coming on and all." He put half his beard into his mouth, all red like the gold of his crown.

"'I'm sorry, Daniel,' says I. "I've done all I could. I've drilled the men and shown the people how to stack their oats better; and I've brought in those tinware rifles from

Ghorband—but I know what you're driving at. I take it Kings always feel oppressed that way."

"'There's another thing too," says Dravot, walking up and down. "The winter's coming and these people won't be giving much trouble, and if they do we can't move about. I want a wife."

"'For Gord's sake leave the women alone!" I says. "We've both got all the work we can, though I *am* a fool. Remember the Contrack, and keep clear o' women."

"'The Contrack only lasted till such time as we was Kings; and Kings we have been these months past," says Dravot, weighing his crown in his hand. "You go get a wife too, Peachey—a nice, strappin', plump girl that'll keep you warm in the winter. They're prettier than English girls, and we can take the pick of 'em. Boil 'em once or twice in hot water and they'll come out like chicken and ham."

"'Don't tempt me!" I says. "I will not have any deal-ings with a woman not till we are a dam' side more settled than we are now. I've been doing the work o' two men, and you've been doing the work o' three. Let's lie off a bit, and see if we can get some better tobacco from Afghan country and run in some good liquor; but no women."

"'Who's talking o' *women*?" says Dravot. "I said *wife*—a Queen to breed a King's son for the King. A Queen out of the strongest tribe, that'll make them your blood-brothers, and that'll lie by your side and tell you all the people thinks about you and their own affairs. That's what I want."

"'Do you remember that Bengali woman I kept at Mogul Serai when I was a plate-layer?" says I. "A fat lot o' good she was to me. She taught me the lingo and one or two other things; but what happened? She ran away with the Station-master's servant and half my month's pay. Then she turned up at Dadur Junction in tow of a half-caste, and had the impidence to say I was her husband—all among the drivers in the running-shed too!"

"'We've done with that," says Dravot; "these women are whiter than you or me, and a Queen I will have for the winter months."

"'For the last time o' asking, Dan, do *not*," I says. "It'll only bring us harm. The Bible says that Kings ain't to waste their strength on women, 'specially when they've got a new raw Kingdom to work over."

"'For the last time of answering I will," said Dravot, and he went away through the pine-trees looking like a big red devil, the sun being on his crown and beard and all.

'But getting a wife was not as easy as Dan thought. He put it before the Council, and there was no answer till Billy Fish said that he'd better ask the girls. Dravot damned them all round. "What's wrong with me?" he shouts, standing by the idol Imbra. "Am I a dog or am I not enough of a man for your wenches? Haven't I put the shadow of my hand over this country? Who stopped the last Afghan raid?" It was me really, but Dravot was too angry to remember. "Who bought your guns? Who repaired the bridges? Who's the Grand-Master of the sign cut in the stone?" says he, and he thumped his hand on the block that he used to sit on in Lodge, and at Council, which opened like Lodge always. Billy Fish said nothing and no more did the others. "Keep your hair on, Dan," said I; "and ask the girls. That's how it's done at Home, and these people are quite English."

"'The marriage of the King is a matter of State,' says Dan, in a white-hot rage, for he could feel, I hope, that he was going against his better mind. He walked out of the Council-room, and the others sat still, looking at the ground.

"'Billy Fish,' says I to the Chief of Bashkai, 'what's the difficulty here? A straight answer to a true friend.'

"'You know,' says Billy Fish. 'How should a man tell you who knows everything? How can daughters of men marry Gods or Devils? It's not proper.'

'I remembered something like that in the Bible; but if, after seeing us as long as they had, they still believed we were Gods, it wasn't for me to undeceive them.

"'A God can do anything,' says I. 'If the King is fond of a girl he'll not let her die.'—'She'll have to,' said Billy Fish. 'There are all sorts of Gods and Devils in these mountains, and now and again a girl marries one of them and isn't seen any more. Besides, you two know the Mark cut in the stone. Only the Gods know that. We thought you were men till you showed the sign of the Master.'

'I wished then that we had explained about the loss of the genuine secrets of a Master-Mason at the first go-off; but I said nothing. All that night there was a blowing of horns in a little dark temple half-way down the hill, and I heard a girl crying fit to die. One of the priests told us that she was being prepared to marry the King.

"'I'll have no nonsense of that kind,' says Dan. 'I don't want to interfere with your customs, but I'll take my own wife.'—'The girl's a little bit afraid,' says the priest. "She thinks she's going to die, and they are a-heartening of her up down in the temple."

"'Hearten her very tender, then," says Dravot, "or I'll hearten you with the butt of a gun so you'll never want to be heartened again." He licked his lips, did Dan, and stayed up walking about more than half the night, thinking of the wife that he was going to get in the morning. I wasn't any means comfortable, for I knew that dealings with a woman in foreign parts, though you was a crowned King twenty times over, could not but be risky. I got up very early in the morning while Dravot was asleep, and I saw the priests talking together in whispers, and the Chiefs talking together too, and they looked at me out of the corners of their eyes.

"'What is up, Fish?" I say to the Bashkai man, who was wrapped up in his furs and looking splendid to behold.

"'I can't rightly say," says he; "but if you can make the King drop all this nonsense about marriage, you'll be doing him and me and yourself a great service."

"'That I do believe," says I. "But sure, you know, Billy, as well as me, having fought against and for us, that the King and me are nothing more than two of the finest men that God Almighty ever made. Nothing more, I do assure you."

"'That may be," said Billy Fish, "and yet I should be sorry if it was." He sinks his head upon his great fur cloak for a minute and thinks. "King," says he, "be you man or God or Devil, I'll stick by you to-day. I have twenty of my men with me, and they will follow me. We'll go to Bashkai until the storm blows over."

'A little snow had fallen in the night, and everything

was white except the greasy fat clouds that blew down and down from the north. Dravot came out with his crown on his head, swinging his arms and stamping his feet, and looking more pleased than Punch.

"'For the last time, drop it, Dan,' says I in a whisper, "Billy Fish here says that there will be a row."

"'A row among my people!' says Dravot. "Not much. Peachey, you're a fool not to get a wife too. Where's the girl?' says he with a voice as loud as the braying of a jackass. "Call up all the Chiefs and priests, and let the Emperor see if his wife suits him."

'There was no need to call any one. They were all there leaning on their guns and spears round the clearing in the centre of the pine wood. A lot of priests went down to the little temple to bring up the girl, and the horns blew fit to wake the dead. Billy Fish saunters round and gets as close to Daniel as he could, and behind him stood his twenty men with matchlocks. Not a man of them under six feet. I was next to Dravot, and behind me was twenty men of the regular Army. Up comes the girl, and a strapping wench she was, covered with silver and turquoises, but white as death, and looking back every minute at the priests.

"'She'll do,' said Dan, looking her over. "What's to be afraid of, lass? Come and kiss me.' He puts his arm round her. She shuts her eyes, gives a bit of a squeak, and down goes her face in the side of Dan's flaming red beard.

"'The slut's bitten me!' says he, clapping his hand to his neck, and, sure enough, his hand was red with blood. Billy Fish and two of his matchlock-men catches hold of Dan by the shoulders and drags him into the Bashkai lot, while the priests howls in their lingo—"Neither God nor Devil but a man!" I was all taken aback, for a priest cut at me in front, and the Army behind began firing into the Bashkai men.

'"God A'mighty!" says Dan. "What is the meaning o' this?"

'"Come back! Come away!" says Billy Fish. "Ruin and Mutiny is the matter. We'll break for Bashkai if we can."

'I tried to give some sort of orders to my men—the men o' the regular Army—but it was no use, so I fired into the brown of 'em with an English Martini and drilled three beggars in a line. The valley was full of shouting, howling creatures, and every soul was shrieking, "Not a God nor a Devil but only a man!" The Bashkai troops stuck to Billy Fish all they were worth, but their match-locks wasn't half as good as the Kabul breechloaders, and four of them dropped. Dan was bellowing like a bull, for he was very wrathy; and Billy Fish had a hard job to prevent him running out at the crowd.

'"We can't stand," says Billy Fish. "Make a run for it down the valley! The whole place is against us." The matchlock-men ran, and we went down the valley in spite of Dravot. He was swearing horrible and crying out he was a King. The priests rolled great stones on us, and the regular Army fired hard, and there wasn't more than six men, not counting Dan, Billy Fish, and Me, that came down to the bottom of the valley alive.

'Then they stopped firing and the horns in the temple blew again. "Come away—for God's sake come away!" says Billy Fish. "They'll send runners out to all the villages before ever we get to Bashkai. I can protect you there, but I can't do anything now."

'My own notion is that Dan began to go mad in his head from that hour. He stared up and down like a stuck pig. Then he was all for walking back alone and killing the priests with his bare hands; which he could have done. "An Emperor am I," says Daniel, "and next year I shall be a Knight of the Queen."

'"All right, Dan," says I; "but come along now while there's time."

'"It's your fault," says he, "for not looking after your Army better. There was mutiny in the midst, and you didn't know—you damned engine-driving, plate-laying, missionary's-pass-hunting hound!" He sat upon a rock and called me every foul name he could lay tongue to. I was too heart-sick to care, though it was all his foolishness that brought the smash.

'"I'm sorry, Dan," says I, "but there's no accounting for natives. This business is our Fifty-Seven. Maybe we'll make something out of it yet, when we've got to Bashkai."

'"Let's get to Bashkai, then," says Dan, "and, by God, when I come back here again I'll sweep the valley so there isn't a bug in a blanket left!"

'We walked all that day, and all that night Dan was stumping up and down on the snow, chewing his beard and muttering to himself.

'"There's no hope o' getting clear," said Billy Fish. "The priests will have sent runners to the villages to say that you are only men. Why didn't you stick on as Gods till things was more settled? I'm a dead man," says Billy Fish, and he throws himself down on the snow and begins to pray to his Gods.

'Next morning we was in a cruel bad country—all up

and down, no level ground at all, and no food either. The six Bashkai men looked at Billy Fish hungry-way as if they wanted to ask something, but they said never a word. At noon we came to the top of a flat mountain all covered with snow, and when we climbed up into it, behold, there was an Army in position waiting in the middle!

'"The runners have been very quick," says Billy Fish, with a little bit of a laugh. "They are waiting for us."

'Three or four men began to fire from the enemy's side, and a chance shot took Daniel in the calf of the leg. That brought him to his senses. He looks across the snow at the Army, and sees the rifles that we had brought into the country.

'"We're done for," says he. "They are Englishmen, these people,—and it's my blasted nonsense that has brought you to this. Get back, Billy Fish, and take your men away; you've done what you could, and now cut for it. Carnehan," says he, "shake hands with me and go along with Billy. Maybe they won't kill you. I'll go and meet 'em alone. It's me that did it., Me, the King!"

'"Go!" says I. "Go to Hell, Dan! I'm with you here. Billy Fish, you clear out, and we two will meet those folk."

'"I'm a Chief," says Billy Fish, quite quiet. "I stay with you. My men can go."

'The Bashkai fellows didn't wait for a second word, but ran off, and Dan and Me and Billy Fish walked across to where the drums were drumming and the horns were horning. It was cold—awful cold. I've got that cold in the back of my head now. There's a lump of it there.'

The punkah-coolies had gone to sleep. Two kerosene lamps were blazing in the office, and the perspiration poured down my face and splashed on the blotter as I leaned forward. Carnehan was shivering, and I feared that his mind might go. I wiped my face, took a fresh grip of the piteously mangled hands, and said: 'What happened after that?'

The momentary shift of my eyes had broken the clear current.

'What was you pleased to say?' whined Carnehan. 'They took them without any sound. Not a little whisper all along the snow, not though the King knocked down the first man that set hand to him—not though old Peachey fired his last cartridge into the brown of 'em. Not a single solitary sound did those swines make. They just closed up tight, and I tell you their furs stunk. There was a man called Billy Fish, a good friend of us all, and they cut his throat, sir, then and there, like a pig; and the King kicks up the bloody snow and says: "We've had a dashed fine run for our money. What's coming next?" But Peachey, Peachey Taliaferro, I tell you, sir, in confidence as betwixt two friends, he lost his head, sir. No, he didn't neither. The King lost his head, so he did, all along o' one of those cunning rope-bridges. Kindly let me have the paper-cutter, sir. It tilted this way. They marched him a mile across that snow to a rope-bridge over a ravine with a river at the bottom. You may have seen such. They prodded him behind like an ox. "Damn your eyes!" says the King. "D'you suppose I can't die like a gentleman?" He turns to Peachey—Peachey that was crying like a child. "I've brought you to this, Peachey," says he. "Brought you out of your happy life to be killed in Kafiristan, where you was late Commander-in-Chief of the Emperor's forces. Say you forgive me, Peachey."—"I do," says Peachey. "Fully and freely do I forgive you, Dan."—"Shake hands, Peachey," says he. "I'm going now." Out he goes, looking neither right nor left, and when he was plumb in the middle of those dizzy dancing ropes—"Cut, you beggars," he shouts; and they cut, and old Dan fell, turning round and round and round, twenty thousand miles, for he took half an hour to fall till he struck the water, and I could see his body caught on a rock with the gold crown close beside.

'But do you know what they did to Peachey between two pine-trees? They crucified him, sir, as Peachey's hand will show. They used wooden pegs for his hands and his feet; and he didn't die. He hung there and screamed, and they took him down next day, and said it was a miracle that he wasn't dead. They took him down—poor old Peachey that hadn't done them any harm—that hadn't done them any——'

He rocked to and fro and wept bitterly, wiping his eyes with the back of his scarred hands and moaning like a child for some ten minutes.

'They was cruel enough to feed him up in the temple, because they said he was more of a God than old Daniel that was a man. Then they turned him out on the snow, and told him to go home, and Peachey came home in about a year, begging along the roads quite safe; for Daniel Dravot he walked before and said: "Come along, Peachey. It's a big thing we're doing." The mountains they danced at night, and the mountains they tried to fall on Peachey's head, but Dan he held up his hand, and Peachey came along bent double. He never let go of Dan's hand, and he never let go of Dan's head. They gave it to him as a present in the temple, to remind him not to come again, and though the crown was pure gold, and Peachey was starving, never would Peachey sell the same. You knew Dravot, sir! You knew Right Worshipful Brother Dravot! Look at him now!'

He fumbled in the mass of rags round his bent waist; brought out a black horsehair bag embroidered with silver thread, and shook therefrom on to my table—the dried, withered head of Daniel Dravot! The morning sun that had long been paling the lamps struck the red beard and blind sunken eyes; struck, too, a heavy circlet of gold studded with raw turquoises, that Carnehan placed tenderly on the battered temples.

'You be'old now,' said Carnehan, 'the Emperor in his 'abit as he lived—the King of Kafiristan with his crown upon his head. Poor old Daniel that was a monarch once!'

I shuddered, for, in spite of defacements manifold, I recognised the head of the man of Marwar Junction. Carnehan rose to go. I attempted to stop him. He was not fit to walk abroad. 'Let me take away the whisky, and give me a little money,' he gasped. 'I was a King once. I'll go to the Deputy Commissioner and ask to set in the Poorhouse till I get my health. No, thank you, I can't wait till you get a carriage for me. I've urgent private affairs—in the South—at Marwar.'

He shambled out of the office and departed in the direction of the Deputy Commissioner's house. That day at noon I had occasion to go down the blinding hot Mall, and I saw a crooked man crawling along the white dust of the roadside, his hat in his hand, quavering dolorously after the fashion of street-singers at Home. There was not a soul in sight, and he was out of all possible earshot of the houses. And he sang through his nose, turning his head from right to left:—

> 'The Son of Man goes forth to war,
>   A golden crown to gain;
>   His blood-red banner streams afar—
>   Who follows in his train?'

I waited to hear no more, but put the poor wretch into my carriage and drove him off to the nearest missionary for eventual transfer to the Asylum. He repeated the hymn twice while he was with me, whom he did not in the least recognise, and I left him singing it to the missionary.

Two days later I inquired after his welfare of the Superintendent of the Asylum.

'He was admitted suffering from sunstroke. He died early yesterday morning,' said the Superintendent. 'Is it true that he was half an hour bareheaded in the sun at mid-day?'

'Yes,' said I, 'but do you happen to know if he had anything upon him by any chance when he died?'

'Not to my knowledge,' said the Superintendent.

And there the matter rests.

A MATTER OF FACT

And if ye doubt the tale I tell,
Steer through the South Pacific well;
Go where the branching coral hives
Unending strife of endless lives,
Where, leagued about the 'wildered boat,
The rainbow jellies fill and float;
And, lilting where the laver lingers,
The starfish trips on all her fingers;
Where, 'neath his myriad spines ashock,
The sea-egg ripples down the rock;
An orange wonder dimly guessed,
From darkness where the cuttles rest,
Moored o'er the darker deeps that hide
The blind white Sea-snake and his bride
Who, drowsing, nose the long-lost ships
Let down through darkness to their lips.

In the Matter of One Compass

Once a priest, always a priest; once a Mason, always a Mason; but once a journalist, always and for ever a journalist.

There were three of us, all newspaper men, the only passengers on a little tramp steamer that ran where her owners told her to go. She had once been in the Bilbao iron-ore business, had been lent to the Spanish Government for service at Manila; and was ending her days in the Cape Town coolie-trade, with occasional trips to Madagascar and even as far as England. We found her going to Southampton in ballast, and shipped in her because the fares were nominal. There was Keller, of an American paper, on his way back to the States from palace executions in Madagascar; there was a burly half-Dutchman, called Zuyland, who owned and edited a paper up country near Johannesburg; and there was myself, who had solemnly put away all journalism, vowing to forget that I had ever known the difference between an imprint and a stereo advertisement.

Ten minutes after Keller spoke to me, as the *Rathmines* cleared Cape Town, I had forgotten the aloofness I desired to feign, and was in heated discussion on the immorality of expanding telegrams beyond a certain fixed point. Then Zuyland came out of his cabin, and we were all at home instantly, because we were men of the same profession needing no introduction. We annexed the boat formally, broke open the passengers' bath-room door—on the Manila lines the Dons do not wash—cleaned out the orange-peel and cigar-ends at the bottom of the bath, hired a Lascar to shave us throughout the voyage, and then asked each other's names.

Three ordinary men would have quarrelled through sheer boredom before they reached Southampton. We, by virtue of our craft, were anything but ordinary men. A large percentage of the tales of the world, the thirty-nine that cannot be told to ladies and the one that can, are common property coming of a common stock. We told them all, as a matter of form, with all their local and specific variants which are surprising. Then came, in the intervals of steady card-play, more personal histories of adventure and things seen and suffered: panics among white folk, when the blind terror ran from man to man on the Brooklyn Bridge, and the people crushed each other to death they knew not why; fires, and faces that opened and shut their mouths horribly at red-hot window-frames; wrecks in frost and snow, reported from the sleet-sheathed rescue-tug at the risk of frostbite; long rides after diamond thieves; skirmishes on the veldt and in municipal committees with the Boers; glimpses of lazy tangled Cape politics and the mule-rule in the Transvaal; card-tales, horse-tales, woman-tales, by the score and the half-hundred; till the first mate, who had seen more than us all put together, but lacked words to clothe his tales with, sat open-mouthed far into the dawn.

When the tales were done we picked up cards till a curious hand or a chance remark made one or other of us say, 'That reminds me of a man who—or a business which—' and the anecdotes would continue while the *Rathmines* kicked her way northward through the warm water.

In the morning of one specially warm night we three were sitting immediately in front of the wheel-house, where an old Swedish boatswain whom we called 'Frithiof the Dane' was at the wheel, pretending that he could not hear our stories. Once or twice Frithiof spun the spokes curiously, and Keller lifted his head from a long chair to ask, 'What is it? Can't you get any steerage-way on her?'

'There is a feel in the water,' said Frithiof, 'that I

cannot understand. I think that we run downhills or somethings. She steers bad this morning.'

Nobody seems to know the laws that govern the pulse of the big waters. Sometimes even a landsman can tell that the solid ocean is atilt, and that the ship is working herself up a long unseen slope; and sometimes the captain says, when neither full steam nor fair wind justifies the length of a day's run, that the ship is sagging downhill; but how these ups and downs come about has not yet been settled authoritatively.

'No, it is a following sea,' said Frithiof; 'and with a following sea you shall not get good steerage-way.'

The sea was as smooth as a duck-pond, except for a regular oily swell. As I looked over the side to see where it might be following us from, the sun rose in a perfectly clear sky and struck the water with its light so sharply that it seemed as though the sea should clang like a burnished gong. The wake of the screw and the little white streak cut by the log-line hanging over the stern were the only marks on the water as far as eye could reach.

Keller rolled out of his chair and went aft to get a pineapple from the ripening stock that was hung inside the after awning.

'Frithiof, the log-line has got tired of swimming. It's coming home,' he drawled.

'What?' said Frithiof, his voice jumping several octaves.

'Coming home,' Keller repeated, leaning over the stern. I ran to his side and saw the log-line, which till then had been drawn tense over the stern railing, slacken, loop, and come up off the port quarter. Frithiof called up the speaking-tube to the bridge, and the bridge answered,

'Yes, nine knots.' Then Frithiof spoke again, and the answer was, 'What do you want of the skipper?' and Frithiof bellowed, 'Call him up.'

By this time Zuyland, Keller, and myself had caught something of Frithiof's excitement, for any emotion on shipboard is most contagious. The captain ran out of his cabin, spoke to Frithiof, looked at the log-line, jumped on the bridge, and in a minute we felt the steamer swing round as Frithiof turned her.

'Going back to Cape Town?' said Keller.

Frithiof did not answer, but tore away at the wheel. Then he beckoned us three to help, and we held the wheel down till the *Rathmines* answered it, and we found ourselves looking into the white of our own wake, with the still oily sea tearing past our bows, though we were not going more than half steam ahead.

The captain stretched out his arm from the bridge and shouted. A minute later I would have given a great deal to have shouted too, for one-half of the sea seemed to shoulder itself above the other half, and came on in the shape of a hill. There was neither crest, comb, nor curl-over to it; nothing but black water with little waves chasing each other about the flanks. I saw it stream past and on a level with the *Rathmines*' bow-plates before the steamer hove up her bulk to rise, and I argued that this would be the last of all earthly voyages for me. Then we lifted for ever and ever and ever, till I heard Keller saying in my ear, 'The bowels of the deep, good Lord!' and the *Rathmines* stood poised, her screw racing and drumming on the slope of a hollow that stretched downwards for a good half-mile.

We went down that hollow, nose under for the most

part, and the air smelt wet and muddy, like that of an emptied aquarium. There was a second hill to climb; I saw that much: but the water came aboard and carried me aft till it jammed me against the wheel-house door, and before I could catch breath or clear my eyes again we were rolling to and fro in torn water, with the scuppers pouring like eaves in a thunderstorm.

'There were three waves,' said Keller; 'and the stoke-hold's flooded.'

The firemen were on deck waiting, apparently, to be drowned. The engineer came and dragged them below, and the crew, gasping, began to work the clumsy Board of Trade pump. That showed nothing serious, and when I understood that the *Rathmines* was really on the water, and not beneath it, I asked what had happened.

'The captain says it was a blow-up under the sea—a volcano,' said Keller.

'It hasn't warmed anything,' I said. I was feeling bitterly cold, and cold was almost unknown in those waters.

I went below to change my clothes, and when I came up everything was wiped out in clinging white fog.

'Are there going to be any more surprises?' said Keller to the captain.

'I don't know. Be thankful you're alive, gentlemen. That's a tidal wave thrown up by a volcano. Probably the bottom of the sea has been lifted a few feet somewhere or other. I can't quite understand this cold spell. Our sea-thermometer says the surface water is 44°, and it should be 68° at least.'

'It's abominable,' said Keller, shivering. 'But hadn't you better attend to the fog-horn? It seems to me that I heard something.'

'Heard! Good heavens!' said the captain from the bridge, 'I should think you did.' He pulled the string of our fog-horn, which was a weak one. It sputtered and choked, because the stokehold was full of water and the fires were half-drowned, and at last gave out a moan. It was answered: from the fog by one of the most appalling steam-sirens I have ever heard. Keller turned as white as I did, for the fog, the cold fog, was upon us, and any man may be forgiven for fearing a death he cannot see.

'Give her steam there!' said the captain to the engine-room. 'Steam for the whistle, if we have to go dead slow.'

We bellowed again, and the damp dripped off the awnings on to the deck as we listened for the reply. It seemed to be astern this time, but much nearer than before.

'The *Pembroke Castle* on us!' said Keller; and then viciously, 'Well, thank God, we shall sink her too.'

'It's a side-wheel steamer,' I whispered. 'Can't you hear the paddles?'

This time we whistled and roared till the steam gave out, and the answer nearly deafened us. There was a sound of frantic threshing in the water, apparently about fifty yards away, and something shot past in the whiteness that looked as though it were grey and red.

'The *Pembroke Castle* bottom up,' said Keller, who, being a journalist, always sought for explanations. 'That's the colours of a Castle liner. We're in for a big thing.'

'The sea is bewitched,' said Frithiof from the wheel-house. 'There are *two* steamers!'

Another siren sounded on our bow, and the little steamer rolled in the wash of something that had passed unseen.

'We're evidently in the middle of a fleet,' said Keller quietly. 'If one doesn't run us down, the other will. Phew! What in creation is that?'

I sniffed, for there was a poisonous rank smell in the cold air—a smell that I had smelt before.

'If I was on land I should say that it was an alligator. It smells like musk,' I answered.

'Not ten thousand alligators could make that smell,' said Zuyland; 'I have smelt them.'

'Bewitched! Bewitched!' said Frithiof. 'The sea she is turned upside down, and we are walking along the bottom.'

Again the *Rathmines* rolled in the wash of some unseen ship, and a silver-grey wave broke over the bow, leaving on the deck a sheet of sediment—the grey broth that has its place in the fathomless deeps of the sea. A sprinkling of the wave fell on my face, and it was so cold that it stung as boiling water stings. The dead and most untouched deep water of the sea had been heaved to the top by the submarine volcano—the chill still water that kills all life and smells of desolation and emptiness. We did not need either the blinding fog or that indescribable smell of musk to make us unhappy—we were shivering with cold and wretchedness where we stood.

'The hot air on the cold water makes this fog,' said the captain; 'it ought to clear in a little time.'

'Whistle, oh! whistle, and let's get out of it,' said Keller.

The captain whistled again, and far and far astern the invisible twin steam-sirens answered us. Their blasting shriek grew louder, till at last it seemed to tear out of the fog just above our quarter, and I cowered while the *Rath-mines* plunged bows under on a double swell that crossed.

'No more,' said Frithiof, 'it is not good any more. Let us get away, in the name of God.'

'Now if a torpedo-boat with a *City of Paris* siren went mad and broke her moorings and hired a friend to help her, it's just conceivable that we might be carried as we are now. Otherwise this thing is—'

The last words died on Keller's lips, his eyes began to start from his head, and his jaw fell. Some six or seven feet above the port bulwarks, framed in fog, and as utterly unsupported as the full moon, hung a Face. It was not human, and it certainly was not animal, for it did not belong to this earth as known to man. The mouth was open, revealing a ridiculously tiny tongue—as absurd as the tongue of an elephant; there were tense wrinkles of white skin at the angles of the drawn lips, white feelers like those of a barbel sprung from the lower jaw, and there was no sign of teeth within the mouth. But the horror of the face lay in the eyes, for those were sight-less—white, in sockets as white as scraped bone, and blind. Yet for all this the face, wrinkled as the mask of a lion is drawn in Assyrian sculpture, was alive with rage and terror. One long white feeler touched our bulwarks. Then the face disappeared with the swiftness of a blind-worm popping into its burrow, and the next thing that I remember is my own voice in my own ears, saying gravely to the mainmast, 'But the air-bladder ought to have been forced out of its mouth, you know.'

Keller came up to me, ashy white. He put his hand into his pocket, took a cigar, bit it, dropped it, thrust his shaking thumb into his mouth and mumbled, 'The giant gooseberry and the raining frogs! Gimme a light—gimme a light! Say, gimme a light.' A little bead of blood dropped from his thumb-joint.

I respected the motive, though the manifestation was absurd. 'Stop, you'll bite your thumb off,' I said, and Keller laughed brokenly as he picked up his cigar. Only Zuyland, leaning over the port bulwarks, seemed self-possessed. He declared later that he was very sick.

'We've seen it,' he said, turning round. 'That is it.'

'What?' said Keller, chewing the unlighted cigar.

As he spoke the fog was blown into shreds, and we saw the sea, grey with mud, rolling on every side of us and empty of all life. Then in one spot it bubbled and became like the pot of ointment that the Bible speaks of. From that wide-ringed trouble a Thing came up—a grey and red Thing with a neck—a Thing that bellowed and writhed in pain. Frithiof drew in his breath and held it till the red letters of the ship's name, woven across his jersey, straggled and opened out as though they had been badly typeset. Then he said with a little cluck in his throat, 'Ah me! It is blind. *Hur illa!* That thing is blind,' and a murmur of pity went through us all, for we could see that the thing on the water was blind and in pain. Something had gashed and cut the great sides cruelly and the blood was spurting out. The grey ooze of the undermost sea lay in the monstrous wrinkles of the back, and poured away in sluices. The blind white head flung back and battered the wounds, and the body in its torment rose clear of the red and grey waves till we saw a pair of quivering shoulders streaked with weed and rough with shells, but as white in the clear spaces as the hairless, maneless, blind, toothless head. Afterwards, came a dot on the horizon and the sound of a shrill scream, and it was as though a shuttle shot all across the sea in one breath, and a second head and neck tore through the levels, driving a whispering wall of water to right and left. The two Things met —the one untouched and the other in its death-throe— male and female, we said, the female coming to the male. She circled round him bellowing, and laid her neck across the curve of his great turtle-back, and he disappeared under water for an instant, but flung up again, grunting in agony while the blood ran. Once the entire head and neck shot clear of the water and stiffened, and I heard Keller saying, as though he was watching a street accident, 'Give him air. For God's sake, give him air.' Then the death-struggle began, with crampings and twistings and jerkings of the white bulk to and fro, till our little steamer rolled again, and each gray wave coated her plates with the grey slime. The sun was clear, there was no wind, and we watched, the whole crew, stokers and all, in wonder and pity, but chiefly pity. The Thing was so helpless, and, save for his mate, so alone. No human eye should have beheld him; it was monstrous and indecent to exhibit him there in trade waters between atlas degrees of latitude. He had been spewed up, mangled and dying, from his rest on the sea-floor, where he might have lived till the Judgment Day, and we saw the tides of his life go from him as an angry tide goes out across rocks in the teeth of a landward gale. His mate lay rocking on the water a little distance off, bellowing continually, and the smell of musk came down upon the ship making us cough.

At last the battle for life ended in a batter of coloured seas. We saw the writhing neck fall like a flail, the carcase turn sideways, showing the glint of a white belly and the inset of a gigantic hind leg or flipper. Then all sank, and sea boiled over it, while the mate swam round and round, darting her head in every direction. Though we might have feared that she would attack the steamer, no power on earth could have drawn any one of us from our places that hour. We watched, holding our breaths. The mate paused in her search; we could hear the wash beating along her sides; reared her neck as high as she could reach, blind and lonely in all that loneliness of the sea, and sent one desperate bellow booming across the swells as an oyster-shell skips across a pond. Then she made off to the westward, the sun shining on the white head and the wake behind it, till nothing was left to see but a little pin point of silver on the horizon. We stood on our course again; and the *Rathmines*, coated with the sea-sediment from bow to stern, looked like a ship made grey with terror.

'We must pool our notes,' was the first coherent remark from Keller. 'We're three trained journalists—we hold absolutely the biggest scoop on record. Start fair.'

I objected to this. Nothing is gained by collaboration in journalism when all deal with the same facts, so we went to work each according to his own lights. Keller triple-headed his account, talked about our 'gallant captain,' and wound up with an allusion to American enterprise in that it was a citizen of Dayton, Ohio, that had seen the sea-serpent. This sort of thing would have discredited the Creation, much more a mere sea tale, but as a specimen of the picture-writing of a half-civilised people it was very interesting. Zuyland took a heavy column and a half, giving approximate lengths and breadths, and the whole list of the crew whom he had sworn on oath to testify to his facts. There was nothing fantastic or flamboyant in Zuyland. I wrote three-quarters of a leaded bourgeois column, roughly speaking, and refrained from putting any journalese into it for reasons that had begun to appear to me.

Keller was insolent with joy. He was going to cable from Southampton to the New York *World*, mail his account to America on the same day, paralyse London with his three columns of loosely knitted headlines, and generally efface the earth. 'You'll see how I work a big scoop when I get it,' he said.

'Is this your first visit to England?' I asked.

'Yes,' said he. 'You don't seem to appreciate the beauty of our scoop. It's pyramidal—the death of the sea-serpent! Good heavens alive, man, it's the biggest thing ever vouchsafed to a paper!'

'Curious to think that it will never appear in any paper, isn't it?' I said.

Zuyland was near me, and he nodded quickly.

'What do you mean?' said Keller. 'If you're enough of a Britisher to throw this thing away, I shan't. I thought you were a newspaper-man.'

'I am. That's why I know. Don't be an ass, Keller. Remember, I'm seven hundred years your senior, and what your grandchildren may learn five hundred years hence, I learned from my grandfathers about five hundred years ago. You won't do it, because you can't.'

This conversation was held in open sea, where everything seems possible, some hundred miles from Southampton. We passed the Needles Light at dawn, and the lifting day showed the stucco villas on the green and the awful orderliness of England—line upon line, wall upon wall, solid stone dock and monolithic pier. We waited an hour in the Customs shed, and there was ample time for the effect to soak in.

'Now, Keller, you face the music. The *Havel* goes out to-day. Mail by her, and I'll take you to the telegraph-office,' I said.

I heard Keller gasp as the influence of the land closed about him, cowing him as they say Newmarket Heath cows a young horse unused to open courses.

'I want to retouch my stuff. Suppose we wait till we get to London?' he said.

Zuyland, by the way, had torn up his account and thrown it overboard that morning early. His reasons were my reasons.

In the train Keller began to revise his copy, and every time that he looked at the trim little fields, the red villas, and the embankments of the line, the blue pencil plunged remorselessly through the slips. He appeared to have dredged the dictionary for adjectives. I could think of none that he had not used. Yet he was a perfectly sound poker-player and never showed more cards than were sufficient to take the pool.

'Aren't you going to leave him a single bellow?' I asked sympathetically. 'Remember, everything goes in the States, from a trouser-button to a double-eagle.'

'That's just the curse of it,' said Keller below his breath. 'We've played 'em for suckers so often that when it comes to the golden truths—I'd like to try this on a London paper. You have first call there, though.'

'Not in the least. I'm not touching the thing in our

papers. I shall be happy to leave 'em all to you; but surely you'll cable it home?'

'No. Not if I can make the scoop here and see the Britishers sit up.'

'You won't do it with three columns of slushy headline, believe me. They don't sit up as quickly as some people.'

'I'm beginning to think that too. Does *nothing* make any difference in this country?' he said, looking out of the window. 'How old is that farmhouse?'

'New. It can't be more than two hundred years at the most.'

'Um. Fields, too?'

'That hedge there must have been clipped for about eighty years.'

'Labour cheap—eh?'

'Pretty much. Well, I suppose you'd like to try the *Times*, wouldn't you?'

'No,' said Keller, looking at Winchester Cathedral. 'Might as well try to electrify a haystack. And to think that the *World* would take three columns and ask for more—with illustrations too! It's sickening.'

'But the *Times* might,' I began.

Keller flung his paper across the carriage, and it opened in its austere majesty of solid type—opened with the crackle of an encyclopædia.

'Might! You *might* work your way through the bowplates of a cruiser. Look at that first page!'

'It strikes you that way, does it?' I said. 'Then I'd recommend you to try a light and frivolous journal.'

'With a thing like this of mine—of ours? It's sacred history!'

I showed him a paper which I conceived would be after his own heart, in that it was modelled on American lines.

'That's homey,' he said, 'but it's not the real thing. Now, I should like one of these fat old *Times* columns. Probably there'd be a bishop in the office, though.'

When we reached London Keller disappeared in the direction of the Strand. What his experiences may have been I cannot tell, but it seems that he invaded the office of an evening paper at 11.45 A.M. (I told him English editors were most idle at that hour), and mentioned my name as that of a witness to the truth of his story.

'I was nearly fired out,' he said furiously at lunch. 'As soon as I mentioned you, the old man said that I was to tell you that they didn't want any more of your practical jokes, and that you knew the hours to call if you had anything to sell, and that they'd see you condemned before they helped to puff one of your infernal yarns in advance. Say, what record do you hold for truth in this country, anyway?'

'A beauty. You ran up against it, that's all. Why don't you leave the English papers alone and cable to New York? Everything goes over there.'

'Can't you see that's just why?' he repeated.

'I saw it a long time ago. You don't intend to cable, then?'

'Yes, I do,' he answered, in the over-emphatic voice of one who does not know his own mind.

That afternoon I walked him abroad and about, over the streets that run between the pavements like channels of grooved and tongued lava, over the bridges that are made of enduring stone, through subways floored and sided with yard-thick concrete, between houses that are never rebuilt, and by river-steps hewn, to the eye, from the living rock. A black fog chased us into Westminster Abbey, and, standing there in the darkness, I could hear the wings of the dead centuries circling round the head of Litchfield A. Keller, journalist, of Dayton, Ohio, U.S.A., whose mission it was to make the Britishers sit up.

He stumbled gasping into the thick gloom, and the roar of the traffic came to his bewildered ears.

'Let's go to the telegraph-office and cable,' I said. 'Can't you hear the New York *World* crying for news of the great sea-serpent, blind, white, and smelling of musk, stricken to death by a submarine volcano, and assisted by his loving wife to die in mid-ocean, as visualised by an American citizen, the breezy, newsy, brainy newspaper man of Dayton, Ohio? 'Rah for the Buckeye State. Step lively! Both gates! Szz! Boom! Aah!' Keller was a Princeton man, and he seemed to need encouragement.

'You've got me on your own ground,' said he, tugging at his overcoat pocket. He pulled out his copy, with the cable forms—for he had written out his telegram—and put them all into my hand, groaning, 'I pass. If I hadn't come to your cursed country—if I'd sent it off at Southampton—if I ever get you west of the Alleghanies, if——'

'Never mind, Keller. It isn't your fault. It's the fault of your country. If you had been seven hundred years older you'd have done what I am going to do.'

'What are you going to do?'

'Tell it as a lie.'

'Fiction?' This with the full-blooded disgust of a journalist for the illegitimate branch of the profession.

'You can call it that if you like. I shall call it a lie.'

And a lie it has become; for Truth is a naked lady, and if by accident she is drawn up from the bottom of the sea, it behoves a gentleman either to give her a print petticoat or to turn his face to the wall and vow that he did not see.

THE HOUSE SURGEON

On an evening after Easter Day, I sat at a table in a home-
ward-bound steamer's smoking-room, where half a dozen
of us told ghost stories. As our party broke up, a man,
playing Patience in the next alcove, said to me: 'I didn't
quite catch the end of that last story about the Curse on
the family's first-born.'

'It turned out to be drains,' I explained. 'As soon as
new ones were put into the house the Curse was lifted, I
believe. I never knew the people myself.'

'Ah! I've had *my* drains up twice; I'm on gravel too.'

'You don't mean to say you've a ghost in your house?
Why didn't you join our party?'

'Any more orders, gentlemen, before the bar closes?'
the steward interrupted.

'Sit down again and have one with me,' said the
Patience player. 'No, it isn't a ghost. Our trouble is more
depression than anything else.'

'How interesting! Then it's nothing any one can see?'

'It's—it's nothing worse than a little depression. And
the odd part is that there hasn't been a death in the house
since it was built—in 1863. The lawyer said so. That
decided me—my good lady, rather—and he made me pay
an extra thousand for it.'

'How curious! Unusual, too!' I said.

'Yes, ain't it? It was built for three sisters—Moultrie

was the name—three old maids. They all lived together; the eldest owned it. I bought it from her lawyer a few years ago, and if I've spent a pound on the place first and last, I must have spent five thousand. Electric light, new servants' wing, garden—all that sort of thing. A man and his family ought to be happy after so much expense, ain't it?' He looked at me through the bottom of his glass.

'Does it affect your family much?'

'My good lady—she's a Greek by the way—and myself are middle-aged. We can bear up against depression; but it's hard on my little girl. I say little; but she's twenty. We send her visiting to escape it. She almost lived at hotels and Hydros last year, but that isn't pleasant for her. She used to be a canary—a perfect canary—always singing. You ought to hear her. She doesn't sing now. That sort of thing's unwholesome for the young, ain't it?'

'Can't you get rid of the place?' I suggested.

'Not except at a sacrifice, and we are fond of it. Just suits us three. We'd love it if we were allowed.'

'What do you mean by not being allowed?'

'I mean because of the depression. It spoils everything.'

'What's it like exactly?'

'I couldn't very well explain. It must be seen to be appreciated, as the auctioneers say. Now, I was much impressed by the story you were telling just now.'

'It wasn't true,' I said.

'My tale is true. If you would do me the pleasure to come down and spend a night at my little place, you'd learn more than you would if I talked till morning. Very likely 'twouldn't touch your good self at all. You might be—immune, ain't it? On the other hand, if this influenza-influence *does* happen to affect you, why, I think it will be an experience.'

While he talked he gave me his card, and I read his name was L. Maxwell M'Leod, Esq., of Holmescroft. A City address was tucked away in a corner.

'My business,' he added, 'used to be furs. If you are interested in furs—I've given thirty years of my life to 'em.'

'You're very kind,' I murmured.

'Far from it, I assure you. I can meet you next Saturday afternoon anywhere in London you choose to name, and I'll be only too happy to motor you down. It ought to be a delightful run at this time of year—the rhododendrons will be out. I mean it. You don't know how truly I mean it. Very probably—it won't affect you at all. And—I think I may say I have the finest collection of narwhal tusks in the world. All the best skins and horns have to go through London, and L. Maxwell M'Leod, he knows where they come from, and where they go to. That's his business.'

For the rest of the voyage up-channel Mr. M'Leod talked to me of the assembling, preparation, and sale of the rarer furs; and told me things about the manufacture of fur-lined coats which quite shocked me. Somehow or other, when we landed on Wednesday, I found myself pledged to spend that week-end with him at Holmescroft.

On Saturday he met me with a well-groomed motor, and ran me out in an hour-and-a-half to an exclusive residential district of dustless roads and elegantly designed country villas, each standing in from three to five acres of perfectly appointed land. He told me land was selling at eight hundred pounds the acre, and the new golf links, whose Queen Anne pavilion we passed, had cost nearly twenty-four thousand pounds to create.

Holmescroft was a large, two-storied, low, creeper-covered residence. A verandah at the south side gave on to a garden and two tennis courts, separated by a tasteful iron fence from a most park-like meadow of five or six acres, where two Jersey cows grazed. Tea was ready in the shade of a promising copper beech, and I could see groups on the lawn of young men and maidens appropriately clothed, playing lawn tennis in the sunshine.

'A pretty scene, ain't it?' said Mr. M'Leod. 'My good lady's sitting under the tree, and that's my little girl in pink on the far court. But I'll take you to your room, and you can see 'em all later.'

He led me through a wide parquet-floored hall furnished in pale lemon, with huge cloisonné vases, an ebonised and gold grand piano, and banks of pot flowers in Benares brass bowls, up a pale oak staircase to a spacious landing, where there was a green velvet settee trimmed with silver. The blinds were down, and the light lay in parallel lines on the floors.

He showed me my room, saying cheerfully: 'You may be a little tired. One often is without knowing it after a run through traffic. Don't come down till you feel quite restored. We shall all be in the garden.'

My room was rather close, and smelt of perfumed soap. I threw up the window at once, but it opened so close to the floor and worked so clumsily that I came within an ace of pitching out, where I should certainly have ruined a rather lopsided laburnum below. As I set about washing off the journey's dust, I began to feel a little tired. But, I reflected, I had not come down here in this weather and among these new surroundings to be depressed, so I began to whistle.

And it was just then that I was aware of a little grey shadow, as it might have been a snow-flake seen against the light, floating at an immense distance in the background of my brain. It annoyed me, and I shook my head to get rid of it. Then my brain telegraphed that it was the forerunner of a swift-striding gloom which there was yet time to escape if I would force my thoughts away from it, as a man leaping for life forces his body forward and away from the fall of a wall. But the gloom overtook me before I could take in the meaning of the message. I moved toward the bed, every nerve already aching with the foreknowledge of the pain that was to be dealt it, and sat down, while my amazed and angry soul dropped, gulf by gulf, into that horror of great darkness which is spoken of in the Bible, and which, as auctioneers say, must be experienced to be appreciated.

Despair upon despair, misery upon misery, fear after fear, each causing their distinct and separate woe, packed in upon me for an unrecorded length of time, until at last they blurred together, and I heard a click in my brain like the click in the ear when one descends in a diving bell, and I knew that the pressures were equalised within and without, and that, for the moment, the worst was at an end. But I knew also that at any moment the darkness might come down anew; and while I dwelt on this speculation precisely as a man torments a raging tooth with his tongue, it ebbed away into the little grey shadow on the brain of its first coming, and once more I heard my brain, which knew what would recur, telegraph to every quarter for help, release, or diversion.

The door opened, and M'Leod reappeared. I thanked him politely, saying I was charmed with my room, anxious to meet Mrs. M'Leod, much refreshed with my wash, and so on and so forth. Beyond a little stickiness at the corners of my mouth, it seemed to me that I was managing my words admirably, the while that I myself cowered at the bottom of unclimbable pits. M'Leod laid his hand on my shoulder, and said: 'You've got it now already, ain't it?'

'Yes,' I answered, 'it's making me sick!'

'It will pass off when you come outside. I give you my word it will then pass off. Come!'

I shambled out behind him, and wiped my forehead in the hall.

'You mustn't mind,' he said. 'I expect the run tired you. My good lady is sitting there under the copper beech.'

She was a fat woman in an apricot-coloured gown, with a heavily powdered face, against which her black long-lashed eyes showed like currants in dough. I was introduced to many fine ladies and gentlemen of those parts. Magnificently appointed landaus and covered motors swept in and out of the drive, and the air was gay with the merry outcries of the tennis players.

As twilight drew on they all went away, and I was left alone with Mr. and Mrs. M'Leod, while tall men-servants and maid-servants took away the tennis and tea things. Miss M'Leod had walked a little down the drive with a light-haired young man, who apparently knew everything about every South American railway stock. He had told me at tea that these were the days of financial specialisation.

'I think it went off beautifully, my dear,' said Mr. M'Leod to his wife; and to me: 'You feel all right now, ain't it? Of course you do.'

Mrs. M'Leod surged across the gravel. Her husband skipped nimbly before her into the south verandah, turned a switch, and all Holmescroft was flooded with light.

'You can do that from your room also,' he said as they went in. 'There is something in money, ain't it?'

Miss M'Leod came up behind me in the dusk. 'We have not yet been introduced,' she said, 'but I suppose you are staying the night?'

'Your father was kind enough to ask me,' I replied.

She nodded. 'Yes, I know; and you know too, don't you? *I* saw your face when you came to shake hands with mamma. You felt the depression very soon. It is simply frightful in that bedroom sometimes. What do you think it is—bewitchment? In Greece, where I was a little girl, it might have been; but not in England, do you think? Or *do* you?'

'I don't know what to think,' I replied. 'I never felt anything like it. Does it happen often?'

'Yes, sometimes. It comes and goes.'

'Pleasant!' I said, as we walked up and down the gravel at the lawn edge. 'What has been your experience of it?'

'That is difficult to say, but—sometimes that—that depression is like as it were'—she gesticulated in most un-English fashion—'a light. Yes, like a light turned into a room—only a light of blackness, do you understand? —into a happy room. For sometimes, we are so happy, all we three,—so very happy. Then this, blackness, it is turned on us just like—ah, I know what I mean now—like the head-lamp of a motor, and we are eclipsed. And there is another thing——'

The dressing gong roared, and we entered the over-lighted hall. My dressing was a brisk athletic performance, varied with outbursts of song—careful attention paid to articulation and expression. But nothing happened. As I hurried downstairs, I thanked Heaven that nothing had happened.

Dinner was served breakfast fashion; the dishes were placed on the sideboard over heaters, and we helped ourselves.

'We always do this when we are alone, so we talk better,' said Mr. M'Leod.

'And we are always alone,' said the daughter.

'Cheer up, Thea. It will all come right,' he insisted.

'No, papa.' She shook her dark head. 'Nothing is right while *it* comes.'

'It is nothing that we ourselves have ever done in our lives—that I will swear to you,' said Mrs. M'Leod suddenly. 'And we have changed our servants several times. So we know it is not *them*.'

'Never mind. Let us enjoy ourselves while we can,' said Mr. M'Leod, opening the champagne.

But we did not enjoy ourselves. The talk failed. There were long silences.

'I beg your pardon,' I said, for I thought some one at my elbow was about to speak.

'Ah! That is the other thing!' said Miss M'Leod. Her mother groaned.

We were silent again, and, in a few seconds it must have been, a live grief beyond words—not ghostly dread or horror, but aching, helpless grief—overwhelmed us, each, I felt, according to his or her nature, and held steady like the beam of a burning-glass. Behind that pain I was conscious there was a desire on somebody's part to explain something on which some tremendously important issue hung.

Meantime I rolled bread pills and remembered my sins; M'Leod considered his own reflection in a spoon; his wife seemed to be praying, and the girl fidgeted desperately with hands and feet, till the darkness passed on—as though the malignant rays of a burning glass had been shifted from us.

'There,' said Miss M'Leod, half rising. 'Now you see what makes a happy home. Oh, sell it—sell it, father mine, and let us go away!'

'But I've spent thousands on it. You shall go to Harrogate next week, Thea dear.'

'I'm only just back from hotels. I am *so* tired of packing.'

'Cheer up, Thea. It is over. You know it does not often come here twice in the same night. I think we shall dare now to be comfortable.'

He lifted a dish-cover, and helped his wife and daughter. His face was lined and fallen like an old man's after debauch, but his hand did not shake, and his voice was clear. As he worked to restore us by speech and action, he reminded me of a grey-muzzled collie herding demoralised sheep.

After dinner we sat round the dining-room fire—the drawing-room might have been under the Shadow for aught we knew—talking with the intimacy of gipsies by the wayside, or of wounded comparing notes after a skirmish. By eleven o'clock the three between them had given me every name and detail they could recall that in any way bore on the house, and what they knew of its history.

We went to bed in a fortifying blaze of electric light. My one fear was that the blasting gust of depression would return—the surest way, of course, to bring it. I lay awake till dawn, breathing quickly and sweating lightly, beneath what De Quincey inadequately describes as 'the oppression of inexpiable guilt.' Now as soon as the lovely day was broken, I fell into the most terrible of all dreams —that joyous one in which all past evil has not only been wiped out of our lives, but has never been committed; and in the very bliss of our assured innocence, before our loves shriek and change countenance, we wake to the day we have earned.

It was a coolish morning, but we preferred to breakfast in the south verandah. The forenoon we spent in the garden, pretending to play games that come out of boxes, such as croquet and clock golf. But most of the time we drew together and talked. The young man who knew all about South American railways took Miss M'Leod for a walk in the afternoon, and at five M'Leod thoughtfully whirled us all up to dine in town.

'Now, don't say you will tell the Psychological Society, and that you will come again,' said Miss M'Leod, as we parted. 'Because I know you will not.'

'You should not say that,' said her mother. 'You should say, "Good-bye, Mr. Perseus. Come again."'

'Not him!' the girl cried. 'He has seen the Medusa's head!'

Looking at myself in the restaurant's mirrors, it seemed to me that I had not much benefited by my week-end. Next morning I wrote out all my Holmescroft notes at fullest length, in the hope that by so doing I could put it all behind me. But the experience worked on my mind, as they say certain imperfectly understood rays work on the body.

I am less calculated to make a Sherlock Holmes than any man I know, for I lack both method and patience, yet the idea of following up the trouble to its source fascinated me. I had no theory to go on, except a vague idea that I had come between two poles of a discharge, and had taken a shock meant for some one else. This was followed by a feeling of intense irritation. I waited cautiously on myself, expecting to be overtaken by horror of the supernatural, but my self persisted in being humanly indignant, exactly as though it had been the victim of a practical joke. It was in great pains and upheavals—that I felt in every fibre—but its dominant idea, to put it coarsely, was to get back a bit of its own. By this I knew that I might go forward if I could find the way.

After a few days it occurred to me to go to the office of Mr. J. M. M. Baxter—the solicitor who had sold Holmescroft to M'Leod. I explained I had some notion of buying the place. Would he act for me in the matter?

Mr. Baxter, a large, greyish, throaty-voiced man, showed no enthusiasm. 'I sold it to Mr. M'Leod,' he said. 'It 'ud scarcely do for me to start on the running-down tack now. But I can recommend——'

'I know he's asking an awful price,' I interrupted, 'and atop of it he wants an extra thousand for what he calls your clean bill of health.'

Mr. Baxter sat up in his chair. I had all his attention.

'Your guarantee with the house. Don't you remember it?'

'Yes, yes. That no death had taken place in the house since it was built. I remember perfectly.'

He did not gulp as untrained men do when they lie, but his jaws moved stickily, and his eyes, turning towards the deed boxes on the wall, dulled. I counted seconds, one, two, three—one, two, three—up to ten. A man, I knew, can live through ages of mental depression in that time.

'I remember perfectly.' His mouth opened a little as though it had tasted old bitterness.

'Of course *that* sort of thing doesn't appeal to me,' I went on. '*I* don't expect to buy a house free from death.'

'Certainly not. No one does. But it was Mr. M'Leod's fancy—his wife's rather, I believe; and since we could meet it—it was my duty to my clients—at whatever cost to my own feelings—to make him pay.'

'That's really why I came to you. I understood from him you knew the place well.'

'Oh yes. Always did. It originally belonged to some connections of mine.'

'The Misses Moultrie, I suppose. How interesting! They must have loved the place before the country round about was built up.'

'They were very fond of it indeed.'

'I don't wonder. So restful and sunny. I don't see how they could have brought themselves to part with it.'

Now it is one of the most constant peculiarities of the English that in polite conversation—and I had striven to be polite—no one ever does or sells anything for mere money's sake.

'Miss Agnes—the youngest—fell ill' (he spaced his

words a little), 'and, as they were very much attached to each other, that broke up the home.'

'Naturally. I fancied it must have been something of that kind. One doesn't associate the Staffordshire Moultries' (my Demon of Irresponsibility at that instant created 'em), 'with—with being hard up.'

'I don't know whether we're related to them,' he answered importantly. 'We may be, for our branch of the family comes from the Midlands.'

I give this talk at length, because I am so proud of my first attempt at detective work. When I left him, twenty minutes later, with instructions to move against the owner of Holmescroft with a view to purchase, I was more bewildered than any Doctor Watson at the opening of a story.

Why should a middle-aged solicitor turn plover's-egg colour and drop his jaw when reminded of so innocent and festal a matter as that no death had ever occurred in a house that he had sold? If I knew my English vocabulary at all, the tone in which he said the youngest sister 'fell ill' meant that she had gone out of her mind. That might explain his change of countenance, and it was just possible that her demented influence still hung about Holmescroft; but the rest was beyond me.

I was relieved when I reached M'Leod's City office, and could tell him what I had done—not what I thought.

M'Leod was quite willing to enter into the game of the pretended purchase, but did not see how it would help if I knew Baxter.

'He's the only living soul I can get at who was connected with Holmescroft,' I said.

'Ah! Living soul is good,' said M'Leod. 'At any rate

our little girl will be pleased that you are still interested in us. Won't you come down some day this week?'

'How is it there now?' I asked.

He screwed up his face. 'Simply frightful!' he said. 'Thea is at Droitwich.'

'I should like it immensely, but I must cultivate Baxter for the present. You'll be sure and keep him busy your end, won't you?'

He looked at me with quiet contempt. 'Do not be afraid. I shall be a good Jew. I shall be my own solicitor.'

Before a fortnight was over, Baxter admitted ruefully that M'Leod was better than most firms in the business. We buyers were coy, argumentative, shocked at the price of Holmescroft, inquisitive, and cold by turns, but Mr. M'Leod the seller easily met and surpassed us; and Mr. Baxter entered every letter, telegram, and consultation at the proper rates in a cinematograph-film of a bill. At the end of a month he said it looked as though M'Leod, thanks to him, were really going to listen to reason. I was many pounds out of pocket, but I had learned something of Mr. Baxter on the human side. I deserved it. Never in my life have I worked to conciliate, amuse, and flatter a human being as I worked over my solicitor.

It appeared that he golfed. Therefore, I was an enthusiastic beginner, anxious to learn. Twice I invaded his office with a bag (M'Leod lent it) full of the spelicans needed in this detestable game, and a vocabulary to match. The third time the ice broke, and Mr. Baxter took me to his links, quite ten miles off, where in a maze of tramway lines, railroads, and nursery-maids, we skelped our divoted way round nine holes like barges plunging through head seas. He played vilely and had never expected to meet any one worse; but as he realised my form, I think he began to like me, for he took me in hand by the two hours together. After a fortnight he could give me no more than a stroke a hole, and when, with this allowance I once managed to beat him by one, he was honestly glad; and assured me that I should be a golfer if I stuck to it. I was sticking to it for my own ends, but now and again my conscience pricked me; for the man was a nice man. Between games he supplied me with odd pieces of evidence, such as that he had known the Moultries all his life, being their cousin, and that Miss Mary, the eldest, was an unforgiving woman who would never let bygones be. I naturally wondered what she might have against him and somehow connected him unfavourably with mad Agnes.

'People ought to forgive and forget,' he volunteered one day, between rounds. 'Specially where, in the nature of things, they can't be sure of their deductions. Don't you think so?'

'It all depends on the nature of the evidence on which one forms one's judgment,' I answered.

'Nonsense!' he cried. 'I'm lawyer enough to know that there's nothing in the world so misleading as circumstantial evidence. Never was.'

'Why? Have you ever seen men hanged on it?'

'Hanged? People have been supposed to be eternally lost on it.' His face turned grey again. 'I don't know how it is with you, but my consolation is that God must know. He *must*! Things that seem on the face of 'em like murder, or say suicide, may appear different to God. Heh?'

'That's what the murderer and the suicide can always hope—I suppose.'

'I have expressed myself clumsily as usual. The facts as God knows 'em—may *be* different—even after the most clinching evidence. I've always said that—both as a lawyer and a man, but some people won't—I don't want to judge 'em—we'll say they can't—believe it; whereas *I* say there's always a working chance—a certainty—that the worst hasn't happened.' He stopped and cleared his throat. 'Now, let's come on! This time next week I shall be taking my holiday.'

'What links?' I asked carelessly, while twins in a perambulator got out of our line of fire.

'A potty little nine-hole affair at a Hydro in the Midlands. My cousins stay there. Always will. Not but what the fourth and the seventh holes take some doing. You could manage it, though,' he said encouragingly. 'You're doing much better. It's only your approach shots that are weak.'

'You're right. I can't approach for nuts! I shall go to pieces while you're away—with no one to coach me,' I said mournfully.

'I haven't taught you anything,' he said, delighted with the compliment.

'I owe all I've learned to you, anyhow. When will you come back?'

'Look here,' he began. 'I don't know your engagements, but I've no one to play with at Burry Mills. Never have. Why couldn't you take a few days off and join me there? I warn you it will be rather dull. It's a throat and gout place—baths, massage, electricity, and so forth. But the fourth and the seventh holes really take some doing.'

'I'm for the game,' I answered valiantly, Heaven well knowing that I hated every stroke and word of it.

'That's the proper spirit. As their lawyer I must ask you not to say anything to my cousins about Holmescroft. It upsets 'em. Always did. But speaking as man to man, it would be very pleasant for me if you could see your way to——'

I saw it as soon as decency permitted, and thanked him sincerely. According to my now well-developed theory he had certainly misappropriated his aged cousins' monies under power of attorney, and had probably driven poor Agnes Moultrie out of her wits, but I wished that he was not so gentle, and good-tempered, and innocent-eyed.

Before I joined him at Burry Mills Hydro, I spent a night at Holmescroft. Miss M'Leod had returned from her Hydro, and first we made very merry on the open lawn in the sunshine over the manners and customs of the English resorting to such places. She knew dozens of Hydros, and warned me how to behave in them, while Mr. and Mrs. M'Leod stood aside and adored her.

'Ah! That's the way she always comes back to us,' he said. 'Pity it wears off so soon, ain't it? You ought to hear her sing "With mirth, thou pretty bird."'

We had the house to face through the evening, and there we neither laughed nor sang. The gloom fell on us as we entered, and did not shift till ten o'clock, when we crawled out, as it were, from beneath it.

'It has been bad this summer,' said Mrs. M'Leod in a whisper after we realised that we were freed. 'Sometimes I think the house will get up and cry out—it is so bad.'

'How?'

'Have you forgotten what comes after the depression?'

So then we waited about the small fire, and the dead air in the room presently filled and pressed down upon us with the sensation (but words are useless here) as though some dumb and bound power were striving against gag and bond to deliver its soul of an articulate word. It passed in a few minutes, and I fell to thinking about Mr. Baxter's conscience and Agnes Moultrie, gone mad in the well-lit bedroom that waited me. These reflections secured me a night during which I rediscovered how, from purely mental causes, a man can be physically sick; but the sickness was bliss compared to my dreams when the birds waked. On my departure, M'Leod gave me a beautiful narwhal's horn, much as a nurse gives a child sweets for being brave at a dentist's.

'There's no duplicate of it in the world,' he said, 'else it would have come to old Max M'Leod,' and he tucked it into the motor. Miss M'Leod on the far side of the car whispered, 'Have you found out anything, Mr. Perseus?'

I shook my head.

'Then I shall be chained to my rock all my life,' she went on. 'Only don't tell papa.'

I supposed she was thinking of the young gentleman who specialised in South American rails, for I noticed a ring on the third finger of her left hand.

I went straight from that house to Burry Mills Hydro, keen for the first time in my life on playing golf, which is guaranteed to occupy the mind. Baxter had taken me a room communicating with his own, and after lunch introduced me to a tall, horse-headed elderly lady of decided manners, whom a white-haired maid pushed along in a bath-chair through the park-like grounds of the Hydro.

She was Miss Mary Moultrie, and she coughed and cleared her throat just like Baxter. She suffered—she told me it was the Moultrie caste-mark—from some obscure form of chronic bronchitis, complicated with spasm of the glottis; and, in a dead flat voice, with a sunken eye that looked and saw not, told me what washes, gargles, pastilles, and inhalations she had proved most beneficial. From her I was passed on to her younger sister, Miss Elizabeth, a small and withered thing with twitching lips, victim, she told me, to very much the same sort of throat, but secretly devoted to another set of medicines. When she went away with Baxter and the bath-chair, I fell across a major of the Indian Army with gout in his glassy eyes, and a stomach which he had taken all round the Continent. He laid everything before me; and him I escaped only to be confided in by a matron with a tendency to follicular tonsillitis and eczema. Baxter waited hand and foot on his cousins till five o'clock, trying, as I saw, to atone for his treatment of the dead sister. Miss Mary ordered him about like a dog.

'I warned you it would be dull,' he said when we met in the smoking-room.

'It's tremendously interesting,' I said. 'But how about a look round the links?'

'Unluckily damp always affects my eldest cousin. I've got to buy her a new bronchitis-kettle. Arthurs broke her old one yesterday.'

We slipped out to the chemist's shop in the town, and he bought a large glittering tin thing whose workings he explained.

'I'm used to this sort of work. I come up here pretty often,' he said. 'I've the family throat too.'

'You're a good man,' I said. 'A very good man.'

He turned towards me in the evening light among the beeches, and his face was changed to what it might have been a generation before.

'You see,' he said huskily, 'there was the youngest— Agnes. Before she fell ill, you know. But she didn't like leaving her sisters. Never would.' He hurried on with his odd-shaped load and left me among the ruins of my black theories. The man with that face had done Agnes Moultrie no wrong.

We never played our game. I was waked between two and three in the morning from my hygienic bed by Baxter in an ulster over orange and white pyjamas, which I should never have suspected from his character.

'My cousin has had some sort of a seizure,' he said. 'Will you come? I don't want to wake the doctor. Don't want to make a scandal. Quick!'

So I came quickly, and led by the white-haired Arthurs in a jacket and petticoat, entered a double-bedded room reeking with steam and Friar's Balsam. The electrics were all on. Miss Mary—I knew her by her height—was at the open window, wrestling with Miss Elizabeth, who gripped her round the knees. Her hand was at her throat, which was streaked with blood.

'She's done it. She's done it too!' Miss Elizabeth panted. 'Hold her! Help me!'

'Oh, I say! Women don't cut their throats,' Baxter whispered.

'My God! Has she cut her throat?' the maid cried, and with no warning rolled over in a faint. Baxter pushed her under the wash-basins, and leaped to hold the gaunt woman who crowed and whistled as she struggled towards the window. He took her by the shoulder, and she struck out wildly.

'All right! She's only cut her hand,' he said. 'Wet towel —quick!'

While I got that he pushed her backward. Her strength seemed almost as great as his. I swabbed at her throat when I could, and found no mark; then helped him to control her a little. Miss Elizabeth leaped back to bed, wailing like a child.

'Tie up her hand somehow,' said Baxter. 'Don't let it drip about the place. She'—he stepped on broken glass in his slippers—'she must have smashed a pane.'

Miss Mary lurched towards the open window again, dropped on her knees, her head on the sill, and lay quiet, surrendering the cut hand to me.

'What did she do?' Baxter turned towards Miss Elizabeth in the far bed.

'She was going to throw herself out of the window,' was the answer. 'I stopped her, and sent Arthurs for you. Oh, we can never hold up our heads again!'

Miss Mary writhed and fought for breath. Baxter found a shawl which he threw over her shoulders.

'Nonsense!' said he. 'That isn't like Mary'; but his face worked when he said it.

'You wouldn't believe about Aggie, John. Perhaps you will now!' said Miss Elizabeth. 'I *saw* her do it, and she's cut her throat too!'

'She hasn't,' I said. 'It's only her hand.'

Miss Mary suddenly broke from us with an indescribable grunt, flew, rather than ran, to her sister's bed, and there shook her as one furious schoolgirl would shake another.

'No such thing,' she croaked. 'How dare you think so, you wicked little fool?'

'Get into bed, Mary,' said Baxter. 'You'll catch a chill.'

She obeyed, but sat up with the grey shawl round her lean shoulders, glaring at her sister. 'I'm better now,' she crowed. 'Arthurs let me sit out too long. Where's Arthurs? The kettle.'

'Never mind Arthurs,' said Baxter. '*You* get the kettle.' I hastened to bring it from the side table. 'Now, Mary, as God sees you, tell me what you've done.'

His lips were dry, and he could not moisten them with his tongue.

Miss Mary applied herself to the mouth of the kettle, and between indraws of steam said: 'The spasm came on just now, while I was asleep. I was nearly choking to death. So I went to the window. I've done it often before, without waking any one. Bessie's such an old maid about draughts. I tell you I was choking to death. I couldn't manage the catch, and I nearly fell out. That window opens too low. I cut my hand trying to save myself. Who has tied it up in this filthy handkerchief? I wish you had had my throat, Bessie. I never was nearer dying!' She scowled on us all impartially, while her sister sobbed.

From the bottom of the bed we heard a quivering voice: 'Is she dead? Have they took her away? Oh, I never could bear the sight o' blood!'

'Arthurs,' said Miss Mary, 'you are an hireling. Go away!'

It is my belief that Arthurs crawled out on all fours, but I was busy picking up broken glass from the carpet.

Then Baxter, seated by the side of the bed, began to cross-examine in a voice I scarcely recognised. No one could for an instant have doubted the genuine rage of Miss Mary against her sister, her cousin, or her maid; and that the doctor should have been called in—for she did me the honour of calling me doctor—was the last drop. She was choking with her throat; had rushed to the window for air; had near pitched out, and in catching at the window bars had cut her hand. Over and over she made this clear to the intent Baxter. Then she turned on her sister and tongue-lashed her savagely.

'You mustn't blame me,' Miss Bessie faltered at last. 'You know what we think of night and day.'

'I'm coming to that,' said Baxter. 'Listen to me. What *you* did, Mary, misled four people into thinking you—you meant to do away with yourself.'

'Isn't one suicide in the family enough? Oh God, help and pity us! You *couldn't* have believed that!' she cried.

'The evidence was complete. Now, don't you think,' Baxter's finger wagged under her nose—'*can't* you think that poor Aggie did the same thing at Holmescroft when she fell out of the window?'

'She had the same throat,' said Miss Elizabeth. 'Exactly the same symptoms. Don't you remember, Mary?'

'Which was her bedroom?' I asked of Baxter in an undertone.

'Over the south verandah, looking on to the tennis lawn.'

'I nearly fell out of that very window when I was at

Holmescroft—opening it to get some air. The sill doesn't come much above your knees,' I said.

'You hear that, Mary? Mary, do you hear what this gentleman says? Won't you believe that what nearly happened to you must have happened to poor Aggie that night? For God's sake—for her sake—Mary, *won't* you believe?'

There was a long silence while the steam-kettle puffed.

'If I could have proof—if I could have proof,' said she, and broke into most horrible tears.

Baxter motioned to me, and I crept away to my room, and lay awake till morning, thinking more specially of the dumb Thing at Holmescroft which wished to explain itself. I hated Miss Mary as perfectly as though I had known her for twenty years, but I felt that, alive or dead, I should not like her to condemn me.

Yet at mid-day, when I saw Miss Mary in her bath-chair, Arthurs behind and Baxter and Miss Elizabeth on either side, in the park-like grounds of the Hydro, I found it difficult to arrange my words.

'Now that you know all about it,' said Baxter aside, after the first strangeness of our meeting was over, 'it's only fair to tell you that my poor cousin did not die in Holmescroft at all. She was dead when they found her under the window in the morning. Just dead.'

'Under that laburnum outside the window?' I asked, for I suddenly remembered the crooked evil thing.

'Exactly. She broke the tree in falling. But no death has ever taken place *in* the house, so far as we were concerned. You can make yourself quite easy on that point. Mr. M'Leod's extra thousand for what you called the "clean bill of health" was something towards my cousin's estate when we sold. It was my duty as their lawyer to get it for them—at any cost to my own feelings.'

I know better than to argue when the English talk about their duty. So I agreed with my solicitor.

'Their sister's death must have been a great blow to your cousins,' I went on. The bath-chair was behind me.

'Unspeakable,' Baxter whispered. 'They brooded on it day and night. No wonder. If their theory of poor Aggie making away with herself was correct, she was eternally lost!'

'Do you believe that she made away with herself?'

'No, thank God! Never have! And after what happened to Mary last night, I see perfectly what happened to poor Aggie. She had the family throat too. By the way, Mary thinks you are a doctor. Otherwise she wouldn't like your having been in her room.'

'Very good. Is she convinced now about her sister's death?'

'She'd give anything to be able to believe it, but she's a hard woman, and brooding along certain lines makes one groovy. I have sometimes been afraid for her reason —on the religious side, don't you know. Elizabeth doesn't matter. Brain of a hen. Always had.'

Here Arthurs summoned me to the bath-chair, and the ravaged face, beneath its knitted Shetland wool hood, of Miss Mary Moultrie.

'I need not remind you, I hope, of the seal of secrecy— absolute secrecy—in your profession,' she began. 'Thanks to my cousin's and my sister's stupidity, you have found out——' she blew her nose.

'Please don't excite her, sir,' said Arthurs at the back.

'But, my dear Miss Moultrie, I only know what I've

seen, of course, but it seems to me that what you thought was a tragedy in your sister's case, turns out, on your own evidence, so to speak, to have been an accident—a dreadfully sad one—but absolutely an accident.'

'Do you believe that too?' she cried. 'Or are you only saying it to comfort me?'

'I believe it from the bottom of my heart. Come down to Holmescroft for an hour—for half an hour—and satisfy yourself.'

'Of what? You don't understand. I see the house every day—every night. I am always there in spirit—waking or sleeping. I couldn't face it in reality.'

'But you must,' I said. 'If you go there in the spirit the greater need for you to go there in the flesh. Go to your sister's room once more, and see the window—I nearly fell out of it myself. It's—it's awfully low and dangerous. That would convince you,' I pleaded.

'Yet Aggie had slept in that room for years,' she interrupted.

'You've slept in your room here for a long time, haven't you? But you nearly fell out of the window when you were choking.'

'That is true. That is one thing true,' she nodded. 'And I might have been killed as—perhaps—Aggie was killed.'

'In that case your own sister and cousin and maid would have said you had committed suicide, Miss Moultrie. Come down to Holmescroft, and go over the place just once.'

'You are lying,' she said quite quietly. 'You don't want me to come down to see a window. It is something else.

92

I warn you we are Evangelicals. We don't believe in prayers for the dead. "As the tree falls——"'

'Yes. I daresay. But you persist in thinking that your sister committed suicide——'

'No! No! I have always prayed that I might have misjudged her.'

Arthurs at the bath-chair spoke up: 'Oh, Miss Mary! you *would* 'ave it from the first that poor Miss Aggie 'ad made away with herself; an', of course, Miss Bessie took the notion from you. Only Master—Mister John stood out, and—and I'd 'ave taken my Bible oath *you* was making away with yourself last night.'

Miss Mary leaned towards me, one finger on my sleeve.

'If going to Holmescroft kills me,' she said, 'you will have the murder of a fellow-creature on your conscience for all eternity.'

'I'll risk it,' I answered. Remembering what torment the mere reflection of her torments had cast on Holmescroft, and remembering, above all, the dumb Thing that filled the house with its desire to speak, I felt that there might be worse things.

Baxter was amazed at the proposed visit, but at a nod from that terrible woman went off to make arrangements. Then I sent a telegram to M'Leod bidding him and his vacate Holmescroft for that afternoon. Miss Mary should be alone with her dead, as I had been alone.

I expected untold trouble in transporting her, but to do her justice, the promise given for the journey, she underwent it without murmur, spasm, or unnecessary word. Miss Bessie, pressed in a corner by the window, wept behind her veil, and from time to time tried to take hold of her sister's hand. Baxter wrapped himself in his newly-found happiness as selfishly as a bridegroom, for he sat still and smiled.

'So long as I know that Aggie didn't make away with herself,' he explained, 'I tell you frankly I don't care what happened. She's as hard as a rock—Mary. Always was. *She* won't die.'

We led her out on to the platform like a blind woman, and so got her into the fly. The half-hour crawl to Holmescroft was the most racking experience of the day. M'Leod had obeyed my instructions. There was no one visible in the house or the gardens; and the front door stood open.

Miss Mary rose from beside her sister, stepped forth first, and entered the hall.

'Come, Bessie,' she cried.

'I daren't. Oh, I daren't.'

'Come!' Her voice had altered. I felt Baxter start. 'There's nothing to be afraid of.'

'Good heavens!' said Baxter. 'She's running up the stairs. We'd better follow.'

'Let's wait below. She's going to the room.'

We heard the door of the bedroom I knew open and shut, and we waited in the lemon-coloured hall, heavy with the scent of flowers.

'I've never been into it since it was sold,' Baxter sighed. 'What a lovely restful place it is! Poor Aggie used to arrange the flowers.'

'Restful?' I began, but stopped of a sudden, for I felt all over my bruised soul that Baxter was speaking truth. It was a light, spacious, airy house, full of the sense of well-being and peace—above all things, of peace. I ventured into the dining-room where the thoughtful M'Leods had left a small fire. There was no terror there, present or lurking; and in the drawing-room, which for good reasons we had never cared to enter, the sun and the peace and the scent of the flowers worked together as is fit in an inhabited house. When I returned to the hall, Baxter was sweetly asleep on a couch, looking most unlike a middle-aged solicitor who had spent a broken night with an exacting cousin.

There was ample time for me to review it all—to felici-tate myself upon my magnificent acumen (barring some errors about Baxter as a thief and possibly a murderer), before the door above opened, and Baxter, evidently a light sleeper, sprang awake.

'I've had a heavenly little nap,' he said, rubbing his eyes with the backs of his hands like a child. 'Good Lord! That's not *their* step!'

But it was. I had never before been privileged to see the Shadow turned backward on the dial—the years ripped bodily off poor human shoulders—old sunken eyes filled and alight—harsh lips moistened and human.

'John,' Miss Mary called, 'I know now. Aggie didn't do it!' and 'She didn't do it!' echoed Miss Bessie, and giggled.

'I did not think it wrong to say a prayer,' Miss Mary continued. 'Not for her soul, but for our peace. Then I was convinced.'

'Then we got conviction,' the younger sister piped.

'We've misjudged poor Aggie, John. But I feel she knows now. Wherever she is, she knows that we know she is guiltless.'

'Yes, she knows. I felt it too,' said Miss Elizabeth.

'I never doubted,' said John Baxter, whose face was beautiful at that hour. 'Not from the first. Never have!'

'You never offered me proof, John. Now, thank God, it will not be the same any more. I can think henceforward of Aggie without sorrow.' She tripped, absolutely tripped, across the hall. 'What ideas these Jews have of arranging furniture!' She spied me behind a big cloisonné vase.

'I've seen the window,' she said remotely. 'You took a great risk in advising me to undertake such a journey. However, as it turns out . . . I forgive you, and I pray you may never know what mental anguish means! Bessie! Look at this peculiar piano! Do you suppose, Doctor, these people would offer one tea? I miss mine.'

'I will go and see,' I said, and explored M'Leod's new-built servants' wing. It was in the servants' hall that I unearthed the M'Leod family, bursting with anxiety.

'Tea for three, quick,' I said. 'If you ask me any questions now, I shall have a fit!' So Mrs. M'Leod got it, and I was butler, amid murmured apologies from Baxter, still smiling and self-absorbed, and the cold disapproval of Miss Mary, who thought the pattern of the china vulgar. However, she ate well, and even asked me whether I would not like a cup of tea for myself.

They went away in the twilight—the twilight that I had once feared. They were going to an hotel in London to rest after the fatigues of the day, and as their fly turned down the drive, I capered on the doorstep, with the all-darkened house behind me.

Then I heard the uncertain feet of the M'Leods, and bade them not to turn on the lights, but to feel—to feel what I had done; for the Shadow was gone, with the dumb desire in the air. They drew short, but afterwards deeper, breaths, like bathers entering chill water, separated one from the other, moved about the hall, tiptoed upstairs, raced down, and then Miss M'Leod, and I believe her mother, though she denies this, embraced me. I know M'Leod did.

It was a disgraceful evening. To say we rioted through the house is to put it mildly. We played a sort of Blind Man's Buff along the darkest passages, in the unlighted drawing-room, and little dining-room, calling cheerily to each other after each exploration that here, and here, and here, the trouble had removed itself. We came up to *the* bedroom—mine for the night again—and sat, the women on the bed, and we men on chairs, drinking in blessed draughts of peace and comfort and cleanliness of soul, while I told them my tale in full, and received fresh praise, thanks, and blessings.

When the servants, returned from their day's outing, gave us a supper of cold fried fish, M'Leod had sense enough to open no wine. We had been practically drunk since nightfall, and grew incoherent on water and milk.

'I like that Baxter,' said M'Leod. 'He's a sharp man. The death wasn't in the house, but he ran it pretty close, ain't it?'

'And the joke of it is that he supposes I want to buy the place from you,' I said. 'Are you selling?'

'Not for twice what I paid for it—now,' said M'Leod. 'I'll keep you in furs all your life, but not our Holmescroft.'

'No—never our Holmescroft,' said Miss M'Leod. 'We'll ask *him* here on Tuesday, mamma.' They squeezed each other's hands.

'Now tell me,' said Mrs. M'Leod—'that tall one I saw out of the scullery window—did *she* tell you she was always here in the spirit? I hate her. She made all this trouble. It was not her house after she had sold it. What do you think?'

'I suppose,' I answered, 'she brooded over what she believed was her sister's suicide night and day—she confessed she did—and her thoughts being concentrated on this place, they felt like a—like a burning glass.'

'Burning glass is good,' said M'Leod.

'I said it was like a light of blackness turned on us,' cried the girl, twiddling her ring. 'That must have been when the tall one thought worst about her sister and the house.'

'Ah, the poor Aggie!' said Mrs. M'Leod. 'The poor Aggie, trying to tell every one it was not so! No wonder we felt Something wished to say Something. Thea, Max, do you remember that night——?'

'We need not remember any more,' M'Leod interrupted. 'It is not our trouble. They have told each other now.'

'Do you think, then,' said Miss M'Leod, 'that those two, the living ones, were actually told something—upstairs—in your—in the room?'

'I can't say. At any rate they were made happy, and they ate a big tea afterwards. As your father says, it is not our trouble any longer—thank God!'

'Amen!' said M'Leod. 'Now, Thea, let us have some music after all these months. "With mirth, thou pretty bird," ain't it? You ought to hear that.'

And in the half-lighted hall, Thea sang an old English song that I had never heard before.

With mirth, thou pretty bird, rejoice,
    Thy Maker's praise enhanced;
Lift up thy shrill and pleasant voice,
    Thy God is high advanced!
Thy food before He did provide,
And gives it in a fitting side,
    Wherewith be thou sufficed!
Why shouldst thou now unpleasant be,
    Thy wrath against God venting,
That He a little bird made thee,
    Thy silly head tormenting,
Because He made thee not a man?
Oh, Peace! He hath well thought thereon,
    Therewith be thou sufficed!

ON THE CITY WALL

> Then she let them down by a cord through the
> window; for her house was upon the town wall,
> and she dwelt upon the wall.   —*Joshua* ii, 15

Lalun is a member of the most ancient profession in the
world. Lilith was her very-great-grand-mamma, and that
was before the days of Eve, as every one knows. In the
West, people say rude things about Lalun's profession,
and write lectures about it, and distribute the lectures to
young persons in order that Morality may be preserved.
In the East, where the profession is hereditary, descend-
ing from mother to daughter, nobody writes lectures or
takes any notice; and that is a distinct proof of the inability of the East to manage its own affairs.

Lalun's real husband, for even ladies of Lalun's profession in the East must have husbands, was a big
jujube-tree. Her Mamma, who had married a fig-tree,
spent ten thousand rupees on Lalun's wedding, which
was blessed by forty-seven clergymen of Mamma's
Church, and distributed five thousand rupees in charity
to the poor. And that was the custom of the land. The
advantages of having a jujube-tree for a husband are obvi-
ous. You cannot hurt his feelings, and he looks imposing.

Lalun's husband stood on the plain outside the City
walls, and Lalun's house was upon the east wall facing

the river. If you fell from the broad window-seat you dropped thirty feet sheer into the City Ditch. But if you stayed where you should and looked forth, you saw all the cattle of the City being driven down to water, the students of the Government College playing cricket, the high grass and trees that fringed the river-bank, the great sand-bars that ribbed the river, the red tombs of dead Emperors beyond the river, and very far away through the blue heat-haze a glint of the snows of the Himalayas.

Wali Dad used to lie in the window-seat for hours at a time watching this view. He was a young Mohammedan who was suffering acutely from education of the English variety and knew it. His father had sent him to a Mission-school to get wisdom, and Wali Dad had absorbed more than ever his father or the Missionaries intended he should. When his father died, Wali Dad was independent and spent two years experimenting with the creeds of the Earth and reading books that are of no use to anybody.

After he had made an unsuccessful attempt to enter the Roman Catholic Church and the Presbyterian fold at the same time (the Missionaries found him out and called him names, but they did not understand his trouble), he discovered Lalun on the City wall and became the most constant of her few admirers. He possessed a head that English artists at home would rave over and paint amid impossible surroundings—a face that female novelists would use with delight through nine hundred pages. In reality he was only a clean-bred young Mohammedan, with pencilled eyebrows, small-cut nostrils, little feet and hands, and a very tired look in his eyes. By virtue of his twenty-two years he had grown a neat black beard which he stroked with pride and kept delicately scented. His life seemed to be divided between borrowing books from me and making love to Lalun in the window-seat. He composed songs about her, and some of the songs are sung to this day in the City from the Street of the Mutton-Butchers to the Copper-Smiths' ward.

One song, the prettiest of all, says that the beauty of Lalun was so great that it troubled the hearts of the British Government and caused them to lose their peace of mind. That is the way the song is sung in the streets; but, if you examine it carefully and know the key to the explanation, you will find that there are three puns in it—on 'beauty,' 'heart,' and 'peace of mind'—so that it runs: 'By the subtlety of Lalun the administration of the Government was troubled and it lost such and such a man.' When Wali Dad sings that song his eyes glow like hot coals, and Lalun leans back among the cushions and throws bunches of jasmine-buds at Wali Dad.

But first it is necessary to explain something about the Supreme Government which is above all and below all and behind all. Gentlemen come from England, spend a few weeks in India, walk round this great Sphinx of the Plains, and write books upon its ways and its works, denouncing or praising it as their own ignorance prompts. Consequently all the world knows how the Supreme Government conducts itself. But no one, not even the Supreme Government, knows everything about the administration of the Empire. Year by year England sends out fresh drafts for the first fighting-line, which is officially called the Indian Civil Service. These die, or kill themselves by overwork, or are worried to death, or broken in health and hope in order that the land may be protected from death and sickness, famine and war, and may eventually become capable of standing alone. It will never stand alone, but the idea is a pretty one, and men are willing to die for it, and yearly the work of pushing and coaxing and scolding and petting the country into good living goes forward. If an advance be made all credit is given to the native, while the Englishmen stand back and wipe their foreheads. If a failure occurs the Englishmen step forward and take the blame. Overmuch tenderness of this kind has bred a strong belief among many natives that the native is capable of administering the country, and many devout Englishmen believe this also, because the theory is stated in beautiful English with all the latest political colours.

There be other men who, though uneducated, see visions and dream dreams, and they, too, hope to administer the country in their own way—that is to say, with a garnish of Red Sauce. Such men must exist among two hundred million people, and, if they are not attended to, may cause trouble and even break the great idol called *Pax Britannica*, which, as the newspapers say, lives between Peshawar and Cape Comorin. Were the Day of Doom to dawn to-morrow, you would find the Supreme Government 'taking measures to allay popular excitement,' and putting guards upon the graveyards that the Dead might troop forth orderly. The youngest Civilian would arrest Gabriel on his own responsibility if the Archangel could not produce a Deputy Commissioner's permission to 'make music or other noises' as the licence says.

Whence it is easy to see that mere men of the flesh who would create a tumult must face badly at the hands of the Supreme Government. And they do so. There is no outward sign of excitement; there is no confusion; there is no knowledge. When due and sufficient reasons have been given, weighed and approved, the machinery moves forward, and the dreamer of dreams and the seer of visions is gone from his friends and following. He enjoys the hospitality of Government; there is no restriction upon his movements within certain limits; but he must not confer any more with his brother dreamers. Once in every six months the Supreme Government assures itself that he is well and takes formal acknowledgment of his existence. No one protests against his detention, because the few people who know about it are in deadly fear of seeming to know him; and never a single newspaper 'takes up his case' or organises demonstrations on his behalf, because the newspapers of India have got behind that lying proverb which says the Pen is mightier than the Sword, and can walk delicately.

So now you know as much as you ought about Wali Dad, the educational mixture, and the Supreme Government.

Lalun has not yet been described. She would need, so Wali Dad says, a thousand pens of gold and ink scented with musk. She has been variously compared to the Moon, the Dil Sagar Lake, a spotted quail, a gazelle, the Sun on the Desert of Kutch, the Dawn, the Stars, and the young bamboo. These comparisons imply that she is beautiful exceedingly according to the native standards, which are practically the same as those of the West. Her eyes are black and her hair is black, and her eyebrows are black as leeches; her mouth is tiny and says witty things; her hands are tiny and have saved much money; her feet are tiny and have trodden on the naked hearts of many men. But, as Wali Dad sings: 'Lalun *is* Lalun, and when you have said that, you have only come to the Beginnings of Knowledge.'

The little house on the City wall was just big enough to hold Lalun, and her maid, and a pussy-cat with a silver collar. A big pink and blue cut-glass chandelier hung from the ceiling of the reception room. A petty Nawab had given Lalun the horror, and she kept it for politeness' sake. The floor of the room was of polished chunam, white as curds. A latticed window of carved wood was set in one wall; there was a profusion of squabby fluffy cushions and fat carpets everywhere, and Lalun's silver *huqa*, studded with turquoises, had a special little carpet all to its shining self. Wali Dad was nearly as permanent a fixture as the chandelier. As I have said, he lay in the window-seat and meditated on Life and Death and Lalun—specially Lalun. The feet of the young men of the City tended to her doorways and then—retired, for Lalun was a particular maiden, slow of speech, reserved of mind, and not in the least inclined to orgies which were nearly certain to end in strife. 'If I am of no value, I am unworthy of this honour,' said Lalun. 'If I am of value, they are unworthy of Me.' And that was a crooked sentence.

In the long nights of latter April and May all the City seemed to assemble in Lalun's little white room to smoke and to talk. Shiahs of the grimmest and most uncompromising persuasion; Sufis who had lost all belief in the Prophet and retained but little in God; wandering Hindu priests passing southward on their way to the Central India fairs and other affairs; Pundits in black gowns, with spectacles on their noses and undigested wisdom in their insides; bearded headmen of the wards; Sikhs with all the details of the latest ecclesiastical scandal in the Golden Temple; red-eyed priests from beyond the Border, looking like trapped wolves and talking like ravens; M.A.s of the University, very superior and very voluble—all these people and more also you might find in the white room. Wali Dad lay in the window-seat and listened to the talk.

'It is Lalun's *salon*,' said Wali Dad to me, 'and it is electic—is not that the word? Outside of a Freemasons' Lodge I have never seen such gatherings. *There* I dined once with a Jew—a Yahoudi!' He spat into the City Ditch with apologies for allowing national feelings to overcome him. 'Though I have lost every belief in the world,' said he, 'and try to be proud of my losing, I cannot help hating a Jew. Lalun admits no Jews here.'

'But what in the world do all these men do?' I asked.

'The curse of our country,' said Wali Dad. 'They talk. It is like the Athenians—always hearing and telling some new thing. Ask the Pearl and she will show you how much she knows of the news of the City and the Province. Lalun knows everything.'

'Lalun,' I said at random—she was talking to a gentleman of the Kurd persuasion who had come in from God-knows-where—'when does the 175th Regiment go to Agra?'

'It does not go at all,' said Lalun, without turning her head. 'They have ordered the 118th to go in its stead. That Regiment goes to Lucknow in three months, unless they give a fresh order.'

'That is so,' said Wali Dad, without a shade of doubt. 'Can you, with your telegrams and your newspapers, do better? Always hearing and telling some new thing,' he went on. 'My friend, has your God ever smitten a European nation for gossiping in the bazaars? India has gossiped for centuries—always standing in the bazaars until the soldiers go by. Therefore—you are here to-day instead of starving in your own country, and I am not a Mohammedan—I am a Product—a Demnition Product. That also I owe to you and yours: that I cannot make an end to my sentence without quoting from your authors.' He pulled at the *huqa* and mourned, half feelingly, half in earnest, for the shattered hopes of his youth. Wali Dad was always mourning over something or other—the country of which he despaired, or the creed in which he had lost faith, or the life of the English which he could by no means understand.

Lalun never mourned. She played little songs on the *sitar*, and to hear her sing, 'O Peacock, cry again,' was always a fresh pleasure. She knew all the songs that have ever been sung, from the war-songs of the South, that make the old men angry with the young men and the young men angry with the State, to the love-songs of the North, where the swords whinny-whicker like angry kites in the pauses between the kisses, and the Passes fill with armed men, and the Lover is torn from his Beloved and cries, *Ai! Ai! Ai!* evermore. She knew how to make up tobacco for the *huqa* so that it smelt like the Gates of Paradise and wafted you gently through them. She could embroider strange things in gold and silver, and dance softly with the moonlight when it came in at the window. Also she knew the hearts of men, and the heart of the City, and whose wives were faithful and whose untrue, and more of the secrets of the Government Offices than are good to be set down in this place. Nasiban, her maid, said that her jewelry was worth ten thousand pounds, and that, some night, a thief would enter and murder her for its possession; but Lalun said that all the City would tear that thief limb from limb, and that he, whoever he was, knew it.

So she took her *sitar* and sat in the window-seat, and sang a song of old days that had been sung by a girl of her profession in an armed camp on the eve of a great battle—the day before the Fords of the Jumna ran red and Sivaji fled fifty miles to Delhi with a Toorkh stallion at his horse's tail and another Lalun on his saddle-bow. It was what men call a Mahratta *laonee*, and it said:—

> Their warrior forces Chimnajee
> Before the Peishwa led,
> The Children of the Sun and Fire
> Behind him turned and fled.

And the chorus said:—

> With them there fought who rides so free
> With sword and turban red,
> The warrior-youth who earns his fee
> At peril of his head

'At peril of his head,' said Wali Dad, in English to me. 'Thanks to your Government, all our heads are protected, and with the educational facilities at my command'— his eyes twinkled wickedly—'I might be a distinguished member of the local administration. Perhaps, in time, I might even be a member of a Legislative Council.'

'Don't speak English,' said Lalun, bending over her *sitar* afresh. The chorus went out from the City wall to the blackened wall of Fort Amara which dominates the City. No man knows the precise extent of Fort Amara. Three kings built it hundreds of years ago, and they say that there are miles of underground rooms beneath its walls. It is peopled with many ghosts, a detachment of Garrison Artillery, and a Company of Infantry. In its prime it held ten thousand men and filled its ditches with corpses.

'At peril of his head,' sang Lalun again and again.

A head moved on one of the ramparts—the grey head of an old man—and a voice, rough as shark-skin on a sword-hilt, sent back the last line of the chorus and broke into a song that I could not understand, though Lalun and Wali Dad listened intently.

'What is it?' I asked. 'Who is it?'

'A consistent man,' said Wali Dad. 'He fought you in '46, when he was a warrior-youth; refought you in '57, and he tried to fight you in '71, but you had learned the trick of blowing men from guns too well. Now he is old; but he would still fight if he could.'

'Is he a Wahabi, then? Why should he answer to a Mahratta *laonee* if he be Wahabi—or Sikh?' said I.

'I do not know,' said Wali Dad. 'He has lost, perhaps, his religion. Perhaps he wished to be a King. Perhaps he is a King. I do not know his name.'

'That is a lie, Wali Dad. If you know his career you must know his name.'

'That is quite true. I belong to a nation of liars. I would rather not tell you his name. Think for yourself.'

Lalun finished her song, pointed to the Fort, and said simply: 'Khem Singh.'

'Hm,' said Wali Dad. 'If the Pearl chooses to tell you the Pearl is a fool.'

I translated to Lalun, who laughed. 'I choose to tell what I choose to tell. They kept Khem Singh in Burma,' said she. 'They kept him there for many years until his mind was changed in him. So great was the kindness of the Government. Finding this, they sent him back to his own country that he might look upon it before he died. He is an old man, but when he looks upon this his country his memory will come. Moreover, there be many who remember him.'

'He is an Interesting Survival,' said Wali Dad, pulling at the *huqa*. 'He returns to a country now full of educational and political reform, but, as the Pearl says, there are many who remember him. He was once a great man. There will never be any more great men in India. They will all, when they are boys, go whoring after strange gods, and they will become citizens—"fellow-citizens"— "illustrious fellow-citizens." What is it that the native papers call them?'

Wali Dad seemed to be in a very bad temper. Lalun looked out of the window and smiled into the dust-haze. I went away thinking about Khem Singh who had once made history with a thousand followers, and would have been a princeling but for the power of the Supreme Government aforesaid.

The Senior Captain Commanding Fort Amara was away on leave, but the Subaltern, his Deputy, had drifted down to the Club, where I found him and inquired of him whether it was really true that a political prisoner had been added to the attractions of the Fort. The Subaltern explained at great length, for this was the first time that

he had held Command of the Fort, and his glory lay
heavy upon him.

'Yes,' said he, 'a man was sent in to me about a week
ago from down the line—a thorough gentleman, whoever
he is. Of course I did all I could for him. He had his two
servants and some silver cooking-pots, and he looked for
all the world like a native officer. I called him Subadar
Sahib; just as well to be on the safe side, y'know. "Look
here, Subadar Sahib," I said, "you're handed over to my
authority, and I'm supposed to guard you. Now I don't
want to make your life hard, but you must make things
easy for me. All the Fort is at your disposal, from the
flagstaff to the dry ditch, and I shall be happy to entertain
you in any way I can, but you mustn't take advantage of
it. Give me your word that you won't try to escape, Subadar Sahib, and I'll give you my word that you shall have
no heavy guard put over you." I thought the best way of
getting at him was by going at him straight, y'know;
and it was, by Jove! The old man gave me his word, and
moved about the Fort as contented as a sick crow. He's
a rummy chap—always asking to be told where he is and
what the buildings about him are. I had to sign a slip of
blue paper when he turned up, acknowledging receipt of
his body and all that, and I'm responsible, y'know, that
he doesn't get away. Queer thing, though, looking after a
Johnnie old enough to be your grandfather, isn't it? Come
to the Fort one of these days and see him?'

For reasons which will appear, I never went to the Fort
while Khem Singh was then within its walls. I knew him
only as a grey head seen from Lalun's window—a grey
head and a harsh voice. But natives told me that, day by
day, as he looked upon the fair lands round Amara, his

memory came back to him and, with it, the old hatred against the Government that had been nearly effaced in far-off Burma. So he raged up and down in the west face of the Fort from morning till noon and from evening till the night, devising vain things in his heart, and croaking war-songs when Lalun sang on the City wall. As he grew more acquainted with the Subaltern he unburdened his old heart of some of the passions that had withered it. 'Sahib,' he used to say, tapping his stick against the parapet, 'when I was a young man I was one of twenty thousand horsemen who came out of the City and rode round the plain here. Sahib, I was the leader of a hundred, then of a thousand, then of five thousand, and now'—he pointed to his two servants. 'But from the beginning to to-day I would cut the throats of all the Sahibs in the land if I could. Hold me fast, Sahib, lest I get away and return to those who would follow me. I forgot them when I was in Burma, but now that I am in my own country again, I remember everything.'

'Do you remember that you have given me your Honour not to make your tendance a hard matter?' said the Subaltern.

'Yes, to you, only to you, Sahib,' said Khem Singh. 'To you because you are of a pleasant countenance. If my turn comes again, Sahib, I will not hang you nor cut your throat.'

'Thank you,' said the Subaltern gravely, as he looked along the line of guns that could pound the City to powder in half an hour. 'Let us go into our own quarters, Khem Singh. Come and talk with me after dinner.'

Khem Singh would sit on his own cushion at the Sub-altern's feet, drinking heavy, scented aniseed brandy in great gulps, and telling strange stories of Fort Amara, which had been a palace in the old days, of Begums and Ranees tortured to death—ay, in the very vaulted chamber that now served as a Mess-room; would tell stories of Sobraon that made the Subaltern's cheeks flush and tingle with pride of race, and of the Kuka rising from which so much was expected and the foreknowledge of which was shared by a hundred thousand souls. But he never told tales of '57 because, as he said, he was the Subaltern's guest, and '57 is a year that no man, Black or White, cares to speak of. Once only, when the aniseed brandy had slightly affected his head, he said: 'Sahib, speaking now of a matter which lay between Sobraon and the affair of the Kukas, it was ever a wonder to us that you stayed your hand at all, and that, having stayed it, you did not make the land one prison. Now I hear from without that you do great honour to all men of our country and by your own hands are destroying the Terror of your Name which is your strong rock and defence. This is a foolish thing. Will oil and water mix? Now in '57——'

'I was not born then, Subadar Singh,' said the Subaltern, and Khem Singh reeled to his quarters.

The Subaltern would tell me of these conversations at the Club, and my desire to see Khem Singh increased. But Wali Dad, sitting in the window-seat of the house on the City wall, said that it would be a cruel thing to do, and Lalun pretended that I preferred the society of a grizzled old Sikh to hers.

'Here is tobacco, here is talk, here are many friends and all the news of the City, and, above all, here is myself. I will tell you stories and sing you songs, and Wali Dad will talk his English nonsense in your ears. Is that worse than watching the caged animal yonder? Go to-morrow then, if you must, but to-day such and such an one will be here, and he will speak of wonderful things.'

It happened that To-morrow never came, and the warm heat of the latter Rains gave place to the chill of early October almost before I was aware of the flight of the year. The Captain Commanding the Fort returned from leave and took over charge of Khem Singh according to the laws of seniority. The Captain was not a nice man. He called all natives 'niggers,' which, besides being extreme bad form, shows gross ignorance.

'What's the use of telling off two Tommies to watch that old nigger?' said he.

'I fancy it soothes his vanity,' said the Subaltern. 'The men are ordered to keep well out of his way, but he takes them as a tribute to his importance, poor old wretch.'

'I won't have Line men taken off regular guards in this way. Put on a couple of Native Infantry.'

'Sikhs?' said the Subaltern, lifting his eyebrows.

'Sikhs, Pathans, Dogras—they're all alike, these black vermin,' and the Captain talked to Khem Singh in a manner which hurt that old gentleman's feelings. Fifteen years before, when he had been caught for the second time, every one looked upon him as a sort of tiger. He liked being regarded in this light. But he forgot that the world goes forward in fifteen years, and many Subalterns are promoted to Captaincies.

'The Captain-pig is in charge of the Fort?' said Khem Singh to his native guard every morning. And the native guard said: 'Yes, Subadar Sahib,' in deference to his age and his air of distinction; but they did not know who he was.

In those days the gathering in Lalun's little white room was always large and talked more than before.

'The Greeks,' said Wali Dad, who had been borrowing my books, 'the inhabitants of the city of Athens, where they were always hearing and telling some new thing, rigorously secluded their women—who were fools. Hence the glorious institution of the heterodox women—is it not?—who were amusing and *not* fools. All the Greek philosophers delighted in their company. Tell me, my friend, how it goes now in Greece and the other places upon the Continent of Europe. Are your women-folk also fools?'

'Wali Dad,' I said, 'you never speak to us about your women-folk and we never speak about ours to you. That is the bar between us.'

'Yes,' said Wali Dad, 'it is curious to think that our common meeting-place should be here, in the house of a common—how do you call *her*?' He pointed with the pipe-mouth to Lalun.

'Lalun is nothing but Lalun,' I said, and that was perfectly true. 'But if you took your place in the world, Wali Dad, and gave up dreaming dreams——'

'I might wear an English coat and trouser. I might be a leading Mohammedan pleader. I might be received even at the Commissioner's tennis-parties where the English stand on one side and the natives on the other, in order to promote social intercourse throughout the Empire. Heart's Heart,' said he to Lalun quickly, 'the Sahib says that I ought to quit you.'

'The Sahib is always talking stupid talk,' returned Lalun with a laugh. 'In this house I am a Queen and thou art a King. The Sahib'—she put her arms above her head and thought for a moment—'the Sahib shall be our Vizier—thine and mine, Wali Dad—because he has said that thou shouldst leave me.'

Wali Dad laughed immoderately, and I laughed too. 'Be it so,' said he. 'My friend, are you willing to take this lucrative Government appointment? Lalun, what shall his pay be?'

But Lalun began to sing, and for the rest of the time there was no hope of getting a sensible answer from her or Wali Dad. When the one stopped, the other began to quote Persian poetry with a triple pun in every other line. Some of it was not strictly proper, but it was all very funny, and it only came to an end when a fat person in black, with gold *pince-nez*, sent up his name to Lalun, and Wali Dad dragged me into the twinkling night to walk in a big rose-garden and talk heresies about Religion and Governments and a man's career in life.

The Mohurrum, the great mourning-festival of the Mohammedan, was close at hand, and the things that Wali Dad said about religious fanaticism would have secured his expulsion from the loosest-thinking Muslim sect. There were the rose-bushes round us, the stars above us, and from every quarter of the City came the boom of the big Mohurrum drums. You must know that the City is divided in fairly equal proportions between the Hindus and the Musulmans, and where both creeds belong to the fighting races, a big religious festival gives ample chance for trouble. When they can—that is to say, when the authorities are weak enough to allow it—the Hindus do their best to arrange some minor feast-day of their own in time to clash with the period of general mourning for the martyrs Hasan and Hussain, the heroes of the Mohurrum. Gilt and painted paper representations of their tombs are borne with shouting and wailing, music, torches, and yells, through the principal thoroughfares of the City; which fakements are called *tazias*. Their passage is rigorously laid down beforehand by the Police, and detachments of Police accompany each *tazia*, lest the Hindus should throw bricks at it and the peace of the Queen and the heads of Her loyal subjects should thereby be broken. Mohurrum time in a 'fighting' town means anxiety to all the officials, because, if a riot breaks out, the officials and not the rioters are held responsible. The former must foresee everything, and while not making their precautions ridiculously elaborate, must see that they are at least adequate.

'Listen to the drums!' said Wali Dad. 'That is the heart of the people—empty and making much noise. How, think you, will the Mohurrum go this year? I think that there will be trouble.'

He turned down a side-street and left me alone with the stars and a sleepy Police patrol. Then I went to bed and dreamed that Wali Dad had sacked the City and I was made Vizier, with Lalun's silver *huqa* for mark of office.

All day the Mohurrum drums beat in the City, and all day deputations of tearful Hindu gentlemen besieged the Deputy Commissioner with assurances that they would be murdered ere next dawning by the Mohammedans. 'Which,' said the Deputy Commissioner, in confidence to the Head of Police, 'is a pretty fair indication that the Hindus are going to make 'emselves unpleasant. I think we can arrange a little surprise for them. I have given the heads of both Creeds fair warning. If they choose to dis-regard it, so much the worse for them.'

There was a large gathering in Lalun's house that night, but of men that I had never seen before, if I except the fat gentleman in black with the gold *pince-nez*. Wali Dad lay in the window-seat, more bitterly scornful of his Faith and its manifestations than I had ever known him. Lalun's maid was very busy cutting up and mixing tobacco for the guests. We could hear the thunder of the drums as the processions accompanying each *tazia* marched to the central gathering-place in the plain out-side the City, preparatory to their triumphant re-entry and circuit within the walls. All the streets seemed ablaze with torches, and only Fort Amara was black and silent.

When the noise of the drums ceased, no one in the white room spoke for a time. 'The first *tazia* has moved off,' said Wali Dad, looking to the plain.

'That is very early,' said the man with the *pince-nez*. 'It is only half-past eight.' The company rose and departed.

'Some of them were men from Ladakh,' said Lalun, when the last had gone. 'They brought me brick-tea such as the Russians sell, and a tea-urn from Peshawer. Show me, now, how the English *Memsahibs* make tea.'

The brick-tea was abominable. When it was finished Wali Dad suggested going into the streets. 'I am nearly sure that there will be trouble to-night,' he said. 'All the City thinks so, and *Vox Populi* is *Vox Dei*, as the Babus say. Now I tell you that at the corner of the Padshahi Gate you will find my horse all this night if you want to go about and to see things. It is a most disgraceful exhib-ition. Where is the pleasure of saying "*Ya Hasan, Ya Hussain*" twenty thousand times in a night?'

All the processions—there were two-and-twenty of them—were now well within the City walls. The drums were beating afresh, the crowd were howling '*Ya Hasan! Ya Hussain!*' and beating their breasts, the brass bands were playing their loudest, and at every corner where space allowed, Mohammedan preachers were telling the lamentable story of the death of the Martyrs. It was impossible to move except with the crowd, for the streets were not more than twenty feet wide. In the Hindu quarters the shutters of all the shops were up and cross-barred. As the first *tazia*, a gorgeous erection ten feet high, was borne aloft on the shoulders of a score of stout men into the semidarkness of the Gully of the Horsemen, a brickbat crashed through its talc and tinsel sides.

'Into thy hands, O Lord!' murmured Wali Dad profanely, as a yell went up from behind, and a native officer of Police jammed his horse through the crowd. Another brickbat followed and the *tazia* staggered and swayed where it had stopped.

'Go on! In the name of the *Sirkar*, go forward!' shouted the Policeman; but there was an ugly cracking and splintering of shutters, and the crowd halted, with oaths and growlings, before the house whence the brickbat had been thrown.

Then, without any warning, broke the storm—not only in the Gully of the Horsemen, but in half-a-dozen other places. The *tazias* rocked like ships at sea, the long pole-torches dipped and rose round them while the men shouted: 'The Hindus are dishonouring the *tazias*! Strike! Strike! Into their temples for the Faith!' The six or eight Policemen with each *tazia* drew their batons, and struck as long as they could in the hope of forcing the mob forward, but they were overpowered, and as contingents of Hindus poured into the streets the fight became general. Half a mile away where the *tazias* were yet untouched the drums and the shrieks of '*Ya Hasan! Ya Hussain!*' continued, but not for long. The priests at the corners of the streets knocked the legs from the bedsteads that supported their pulpits and smote for the Faith, while stones fell from the silent houses upon friend and foe, and the packed streets bellowed: '*Din! Din! Din!*' A *tazia* caught fire, and was dropped for a flaming barrier between Hindu and Musulman at the corner of the Gully. Then the crowd surged forward, and Wali Dad drew me close to the stone pillar of a well.

'It was intended from the beginning!' he shouted in my ear, with more heat than blank unbelief should be guilty of. 'The bricks were carried up to the houses beforehand. These swine of Hindus! We shall be gutting kine in their temples to-night!'

Tazia after *tazia*, some burning, others torn to pieces, hurried past us and the mob with them, howling, shrieking, and striking at the house doors in their flight. At last we saw the reason of the rush. Hugonin, the Assistant District Superintendent of Police, a boy of twenty, had got together thirty constables and was forcing the crowd through the streets. His old grey Police-horse showed no sign of uneasiness as it was spurred breast-on into the crowd, and the long dog-whip with which he had armed himself was never still.

'They know we haven't enough Police to hold 'em,' he cried as he passed me, mopping a cut on his face. 'They *know* we haven't! Aren't any of the men from the Club coming down to help? Get on, you sons of burnt fathers!'

The dog-whip cracked across the writhing backs, and the constables smote afresh with baton and gun-butt. With these passed the lights and the shouting, and Wali Dad began to swear under his breath. From Fort Amara shot up a single rocket; then two side by side. It was the signal for troops.

Petitt, the Deputy Commissioner, covered with dust and sweat, but calm and gently smiling, cantered up the clean-swept street in rear of the main body of the rioters. 'No one killed yet,' he shouted. 'I'll keep 'em on the run till dawn! Don't let 'em halt, Hugonin! Trot 'em about till the troops come.'

The science of the defence lay solely in keeping the mob on the move. If they had breathing-space they would halt and fire a house, and then the work of restoring order would be more difficult, to say the least of it. Flames have the same effect on a crowd as blood has on a wild beast.

Word had reached the Club and men in evening-dress were beginning to show themselves and lend a hand in heading off and breaking up the shouting masses with stirrup-leathers, whips, or chance-found staves. They were not very often attacked, for the rioters had sense enough to know that the death of a European would not mean one hanging but many, and possibly the appearance of the thrice-dreaded Artillery. The clamour in the City redoubled. The Hindus had descended into the streets in real earnest and ere long the mob returned. It was a strange sight. There were no *tazias*—only their riven platforms—and there were no Police. Here and there a City dignitary, Hindu or Mohammedan, was vainly imploring his co-religionists to keep quiet and behave themselves—advice for which his white beard was pulled. Then a native officer of Police, unhorsed but still using his spurs with effect, would be borne along, warning all the crowd of the danger of insulting the Government. Everywhere men struck aimlessly with sticks, grasping each other by the throat, howling and foaming with rage, or beat with their bare hands on the doors of the houses.

'It is a lucky thing that they are fighting with natural weapons,' I said to Wali Dad, 'else we should have half the City killed.'

I turned as I spoke and looked at his face. His nostrils were distended, his eyes were fixed, and he was smiting himself softly on the breast. The crowd poured by with renewed riot—a gang of Musulmans hard pressed by some hundred Hindu fanatics. Wali Dad left my side with an oath, and shouting: '*Ya Hasan! Ya Hussain!*' plunged into the thick of the fight, where I lost sight of him.

I fled by a side alley to the Padshahi Gate where I found Wali Dad's horse, and thence rode to the Fort. Once outside the City wall, the tumult sank to a dull roar, very impressive under the stars and reflecting great credit on the fifty thousand angry able-bodied men who were making it. The troops who, at the Deputy Commissioner's instance, had been ordered to rendezvous quietly near the Fort, showed no signs of being impressed. Two companies of Native Infantry, a squadron of Native Cavalry, and a company of British Infantry were kicking their heels in the shadow of the east face, waiting for orders to march in. I am sorry to say that they were all pleased, unholily pleased, at the chance of what they called 'a little fun.' The senior officers, to be sure, grumbled at having been kept out of bed, and the English troops pretended to be sulky, but there was joy in the hearts of all the sub-alterns, and whispers ran up and down the line: 'No ball-cartridge—what a beastly shame!' 'D'you think the beggars will really stand up to us!' 'Hope I shall meet my moneylender there. I owe him more than I can afford.' 'Oh, they won't let us even unsheath swords.' 'Hurrah! Up goes the fourth rocket. Fall in, there!'

The Garrison Artillery, who to the last cherished a wild hope that they might be allowed to bombard the City at a hundred yards' range, lined the parapet above the east gateway and cheered themselves hoarse as the British Infantry doubled along the road to the main gate of the City. The Cavalry cantered on to the Padshahi Gate, and the Native Infantry marched slowly to the Gate of the Butchers. The surprise was intended to be of a distinctly unpleasant nature, and to come on top of the defeat of the Police, who had been just able to keep the Mohammedans from firing the houses of a few leading Hindus. The bulk of the riot lay in the north and north-west wards. The east and south-east were by this time dark and silent, and I rode hastily to Lalun's house, for I wished to tell her to send some one in search of Wali Dad. The house was unlighted, but the door was open, and I climbed upstairs in the darkness. One small lamp in the white room showed Lalun and her maid leaning half out of the window, breathing heavily and evidently pulling at something that refused to come.

'Thou art late—very late,' gasped Lalun without turn-ing her head. 'Help us now, O Fool, if thou hast not spent thy strength howling among the *tazias*. Pull! Nasiban and I can do no more! O Sahib, is it you? The Hindus have been hunting an old Mohammedan round the Ditch with clubs. If they find him again they will kill him. Help us to pull him up.'

I put my hands to the long red silk waist-cloth that was hanging out of the window, and we three pulled and pulled with all the strength at our command. There was something very heavy at the end, and it swore in an unknown tongue as it kicked against the City wall.

'Pull, oh, pull!' said Lalun at the last. A pair of brown hands grasped the window-sill and a venerable Mohammedan tumbled upon the floor, very much out of breath. His jaws were tied up, his turban had fallen over one eye, and he was dusty and angry.

Lalun hid her face in her hands for an instant and said something about Wali Dad that I could not catch.

Then, to my extreme gratification, she threw her arms round my neck and murmured pretty things. I was in no haste to stop her; and Nasiban, being a handmaiden of tact, turned to the big jewel-chest that stands in the corner of the white room and rummaged among the contents. The Mohammedan sat on the floor and glared.

'One service more, Sahib, since thou hast come so opportunely,' said Lalun. 'Wilt thou'—it is very nice to be thou-ed by Lalun—'take this old man across the City—the troops are everywhere, and they might hurt him for he is old—to the Kumharsen Gate? There I think he may find a carriage to take him to his house. He is a friend of mine, and thou art—more than a friend—therefore I ask this.'

Nasiban bent over the old man, tucked something into his belt, and I raised him up, and led him into the streets. In crossing from the east to the west of the City there was no chance of avoiding the troops and the crowd. Long before I reached the Gully of the Horsemen I heard the shouts of the British Infantry crying cheerily: 'Hutt, ye beggars! Hutt, ye devils! Get along! Go forward, there!' Then followed the ringing of rifle-butts and shrieks of pain. The troops were banging the bare toes of the mob with their gun-butts—for not a bayonet had been fixed. My companion mumbled and jabbered as we walked on until we were carried back by the crowd and had to force our way to the troops. I caught him by the wrist and felt a bangle there—the iron bangle of the Sikhs—but I had no suspicions, for Lalun had only ten minutes before put her arms round me. Thrice we were carried back by the crowd, and when we made our way past the British Infantry it was to meet the Sikh Cavalry driving another mob before them with the butts of their lances.

'What are these dogs?' said the old man.

'Sikhs of the Cavalry, Father,' I said, and we edged our way up the line of horses two abreast and found the Deputy Commissioner, his helmet smashed on his head, surrounded by a knot of men who had come down from the Club as amateur constables and had helped the Police mightily.

'We'll keep 'em on the run till dawn,' said Petitt. 'Who's your villainous friend?'

I had only time to say: 'The Protection of the *Sirkar*!' when a fresh crowd flying before the Native Infantry carried us a hundred yards nearer to the Kumharsen Gate, and Petitt was swept away like a shadow.

'I do not know—I cannot see—this is all new to me!' moaned my companion. 'How many troops are there in the City?'

'Perhaps five hundred,' I said.

'A lakh of men beaten by five hundred—and Sikhs among them! Surely, surely, I am an old man, but—the Kumharsen Gate is new. Who pulled down the stone lions? Where is the conduit? Sahib, I am a very old man, and, alas, I—I cannot stand.' He dropped in the shadow of the Kumharsen Gate where there was no disturbance. A fat gentleman wearing gold *pince-nez* came out of the darkness.

'You are most kind to bring my old friend,' he said suavely. 'He is a landholder of Akala. He should not be in a big City when there is religious excitement. But I have a carriage here. You are quite truly kind. Will you help me to put him into the carriage? It is very late.'

We bundled the old man into a hired victoria that stood close to the gate, and I turned back to the house on the City wall. The troops were driving the people to and fro, while the Police shouted, 'To your houses! Get to your houses!' and the dog-whip of the Assistant District Superintendent cracked remorselessly. Terror-stricken *bunnias* clung to the stirrups of the cavalry, crying that their houses had been robbed (which was a lie), and the burly Sikh horsemen patted them on the shoulder and bade them return to those houses lest a worse thing should happen. Parties of five or six British soldiers, joining arms, swept down the side-gullies, their rifles on their backs, stamping, with shouting and song, upon the toes of Hindu and Musulman. Never was religious enthusiasm more systematically squashed; and never were poor breakers of the peace more utterly weary and footsore. They were routed out of holes and corners, from behind well-pillars, and byres, and bidden to go to their houses.

If they had no houses to go to, so much the worse for their toes.

On returning to Lalun's door I stumbled over a man at the threshold. He was sobbing hysterically and his arms flapped like the wings of a goose. It was Wali Dad, Agnostic and Unbeliever, shoeless, turbanless, and frothing at the mouth, the flesh on his chest bruised and bleeding from the vehemence with which he had smitten himself. A broken torch-handle lay by his side, and his quivering lips murmured, '*Ya Hasan! Ya Hussain!*' as I stooped over him. I pushed him a few steps up the staircase, threw a pebble at Lalun's City window and hurried home.

Most of the streets were very still, and the cold wind that comes before the dawn whistled down them. In the centre of the Square of the Mosque a man was bending over a corpse. The skull had been smashed in by gun-butt or bamboo-stave.

'It is expedient that one man should die for the people,' said Petitt grimly, raising the shapeless head. 'These brutes were beginning to show their teeth too much.'

And from afar we could hear the soldiers singing 'Two Lovely Black Eyes,' as they drove the remnant of the rioters within doors.

Of course you can guess what happened? I was not so clever. When the news went abroad that Khem Singh had escaped from the Fort, I did not, since I was then living this story, not writing it, connect myself, or Lalun, or the fat gentleman of the gold *pince-nez*, with his disappearance. Nor did it strike me that Wali Dad was the man who should have convoyed him across the City, or that Lalun's arms round my neck were put there to hide the money that Nasiban gave to Khem Singh, and that Lalun had used me and my white face as even a better safeguard than Wali Dad, who proved himself so untrustworthy. All that I knew at the time was that, when Fort Amara was taken up with the riots, Khem Singh profited by the confusion to get away, and that his two Sikh guards also escaped.

But later on I received full enlightenment; and so did Khem Singh. He fled to those who knew him in the old days, but many of them were dead and more were changed, and all knew something of the Wrath of the Government. He went to the young men, but the glamour of his name had passed away, and they were entering native regiments or Government offices, and Khem Singh could give them neither pension, decorations, nor influence—nothing but a glorious death with their back to the mouth of a gun. He wrote letters and made promises, and the letters fell into bad hands, and a wholly insignificant subordinate officer of Police tracked them down and gained promotion thereby. Moreover, Khem Singh was old, and aniseed brandy was scarce, and he had left his silver cooking-pots in Fort Amara with his nice warm bedding, and the gentleman with the gold *pince-nez* was told by Those who had employed him that Khem Singh as a popular leader was not worth the money paid.

'Great is the mercy of these fools of English!' said Khem Singh when the situation was put before him. 'I will go back to Fort Amara of my own free will and gain honour. Give me good clothes to return in.'

So, at his own time, Khem Singh knocked at the

wicket-gate of the Fort and walked to the Captain and the Subaltern, who were nearly grey-headed on account of correspondence that daily arrived from Simla marked 'Private.'

'I have come back, Captain Sahib,' said Khem Singh. 'Put no more guards over me. It is no good out yonder.'

A week later I saw him for the first time to my knowledge, and he made as though there were an understanding between us.

'It was well done, Sahib,' said he, 'and greatly I admired your astuteness in thus boldly facing the troops when I, whom they would have doubtless torn to pieces, was with you. Now there is a man in Fort Ooltagarh whom a bold man could with ease help to escape. This is the position of the Fort as I draw it on the sand—'

But I was thinking how I had become Lalun's Vizier after all.

'BREAD UPON THE WATERS'

If you remember my improper friend Brugglesmith, you will also bear in mind his friend McPhee, Chief Engineer of the *Breslau*, whose dingey Brugglesmith tried to steal. His apologies for the performances of Brugglesmith may one day be told in their proper place: the tale before us concerns McPhee. He was never a racing engineer, and took special pride in saying as much before the Liverpool men; but he had a thirty-two years' knowledge of machinery and the humours of ships. One side of his face had been wrecked through the bursting of a water-gauge in the days when men knew less than they do now; and his nose rose grandly out of the wreck, like a club in a public riot. There were cuts and lumps on his head, and he would guide your forefinger through his short iron-grey hair and tell you how he had come by his trade-marks. He owned all sorts of certificates of extra-competency, and at the bottom of his cabin chest of drawers, where he kept the photograph of his wife, were two or three Royal Humane Society medals for saving lives at sea. Professionally—it was different when crazy steerage-passengers jumped overboard—professionally, McPhee does not approve of saving life at sea, and he has often told me that a new hell is awaiting stokers and trimmers who sign for a strong man's pay and fall sick the second day out. He believes in throwing boots at fourth and fifth engineers when they wake him up at night with word that a bearing is red-hot, all because a lamp's glare is reflected red from the twirling metal. He believes that there are only two poets in the world: one being Robert Burns of course, and the other Gerald Massey. When he has time for novels he reads Wilkie Collins and Charles Reade— chiefly the latter—and knows whole pages of *Hard Cash* by heart. In the saloon his table is next to the captain's, and he drinks only water while his engines work.

He was good to me when we first met, because I did not ask questions, and believed in Charles Reade as a most shamefully neglected author. Later he approved of my writings to the extent of one pamphlet of twenty-four pages that I wrote for Holdock, Steiner, and Chase, owners of the line, when they bought some ventilating patent and fitted it to the cabins of the *Breslau*, *Spandau*, and *Koltzau*. The purser of the *Breslau* recommended me to Holdock's secretary for the job; and Holdock, who is a Wesleyan Methodist, invited me to his house, and gave me dinner with the governess when the others had finished, and placed the plans and specifications in my hand, and I wrote the pamphlet that same afternoon. It was called 'Comfort in the Cabin,' and brought me seven pound ten, cash down—an important sum of money in those days; and the governess, who was teaching Master John Holdock his scales, told me that Mrs. Holdock had told her to keep an eye on me, in case I went away with coats from the hat-rack. McPhee liked that pamphlet enormously, for it was composed in the Bouverie-Byzantine style, with baroque and rococo embellishments; and afterward he introduced me to Mrs. McPhee, who succeeded Dinah in my heart; for Dinah was half a world away, and it is wholesome and antiseptic to love such a woman as Janet McPhee. They lived in a little twelve-pound house, close to the shipping. When McPhee was away Mrs. McPhee read the Lloyd's column in the papers, and called on the wives of senior engineers of equal social standing. Once or twice, too, Mrs. Holdock visited Mrs. McPhee in a brougham with celluloid fittings, and I have reason to believe that, after she had played owner's wife long enough, they talked scandal. The Holdocks lived in an old-fashioned house with a big brick garden not a mile from the McPhees, for they stayed by their money as their money stayed by them; and in summer you met their brougham solemnly junketing by Theydon Bois or Loughton. But I was Mrs. McPhee's friend, for she allowed me to convoy her westward, sometimes, to theatres, where she sobbed or laughed or shivered with a simple heart; and she introduced me to a new world of doctors' wives, captains' wives, and engineers' wives, whose whole talk and thought centred in and about ships and lines of ships you have never heard of. There were sailing-ships, with stewards and mahogany and maple saloons, trading to Australia, taking cargoes of consumptives and hopeless drunkards for whom a sea-voyage was recommended; there were frowzy little West African boats, full of rats and cockroaches, where men died anywhere but in their bunks; there were Brazilian boats whose cabins could be hired for merchandise that went out loaded nearly awash; there were Zanzibar and Mauritius steamers, and wonderful reconstructed boats that plied to the other side of Borneo. These were loved and known, for they earned our bread and a little butter, and we despised the big Atlantic boats, and made fun of the P. & O. and Orient liners, and swore by our respected owners—Wesleyan, Baptist or Presbyterian, as the case might be.

I had only just come back to England when Mrs. McPhee invited me to dinner at three o'clock in the afternoon, and the notepaper was almost bridal in its scented creaminess. When I reached the house I saw that there were new curtains in the window that must have cost forty-five shillings a pair; and as Mrs. McPhee drew me into the little marble-paper hall, she looked at me keenly, and cried:

'Have ye not heard? What d'ye think o' the hat-rack?'

Now, that hat-rack was oak—thirty shillings at least. McPhee came downstairs with a sober foot—he steps as lightly as a cat, for all his weight, when he is at sea—and shook hands in a new and awful manner—a parody of old Holdock's style when he says good-bye to his skippers. I perceived at once that a legacy had come to him, but I held my peace, though Mrs. McPhee begged me every thirty seconds to eat a great deal and say nothing. It was rather a mad sort of meal, because McPhee and his wife took hold of hands like little children (they always do after voyages), and nodded and winked and choked and gurgled, and hardly ate a mouthful.

A female servant came in and waited; though Mrs. McPhee had told me time and again that she would thank no one to do her housework while she had her health. But this was a servant with a cap, and I saw Mrs. McPhee swell and swell under her *garance*-coloured gown. There is no small free-board to Janet McPhee, nor is *garance* any subdued tint; and with all this unexplained pride and glory in the air I felt like watching fireworks without knowing the festival. When the maid had removed the cloth she brought a pineapple that would have cost half a guinea at that season (only McPhee has his own way of getting such things), and a Canton china bowl of dried lichis, and a glass plate of preserved ginger, and a small jar of sacred and imperial chow-chow that perfumed the room. McPhee gets it from a Dutchman in Java, and I think he doctors it with liqueurs. But the crown of the feast was some Madeira of the kind you can only come by if you know the wine and the man. A little maize-wrapped fig of clotted Madeira cigars went with the wine, and the rest was a pale-blue smoky silence; Janet, in her splendour, smiling on us two, and patting McPhee's hand.

'We'll drink,' said McPhee slowly, rubbing his chin, 'to the eternal damnation o' Holdock, Steiner, and Chase.'

Of course I answered 'Amen,' though I had made seven pound ten shillings out of the firm. McPhee's enemies were mine, and I was drinking his Madeira.

'Ye've heard nothing?' said Janet. 'Not a word, not a whisper?'

'Not a word, nor a whisper. On my word, I have not.'

'Tell him, Mac,' said she; and that is another proof of Janet's goodness and wifely love. A smaller woman would have babbled first, but Janet is five feet nine in her stockings.

'We're rich,' said McPhee. I shook hands all round.

'We're damned rich,' he added. I shook hands all round a second time.

'I'll go to sea no more—unless—there's no sayin'—a private yacht, maybe—wi' a small an' handy auxiliary.'

'It's not enough for *that*,' said Janet. 'We're fair rich—well-to-do, but no more. A new gown for church, and one for the theatre. We'll have it made west.'

'How much is it?' I asked.

'Twenty-five thousand pounds.' I drew a long breath. 'An' I've been earnin' twenty-five an' twenty pound a month!' The last words came away with a roar, as though the wide world was conspiring to beat him down.

'All this time I'm waiting,' I said. 'I know nothing since last September. Was it left you?'

They laughed aloud together. 'It was left,' said McPhee, choking. 'Ou, ay, it was left. That's vara good. Of course it was left. Janet, d'ye note that? It was left. Now if you'd put *that* in your pamphlet it would have been vara jocose. It *was* left.' He slapped his thigh and roared till the wine quivered in the decanter.

The Scotch are a great people, but they are apt to hang over a joke too long, particularly when no one can see the point but themselves.

'When I rewrite my pamphlet I'll put it in, McPhee. Only I must know something more first.'

McPhee thought for the length of half a cigar, while Janet caught my eye and led it round the room to one new thing after another—the new vine-pattern carpet, the new chiming rustic clock between the models of the Colombo outrigger-boats, the new inlaid sideboard with a purple cut-glass flower-stand, the fender of gilt and brass, and last, the new black-and-gold piano.

'In October o' last year the Board sacked me,' began McPhee. 'In October o' last year the *Breslau* came in for winter overhaul. She'd been runnin' eight months—two hunder an' forty days—an' I was three days makin' up my indents, when she went to dry-dock. All told, mark you, it was this side o' three hunder pound—to be preceese, two hunder an' eighty-six pound four shillings. There's not another man could ha' nursed the *Breslau* for eight months to that tune. Never again—never again! They may send their boats to the bottom, for aught I care.'

'There's no need,' said Janet softly. 'We're done wi' Holdock, Steiner, and Chase.'

'It's irritatin', Janet, it's just irritatin'. I ha' been justified from first to last, as the world knows, but—but I canna' forgie 'em. Ay, wisdom is justified o' her children; an' any other man than me wad ha' made the indent eight hunder. Hay was our skipper—ye'll have met him. They shifted him to the *Torgau*, an' bade me wait for the *Breslau* under young Bannister. Ye'll obsairve there'd been a new election on the Board. I heard the shares were sellin' hither an' yon, an' the major part of the Board was new to me. The old Board would ne'er ha' done it. They trusted me. But the new Board was all for reorganisation. Young Steiner—Steiner's son—the Jew, was at the bottom of it, an' they did not think it worth their while to send me word. The first *I* knew—an' I was Chief Engineer—was the notice of the Line's winter sailin's, and the *Breslau* timed for sixteen days between port an' port! Sixteen days, man! She's a good boat, but eighteen is her summer time, mark you. Sixteen was sheer flytin', kitin' nonsense, an' so I told young Bannister.

'"We've got to make it," he said. "Ye should not ha' sent in a three hunder pound indent."

'"Do they look for their boats to be run on air?" I said. "The Board is daft."

"'E'en tell 'em so," he says. "I'm a married man, an' my fourth's on the ways now, she says.'"

'A boy—wi' red hair,' Janet put in. Her own hair is the splendid red-gold that goes with a creamy complexion.

'My word, I was an angry man that day! Forbye I was fond o' the old *Breslau*, I look for a little consideration from the Board after twenty years' service. There was Board meetin' on Wednesday; an' I sat overnight in the engine-room, takin' figures to support my case. Well, I put it fair and square before them all. "Gentlemen," I said, "I've run the *Breslau* eight seasons, an' I believe there's no fault to find wi' my wark. But if ye haud to this"—I waggled the advertisement at 'em—"this that I've never heard of till I read it at breakfast, I do assure you on my professional reputation, she can never do it. That is to say, she can for a while, but at a risk no thinkin' man would run."

"'What the deil d'ye suppose we pass your indent for?" says old Holdock. "Man, we're spendin' money like watter."

"'I'll leave it in the Board's hands," I said, "if two hunder an' eighty-seven pound is anything beyond right and reason for eight months." I might ha' saved my breath, for the Board was new since the last election, an' there they sat, the damned deevidend-huntin' ship-chandlers, deaf as the adders o' Scripture.

"'We must keep faith wi' the public," said young Steiner.

"'Keep faith wi' the *Breslau* then," I said. "She's served you well, an' your father before you. She'll need her bottom restiffenin', an' new bed-plates, an' turnin' out the forward boilers, an' re-borin' all three cylinders, an' refacin' all guides, to begin with. It's a three months' job."

"'Because one employé is afraid?' says young Steiner. "Maybe a piano in the Chief Engineer's cabin would be more to the point."

'I crushed my cap in my hands, an' thanked God we'd no bairns an' a bit put by.

"'Understand, gentlemen,' I said. "If the *Breslau* is made a sixteen-day boat, ye'll find another engineer."

"'Bannister makes no objection,' said Holdock.

"'I'm speakin' for myself,' I said. "Bannister has bairns." An' then I lost my temper. "Ye can run her into Hell an' out again if ye pay pilotage," I said, "but ye run without me."

"'That's insolence,' said young Steiner.

"'At your pleasure,' I said, turnin' to go.

"'Ye can consider yourself dismissed. We must preserve discipline among our employés,' said old Holdock, an' he looked round to see that the Board was with him. They knew nothin'—God forgie 'em—an' they nodded me out o' the Line after twenty years—after twenty years.

'I went out an' sat down by the hall porter to get my wits again. I'm thinkin' I swore at the Board. Then auld McRimmon—o' McNaughton and McRimmon—came oot o' his office, that's on the same floor, an' looked at me, proppin' up one eyelid wi' his forefinger. Ye know they call him the Blind Deevil, forbye he's onythin' but blind, an' no deevil in his dealin's wi' me—McRimmon o' the Black Bird Line.

"'What's here, Mister McPhee?' said he.

'I was past prayin' for by then. "A Chief Engineer sacked after twenty years' service because he'll not risk the *Breslau* on the new timin', an' be damned to ye, McRimmon," I said.

'The auld man sucked in his lips an' whistled. "Ah," said he, "the new timin'. I see!" He doddered into the Board-room I'd just left, an' the Dandie-dog that is just his blind man's leader stayed wi' me. *That* was providential. In a minute he was back again. "Ye've cast your bread on the watter, McPhee, an' be damned to you," he says. "Whaur's my dog? My word, is he on your knee? What garred ye curse your Board, McPhee? It's expensive."

'"They'll pay more for the *Breslau*," I said. "Get off my knee, ye smotherin' beastie."

'"Bearin's hot, eh?" said McRimmon. "It's thirty year since a man daur curse me to my face. Time was I'd ha' cast ye doon the stairway for that."

'"Forgie's all!" I said. He was wearin' to eighty, as I knew. "I was wrong, McRimmon; but when a man's shown the door for doin' his plain duty he's not always ceevil."

'"So I hear," says McRimmon. "Ha' ye any objection to a tramp freighter? It's only fifteen a month, but they say the Blind Deevil feeds a man better than others. She's my *Kite*. Come ben. Ye can thank Dandie, here. I'm no used to thanks. An' noo," says he, "what possessed ye to throw up your berth wi' Holdock?"

'"The new timin'," said I. "The *Breslau* will not stand it."

'"Hoot, oot," said he. "Ye might ha' crammed her a little—enough to show ye were drivin' her—an' brought her in twa days behind. What's easier than to say ye slowed for bearin's, eh? All my men do it, and—I believe 'em.'

"'McRimmon,' says I, 'what's her virginity to a lassie?'

'He puckered his dry face an' twisted in his chair. "The warld an' a',' says he. "My God, the vara warld an' a'! But what ha' you or me to do wi' virginity, this late along?'

"'This,' I said. 'There's just one thing that each one of us in his trade or profession will *not* do for ony consideration whatever. If I run to time I run to time, barrin' always the risks o' the high seas. Less than that, under God, I have not done. More than that, by God, I will not do! There's no trick o' the trade I'm not acquaint wi'—'

"'So I've heard,' says McRimmon, dry as a biscuit.

"'But yon matter o' fair runnin's just my Shekinah, ye'll understand. I daurna tamper wi' *that*. Nursing weak engines is fair craftsmanship; but what the Board ask is cheatin', wi' the risk o' manslaughter addeetional. Ye'll note I know my business.'

'There was some more talk, an' next week I went aboard the *Kite*, twenty-five hunder ton, ordinary compound, a Black Bird tramp. The deeper she rode, the better she'd steam. I've snapped as much as nine out of her, but eight point three was her fair normal. Good food forward an' better aft, all indents passed wi'out marginal remarks, the best coal, new donkeys, and good crews. There was nothin' the old man would not do, except paint. That was his deeeficulty. Ye could no more draw paint than his last teeth from him. He'd come down to dock, an' his boats a scandal all along the watter, an' he'd whine an' cry an' say they looked all he could desire.

Every owner has his *non plus ultra*, I've obsairved. Paint was McRimmon's. But you could get round his engines without riskin' your life, an', for all his blindness, I've seen him reject five flawed intermediates, one after the other, on a nod from me; an' his cattle-fittin's were guaranteed for North Atlantic winter weather. Ye ken what *that* means? McRimmon an' the Black Bird Line, God bless him!

'Oh, I forgot to say she would lie down an' fill her forward deck green, an' snore away into a twenty-knot gale forty-five to the minute, three an' a half knots an hour, the engines runnin' sweet an' true as a bairn breathin' in its sleep. Bell was skipper; an' forbye there's no love lost between crews an' owners, we were fond o' the auld Blind Deevil an' his dog, an' I'm thinkin' he liked us. He was worth the windy side o' twa million sterlin', an' no friend to his own blood-kin. Money's an awfu' thing—overmuch—for a lonely man.

'I'd taken her out twice, there an' back again, when word came o' the *Breslau*'s breakdown, just as I prophesied. Calder was her engineer—he's not fit to run a tug down the Solent—and he fairly lifted the engines off the bed-plates, an' they fell down in heaps, by what I heard. So she filled from the after-stuffin'-box to the after-bulkhead, an' lay star-gazing, with seventy-nine squealin' passengers in the saloon, till the *Camaralzaman* o' Ramsey and Gold's Carthagena Line gave her a tow to the tune o' five thousand seven hunder an' forty pound, wi' costs in the Admiralty Court. She was helpless, ye'll understand, an' in no case to meet ony weather. Five thousand seven hunder an' forty pounds, *with* costs, an' exclusive o' new engines! They'd ha' done better to ha' kept me—on the old timin'.

'But, even so, the new Board were all for retrench-ment. Young Steiner, the Jew, was at the bottom of it. They sacked men right an' left that would not eat the dirt the Board gave 'em. They cut down repairs; they fed crews wi' leavin's and scrapin's; and, reversin' McRim-mon's practice, they hid their defeeciencies wi' paint an' cheap gildin'. *Quem Deus vult perrdere prrius dementat*, ye remember.

'In January we went to dry-dock, an' in the next dock lay the *Grotkau*, their big freighter that was the *Dolabella* o' Piegan, Piegan, and Walsh's Line in '84—a Clyde-built iron boat, a flat-bottomed, pigeon-breasted, under-engined, bull-nosed bitch of a five thousand ton freighter, that would neither steer, nor steam, nor stop when ye asked her. Whiles she'd attend to her helm, whiles she'd take charge, whiles she'd wait to scratch herself, an' whiles she'd buttock into a dockhead. But Holdock and Steiner had bought her cheap, and painted her all over like the Hoor o' Babylon, an' we called her the *Hoor* for short.' (By the way, McPhee kept to that name through-out the rest of his tale; so you must read accordingly.) 'I went to see young Bannister—he had to take what the Board gave him, an' he an' Calder were shifted together from the *Breslau* to this abortion—an' talkin' to him I went into the dock under her. Her plates were pitted till the men that were paint, paint, paintin' her laughed at it. But the warst was at the last. She'd a great clumsy iron nineteen-foot Thresher propeller—Aitcheson designed the *Kite*'s—and just on the tail o' the shaft, before the

143

boss, was a red weepin' crack ye could ha' put a penknife to. Man, it was an awful crack!

"'When d'ye ship a new tail-shaft?' I said to Bannister.

'He knew what I meant. "Oh, yon's a superfeecial flaw," says he, not lookin' at me.

"'Superfeecial Gehenna!' I said. "Ye'll not take her oot wi' a solution o' continuity that like."

"'They'll putty it up this evening,' he said. "I'm a married man, an'—ye used to know the Board."

'I e'en said what was gie'd me in that hour. Ye know how a dry-dock echoes. I saw young Steiner standin' listenin' above me, an', man, he used language provocative of a breach o' the peace. I was a spy and a disgraced employé, an' a corrupter o' young Bannister's morals, an' he'd prosecute me for libel. He went away when I ran up the steps—I'd ha' thrown him into the dock if I'd caught him—an' there I met McRimmon, wi' Dandie pullin' on the chain, guidin' the auld man among the railway lines.

"'McPhee,' said he, "ye're no paid to fight Holdock, Steiner, Chase, and Company, Limited, when ye meet. What's wrong between you?'

"'No more than a tail-shaft rotten as a kail-stump. For ony sakes go and look, McRimmon. It's a comedietta.'

"'I'm feared o' yon conversational Hebrew," said he. "Whaur's the flaw, an' what like?'

"'A seven-inch crack just behind the boss. There's no power on earth will fend it just jarrin' off.'

"'When?'

"'That's beyon' my knowledge," I said.

"'So it is; so it is," said McRimmon. "We've all oor leemitations. Ye're certain it was a crack?'

"'Man, it's a crevasse," I said, for there were no words

to describe the magnitude of it. "An' young Bannister's sayin' it's no more than a superfeecial flaw!"

"'Weel, I tak' it oor business is to mind oor business. If ye've ony friends aboard her, McPhee, why not bid them to a bit dinner at Radley's?"

"'I was thinkin' o' tea in the cuddy," I said. "Engineers o' tramp freighters cannot afford hotel prices."

"'Na! na!" says the auld man, whimperin'. "Not the cuddy. They'll laugh at my *Kite*, for she's no plastered with paint like the *Hoor*. Bid them to Radley's, McPhee, an' send me the bill. Thank Dandie here, man. I'm no used to thanks." Then he turned him round. (I was just thinkin' the vara same thing.)

"'Mister McPhee," said he, "this is *not* senile dementia."

"'Preserve's!" I said, clean jumped oot o' mysel'. "I was but thinkin' you're fey, McRimmon."

'Dod, the auld deevil laughed till he nigh sat down on Dandie. "Send me the bill," says he. "I'm lang past champagne, but tell me how it tastes the morn."

'Bell and I bid young Bannister and Calder to dinner at Radley's. They'll have no laughin' an' singin' there, but we took a private room—like yacht-owners fra' Cowes.'

McPhee grinned all over, and lay back to think.

'And then?' said I.

'We were no drunk in ony preceese sense o' the word, but Radley's showed me the dead men. There were six magnums o' dry champagne an' maybe a bottle o' whisky.'

'Do you mean to tell me that you four got away with a magnum and a half apiece, besides whisky?' I demanded.

McPhee looked down upon me from between his shoulders with toleration.

'Man, we were not settin' down to drink,' he said. 'They no more than made us wutty. To be sure, young Bannister laid his head on the table an' greeted like a bairn, an' Calder was all for callin' on Steiner at two in the morn' an' painting him galley-green; but they'd been drinkin' the afternoon. Lord, how they twa cursed the Board, an' the *Grotkau*, an' the tailshaft, an' the engines, an' a'! They didna talk o' superfeecial flaws that night. I mind young Bannister an' Calder shakin' hands on a bond to be revenged on the Board at ony reasonable cost this side o' losing their certificates. Now mark ye how false economy ruins business. The Board fed them like swine (I have good reason to know it), an' I've obsairved wi' my ain people that if ye touch his stomach ye wauken the deil in a Scot. Men will tak' a dredger across the Atlantic if they're well fed, and fetch her somewhere on the broadside o' the Americas; but bad food's bad service the warld over.

'The bill went to McRimmon, an' he said no more to me till the week-end, when I was at him for more paint, for we'd heard the *Kite* was chartered Liverpool-side.

'"Bide whaur ye're put," said the Blind Deevil. "Man, do ye wash in champagne? The *Kite*'s no leavin' here till I gie the order, an'—how am I to waste paint on her, wi' the *Lammergeyer* docked for who knows how long, an' a'!"

'She was our big freighter—McIntyre was engineer—an' I knew she'd come from overhaul not three months. That morn I met McRimmon's head-clerk—ye'll not know him—fair bitin' his nails off wi' mortification.

'"The auld man's gone gyte," says he. "He's with-drawn the *Lammergeyer*."

'"Maybe he has reasons," says I.

'"Reasons! He's daft!"

'"He'll no be daft till he begins to paint," I said.

'"That's just what he's done—and South American freights higher than we'll live to see them again. He's laid her up to paint her—to paint her—to paint her!" says the little clerk, dancin' like a hen on a hot plate. "Five thousand ton o' potential freight rottin' in dry-dock, man; an' he dolin' the paint out in quarter-pound tins, for it cuts him to the heart, mad though he is. An' the *Grotkau*— the *Grotkau* of all conceivable bottoms—soaking up every pound that should be ours at Liverpool!"

'I was staggered wi' this folly—considerin' the dinner at Radley's in connection wi' the same.

'"Ye may well stare, McPhee," says the head-clerk. "There's engines, an' rollin' stock, an' iron bridges—d'ye know what freights are noo?—an' pianos, an' millinery, an' fancy Brazil cargo o' every species pourin' into the *Grotkau*—the *Grotkau* o' the Jerusalem firm—and the *Lammergeyer*'s bein' painted!"

'Losh, I thought he'd drop dead wi' the fits.

'I could say no more than "Obey orders, if ye break owners," but on the *Kite* we believed McRimmon was mad; an' McIntyre of the *Lammergeyer* was for lockin' him up by some patent legal process he'd found in a book o' maritime law. An' a' that week South American freights rose an' rose. It was sinfu'!

'Syne Bell got orders to tak' the *Kite* round to Liver-pool in water-ballast, and McRimmon came to bid's good-bye, yammerin' an' whinin' o'er the acres o' paint he'd lavished on the *Lammergeyer*.

"'I look to you to retrieve it," says he. "I look to you to reimburse me! 'Fore God, why are ye not cast off? Are ye dawdlin' in dock for a purpose?"

"'What odds, McRimmon?" says Bell. "We'll be a day behind the fair at Liverpool. The *Grotkau*'s got all the freight that might ha' been ours an' the *Lammergeyer*'s." McRimmon laughed an' chuckled—the pairfect eemage o' senile dementia. Ye ken his eyebrows wark up an' down like a gorilla's.

"'Ye're under sealed orders," said he, tee-heein' an' scratchin' himself. "Yon's they—to be opened *seriatim*."

'Says Bell, shufflin' the envelopes when the auld man had gone ashore: "We're to creep round a' the south coast, standin' in for orders—this weather, too. There's no question o' his lunacy now."

'Well, we buttocked the auld *Kite* along—vara bad weather we made—standin' in alongside for telegraphic orders, which are the curse o' skippers. Syne we made over to Holyhead, an' Bell opened the last envelope for the last instructions. I was wi' him in the cuddy, an' he threw it over to me, cryin': "Did ye ever know the like, Mac?"

'I'll no say what McRimmon had written, but he was far from mad. There was a sou'-wester brewin' when we made the mouth o' the Mersey, a bitter cold morn wi' a grey-green sea and a grey-green sky—Liverpool weather, as they say; an' there we lay choppin', an' the men swore. Ye canna keep secrets aboard ship. They thought McRimmon was mad, too.

'Syne we saw the *Grotkau* rollin' oot on the top o'

flood, deep an' double deep, wi' her new-painted funnel an' her new-painted boats an' a'. She looked her name, an', moreover, she coughed like it. Calder tauld me at Radley's what ailed his engines, but my own ear would ha' told me twa mile awa', by the beat o' them. Round we came, plungin' an' squatterin' in her wake, an' the wind cut *wi'* good promise o' more to come. By six it blew hard but clear, an' before the middle watch it was a sou'wester in airnest.

"'She'll edge into Ireland, this gait,' says Bell. I was with him on the bridge, watchin' the *Grotkau*'s port light. Ye canna see green so far as red, or we'd ha' kept to lee-ward. We'd no passengers to consider, an' (all eyes being on the *Grotkau*) we fair walked into a liner rampin' home to Liverpool. Or, to be preceese, Bell no more than twisted the *Kite* oot from under her bows, and there was a little damnin' betwix' the twa bridges. Noo a passenger'—McPhee regarded me benignantly—'wad ha' told the papers that as soon as he got to the Customs. We stuck to the *Grotkau*'s tail that night an' the next twa days—she slowed down to five knots by my reckonin'— and we lapped along the weary way to the Fastnet.'

'But you don't go by the Fastnet to get to any South American port, do you?' I said.

'*We* do not. We prefer to go as direct as may be. But we were followin' the *Grotkau*, an' she'd no walk into that gale for ony consideration. Knowin' what I did to her discredit, I couldna' blame young Bannister. It was warkin' up to a North Atlantic winter gale, snow an' sleet an' a perishin' wind. Eh, it was like the Deil walkin' abroad o' the surface o' the deep, whuppin' off the top o' the waves before he made up his mind. They'd bore up against it so far, but the minute she was clear o' the Skelligs she fair tucked up her skirts an' ran for it by Dunmore Head. Wow, she rolled!

"'She'll be makin' Smerwick," says Bell.

"'She'd ha' tried for Ventry by noo if she meant that," I said.

"'They'll roll the funnel oot o' her, this gait," says Bell. "Why canna Bannister keep her head to sea?"

"'It's the tail-shaft. Ony rollin's better than pitchin' wi' superfeecial cracks in the tail-shaft. Calder knows that much," I said.

"'It's ill wark retreevin' steamers this weather," said Bell. His beard and whiskers were frozen to his oilskin, an' the spray was white on the weather side of him. Pairfect North Atlantic winter weather!

'One by one the sea raxed away our three boats, an' the davits were crumpled like rams' horns.

"'Yon's bad," said Bell, at the last. "Ye canna pass a hawser wi'oot a boat." Bell was a vara judeecious man—for an Aberdonian.

'I'm not one that fashes himself for eventualities outside the engine-room, so I e'en slipped down betwixt waves to see how the *Kite* fared. Man, she's the best geared boat of her class that ever left the Clyde! Kinloch, my second, knew her as well as I did. I found him dryin' his socks on the mainsteam, an' combin' his whiskers wi' the comb Janet gied me last year, for the warld an' a' as though we were in port. I tried the feed, speered into the stoke-hole, thumbed all bearin's, spat on the thrust for luck, gied 'em my blessin', an' took Kinloch's socks before I went up to the bridge again.

'Then Bell handed me the wheel, an' went below to

warm himself. When he came up my gloves were frozen to the spokes, an' the ice clicked over my eyelids. Pairfect North Atlantic winter weather, as I was sayin'.

'The gale blew out by night, but we lay in smotherin' cross-seas that made the auld *Kite* chatter from stem to stern. I slowed to thirty-four, I mind—no, thirty-seven. There was a long swell the morn, an' the *Grotkau* was headin' into it west awa'.

'"She'll win to Rio yet, tail-shaft or no tail-shaft," says Bell.

'"Last night shook her," I said. "She'll jar it off yet, mark my word."

'We were then, maybe, a hunder and fifty mile west-sou'west o' Slyne Head, by dead reckonin'. Next day we made a hunder an' thirty—ye'll note we were not racin' boats—an' the day after a hunder and sixty-one, an' that made us, we'll say, Eighteen an' a bittock west, an' maybe Fifty-one an' a bittock north, crossin' all the North Atlantic liner lanes on the long slant, always in sight o' the *Grotkau*, creepin' up by night and fallin' awa' by day. After the gale, it was cold weather wi' dark nights.

'I was in the engine-room on Friday night, just before the middle watch, when Bell whustled doon the tube: "She's done it"; an' up I came.

'The *Grotkau* was just a fair distance south, an' one by one she ran up the three red lights in a vertical line—the sign of a steamer not under control.

'"Yon's a tow for us," said Bell, lickin' his chops. "She'll be worth more than the *Breslau*. We'll go down to her, McPhee!"

'"Bide a while," I said. "The sea's fair throng wi' ships here."

"'Reason why,'" said Bell. "It's a fortune gaun beggin'. What d'ye think, man?"

"'Gie her till daylight. She knows we're here. If Bannister needs help he'll loose a rocket."

"'Wha told ye Bannister's need? We'll ha' some ragan'-bone tramp snappin' her up under oor nose," said he; an' he put the wheel over. We were gaun slow.

"'Bannister wad like better to go home on a liner an' eat in the saloon. Mind ye what they said o' Holdock and Steiner's food that night at Radley's? Keep her awa', man—keep her awa'. A tow's a tow, but a derelict's big salvage."

"'E-eh!' said Bell. "Yon's an inshot o' yours, Mac. I love ye like a brother. We'll bide whaur we are till daylight"; an' he kept her awa'.

'Syne up went a rocket forward, an' twa on the bridge, an' a blue light aft. Syne a tar-barrel forward again.

"'She's sinkin','" said Bell. "It's all gaun, an' I'll get no more than a pair o' night-glasses for pickin' up young Bannister—the fool!"

"'Fair an' soft again,'" I said. "She's signallin' to the south of us. Bannister knows as well as I that one rocket would bring the *Kite*. He'll no be wastin' fireworks for nothin'. Hear her ca'!"

'The *Grotkau* whustled an' whustled for five minutes, an' then there were more fireworks—a regular exhibeetion.

"'That's no for men in the regular trade,'" says Bell. "Ye're right, Mac. That's for a cuddy full o' passengers." He blinked through the night-glasses where it lay a bit thick to southward.

"'What d'ye make of it?'" I said.

"'Liner,' he says. "Yon's her rocket. Ou, ay; they've waukened the gold-strapped skipper, an'—noo they've waukened the passengers. They're turnin' on the electrics, cabin by cabin. Yon's anither rocket. They're comin' up to help the perishin' in deep watters."

"'Gie me the glass,' I said. But Bell danced on the bridge, clean dementit. "Mails—mails—mails!" said he. "Under contract wi' the Government for the due conveyance o' the mails; an' as such, Mac, ye'll note, she may rescue life at sea, but she canna tow!—she canna tow! Yon's her night-signal. She'll be up in half an hour!"

"'Gowk!' I said, "an' we blazin' here wi' all oor lights. Oh, Bell, but ye're a fool."

'He tumbled off the bridge forward, an' I tumbled aft, an' before ye could wink our lights were oot, the engine-room hatch was covered, an' we lay pitch-dark, watchin' the lights o' the liner come up that the *Grotkau*'d been signallin' for. Twenty knot she came, every cabin lighted, an' her boats swung awa'. It was grandly done, an' in the inside of an hour. She stopped like Mrs. Holdock's machine; doon went the gangway, doon went the boats, an' in ten minutes we heard the passengers cheerin', an' awa' she fled.

"'They'll tell o' this all the days they live," said Bell. "A rescue at sea by night, as pretty as a play. Young Bannister an' Calder will be drinkin' in the saloon, an' six months hence the Board o' Trade'll gie the skipper a pair o' binoculars. It's vara philanthropic all round."

'We lay by till day—ye may think we waited for it wi' sore eyes—an' there sat the *Grotkau*, her nose a bit cocked, just leerin' at us. She looked pairfectly rideeculous.

"'She'll be fillin' aft," says Bell; "for why is she doon by the stern? The tail-shaft's punched a hole in her, an'—we've no boats. There's three hunder thousand pound sterlin', at a conservative estimate, droonin' before our eyes. What's to do?" An' his bearin's got hot again in a minute; for he was an incontinent man.

"'Run her as near as ye daur," I said. "Gie me a jacket an' a life-line, an' I'll swum for it." There was a big lump of a sea, an' it was cold in the wind—vara cold; but they'd gone overside like passengers, young Bannister an' Calder an' a', leaving the gangway doon on the lee-side. It would ha' been a flyin' in the face o' manifest Providence to overlook the invitation. We were within fifty yards o' her while Kinloch was garmin' me all over wi' oil behind the galley; an' as we ran past I went outboard for the salvage o' three hunder thousand pound. Man, it was perishin' cold, but I'd done my job judgmatically, an came scrapin' all along her side slap on to the lower gratin' o' the gangway. No one more astonished than me, I assure ye. Before I'd caught my breath I'd skinned both my knees on the gratin', an' was climbin' up before she rolled again. I made my line fast to the rail, an' squattered aft to young Bannister's cabin, whaur I dried me wi' everything in his bunk, an' put on every conceivable sort o' rig I found till the blood was circulatin'. Three pair drawers, I mind I found—to begin upon—an' I needed them all. It was the coldest cold I remember in all my experience.

'Syne I went aft to the engine-room. The *Grotkau* sat on her own tail, as they say. She was vara short-shafted, an' her gear was all aft. There was four or five foot o' watter in the engine-room slummockin' to and fro, black an' greasy; maybe there was six foot. The stokehold doors were screwed home, an' the stokehold was tight enough, but for a minute the mess in the engine-room deceived me. Only for a minute, though, an' that was because I was not, in a manner o' speakin', as calm as ordinar'. I looked again to mak' sure. 'Twas just black wi' bilge: dead watter that must ha' come in fortuitously, ye ken.'

'McPhee, I'm only a passenger,' I said, 'but you don't persuade me that six foot o' water can come into an engine-room fortuitously.'

'Wha's tryin' to persuade one way or the other?' McPhee retorted. 'I'm statin' the facts o' the case—the simple, natural facts. Six or seven foot o' dead watter in the engine-room is a vara depressin' sight if ye think there's like to be more comin'; but I did not consider that such was likely, and so, ye'll note, I was not depressed.'

'That's all very well, but I want to know about the water,' I said.

'I've told ye. There was six feet or more there, wi' Calder's cap floatin' on top.'

'Where did it come from?'

'Weel, in the confusion o' things after the propeller had dropped off an' the engines were racin' an' a', it's vara possible that Calder might ha' lost it off his head an' no troubled himself to pick it up again. I remember seein' that cap on him at Southampton.'

'I don't want to know about the cap. I'm asking where the water came from, and what it was doing there, and why you were so certain that it wasn't a leak, McPhee?'

'For good reason—for good an' sufficient reason.'

'Give it to me, then.'

'Weel, it's a reason that does not properly concern

myself only. To be preceese, I'm of opinion that it was due, the watter, in part to an error o' judgment in another man. We can a' mak' mistakes.'

'Oh, I beg your pardon! Go on.'

'I got me to the rail again, an', "What's wrang?" said Bell, hailin'.

'"She'll do," I said. "Send's o'er a hawser, an' a man to help steer. I'll pull him in by the life-line."

'I could see heads bobbin' back an' forth, an' a whuff or two o' strong words. Then Bell said: "They'll not trust themselves—one of 'em—in this watter—except Kinloch, an' I'll no spare him."

'"The more salvage to me, then," I said. "I'll make shift *solo*."

'Says one dock-rat at this: "D'ye think she's safe?"

'"I'll guarantee ye nothing," I said, "except, maybe, a hammerin' for keepin' me this long."

'Then he sings out: "There's no more than one life-belt, an' they canna find it, or I'd come."

'"Throw him over, the Jezebel," I said, for I was oot o' patience; an' they took haud o' that volunteer before he knew what was in store, and hove him over in the bight of the life-line. So I e'en hauled him upon the sag of it, hand-over-fist—a vara welcome recruit when I'd tilted the salt watter oot of him; for, by the way, he could not swum.

'Syne they bent a twa-inch rope to the life-line, an' a hawser to that, an' I led the rope o'er the drum of a hand-winch forward, an' we sweated the hawser inboard an' made it fast to the *Grotkau*'s bitts.

'Bell brought the *Kite* so close I feared she'd roll in an' do the *Grotkau*'s plates a mischief. He hove anither life-line to me, an' went astern, an' we had all the weary winch-work to do again wi' a second hawser. For all that, Bell was right: we'd a long tow before us, an' though Providence had helped us that far, there was no sense in leavin' too much to its keepin'. When the second hawser was fast, I was wet wi' sweat, an' I cried Bell to tak' up his slack an' go home. The other man was by way o' helpin' the work wi' askin' for drinks, but I e'en told him he must hand, reef an' steer, beginnin' with steerin', for I was goin' to turn in. He steered—ou, ay, he steered, in a manner o' speakin'. At the least, he grippit the spokes an' twiddled 'em an' looked wise, but I doubt if the *Hoor* ever felt it. I turned in there an' then to young Bannister's bunk, an' slept past expression. I waukened ragin' wi' hunger, a fair lump o' sea runnin', the *Kite* snorin' awa' four knots; an' the *Grotkau* slappin' her nose under, an' yawin' an' standin' over at discretion. She was a most disgracefu' tow. But the shameful thing of all was the food. I raxed me a meal fra galley-shelves an' pantries an' lazareetes an' cubby-holes that I would not ha' gied to the mate of a Cardiff collier; an' ye ken we say a Cardiff mate will eat clinkers to save waste. I'm sayin' it was simply vile! The crew had written what *they* thought of it on the new paint o' the fo'c'sle, but I had not a decent soul wi' me to complain on. There was nothing for me to do save watch the hawsers an' the *Kite*'s tail squatterin' down in white watter when she lifted to a sea; so I got steam on the after donkey-pump, an' pumped oot the engine-room. There's no sense in leavin' watter loose in a ship. When she was dry, I went doon the shaft-tunnel, an' found she was leakin' a little through the stuffin'-box, but nothin' to make wark. The propeller had e'en jarred off, as I knew it must, an' Calder had been waitin' for it to go wi' his hand on the gear. He told me as much when I met him ashore. There was nothin' started or strained. It had just slipped awa' to the bed o' the Atlantic as easy as a man dyin' wi' due warnin'—a most providential business for all concerned. Syne I took stock o' the *Grotkau*'s upper works. Her boats had been smashed on the davits, an' here an' there was the rail missin', an' a ventilator or two had fetched awa', an' the bridge-rails were bent by the seas; but her hatches were tight, and she'd taken no sort of harm. Dod, I came to hate her like a human bein', for I was eight weary days aboard, starvin'—ay, starvin'— within a cable's length o' plenty. All day I lay in the bunk reading the *Woman-Hater*, the grandest book Charlie Reade ever wrote, an' pickin' a toothful here an' there. It was weary, weary work. Eight days, man, I was aboard the *Grotkau*, an' not one full meal did I make. Sma' blame her crew would not stay by her. The other man? Oh, I warked him to keep him crack. I warked him wi' a vengeance.

'It came on to blow when we fetched soundin's, an' that kept me standin' by the hawsers, lashed to the capstan, breathin' betwixt green seas. I near died o' cauld an' hunger, for the *Grotkau* towed like a barge, an' Bell how-kit her along through or over. It was vara thick up-Channel, too. We were standin' in to make some sort o' light, and we near walked over twa three fishin'-boats, an' they cried us we were o'erclose to Falmouth. Then we were near cut down by a drunken foreign fruiter that was blunderin' between us an' the shore, and it got thicker and thicker that night, an' I could feel by the tow Bell did not know whaur he was. Losh, we knew in the morn, for the wind blew the fog oot like a candle, an' the sun came clear; and as surely as McRimmon gied me my cheque, the shadow o' the Eddystone lay across our tow-rope! We were that near—ay, we were that near! Bell fetched the *Kite* round with a jerk that came close to tearin' the bitts out o' the *Grotkau*; an' I mind I thanked my Maker in young Bannister's cabin when we were inside Plymouth breakwater.

'The first to come aboard was McRimmon, wi' Dandie. Did I tell you our orders were to take anything found into Plymouth? The auld deil had just come down overnight, puttin' two an' two together from what Calder had told him when the liner landed the *Grotkau*'s men. He had preceesely hit oor time. I'd hailed Bell for something to eat, an' he sent it o'er in the same boat wi' McRimmon, when the auld man came to me. He grinned an' slapped his legs and worked his eyebrows the while I ate.

'"How do Holdock, Steiner, and Chase feed their men?" said he.

'"Ye can see," I said, knockin' the top off another beer-bottle. "I did not take to be starved, McRimmon."

'"Nor to swim, either," said he, for Bell had tauld him how I carried the line aboard. "Well, I'm thinkin' you'll be no loser. What freight could we ha' put into the *Lammergeyer* would equal salvage on four hunder thousand pounds—hull and cargo? Eh, McPhee? This cuts the liver out o' Holdock, Steiner, Chase, and Company, Limited. Eh, McPhee? An' I'm sufferin' from senile dementia now? Eh, McPhee? An' I'm not daft, am I, till I begin to paint the *Lammergeyer*? Eh, McPhee? Ye may weel lift your leg, Dandie! I ha' the laugh o' them all. Ye found watter in the engine-room?"

"'To speak wi'oot prejudice," I said, "there was some watter."

"'They thought she was sinkin' after the propeller went. She filled with extraordinary rapeedity. Calder said it grieved him an' Bannister to abandon her."

'I thought o' the dinner at Radley's, an' what like o' food I'd eaten for eight days.

"'It would grieve them sore," I said.

"'But the crew would not hear o' stayin' an' takin' their chances. They're gaun up an' down sayin' they'd ha' starved first."

"'They'd ha' starved if they'd stayed," said I.

"'I tak' it, fra Calder's account, there was a mutiny a'most."

"'Ye know more than I, McRimmon," I said. "Speakin' wi'oot prejudice, for we're all in the same boat, *who* opened the bilge-cock?"

"'Oh, that's it—is it?" said the auld man, an' I could see he was surprised. "A bilge-cock, ye say?"

"'I believe it was a bilge-cock. They were all shut when I came aboard, but some one had flooded the engine-room eight feet over all, and shut it off with the worm-an'-wheel gear from the second gratin' afterwards."

"'Losh!" said McRimmon. "The ineequity o' man's beyond belief. But it's awfu' discreditable to Holdock, Steiner, and Chase, if that came oot in court."

"'It's just my own curiosity," I said.

"'Aweel, Dandie's afflicted wi' the same disease. Dandie, strive against curiosity, for it brings a little dog into traps an' suchlike. Whaur was the *Kite* when yon painted liner took off the *Grotkau*'s people?"

"'Just there or thereabouts,' I said.

"'An' which o' you twa thought to cover your lights?" said he, winkin'.

"'Dandie,' I said to the dog, "we must both strive against curiosity. It's an unremunerative business. What's our chance o' salvage, Dandie?"

'He laughed till he choked. "Tak' what I gie you, McPhee, an' be content," he said. "Lord, how a man wastes time when he gets old. Get aboard the *Kite*, mon, as soon as ye can. I've clean forgot there's a Baltic charter yammerin' for you at London. That'll be your last voyage, I'm thinkin', excep' by way o' pleasure."

'Steiner's men were comin' aboard to take charge an' tow her round, an' I passed young Steiner in a boat as I went to the *Kite*. He looked down his nose; but McRimmon pipes up: "Here's the man ye owe the *Grotkau* to—at a price, Steiner—at a price! Let me introduce Mister McPhee to you. Maybe ye've met before; but ye've vara little luck in keeping your men—ashore or afloat!"

'Young Steiner looked angry enough to eat him as he chuckled an' whustled in his dry old throat.

"'Ye've not got your award yet," Steiner says.

"'Na, na," says the auld man, in a screech ye could hear to the Hoe, "but I've twa million sterlin', an' no bairns, ye Judeeas Apella, if ye mean to fight; an' I'll match ye p'und for p'und till the last p'und's oot. Ye ken *me*, Steiner? I'm McRimmon o' McNaughton and McRimmon!"

"'Dod," he said betwix' his teeth, sittin' back in the

boat, "I've waited fourteen year to break that Jew-firm, an' God be thankit I'll do it now."

'The *Kite* was in the Baltic while the auld man was warkin his warks, but I know the assessors valued the *Grotkau*, all told, at over three hunder and sixty thousand —her manifest was a treat o' richness—and McRimmon got a third for salvin' an abandoned ship. Ye see, there's vast deeference between towin' a ship wi' men on her and pickin' up a derelict—a vast deeference—in pounds sterlin'. Moreover, twa three o' the *Grotkau*'s crew were burnin' to testify about food, an' there was a note o' Calder to the Board in regard to the tail-shaft that would ha' been vara damagin' if it had come into court. They knew better than to fight.

'Syne the *Kite* came back, and McRimmon paid off me an' Bell personally, and the rest of the crew *pro rata*, I believe it's ca'ed. My share—oor share, I should say—was just twenty-five thousand pounds sterlin'.'

At this point Janet jumped up and kissed him.

'Five-and-twenty thousand pound sterlin'. Noo, I'm fra the North, and I'm not the like to fling money awa' rashly, but I'd gie six months' pay—one hunder an' twenty pound—to know *who* flooded the engine-room of the *Grotkau*. I'm fairly well acquaint wi' McRimmon's eediosyncrasies, and *he*'d no hand in it. It was not Calder, for I've asked him, an' he wanted to fight me. It would be in the highest degree unprofessional o' Calder —not fightin', but openin' bilge-cocks—but for a while I thought it was him. Ay, I judged it might be him—under temptation.'

'What's your theory?' I demanded.

'Weel, I'm inclined to think it was one o' those singular providences that remind us we're in the hands o' Higher Powers.'

'It couldn't open and shut itself?'

'I did not mean that; but some half-starvin' oiler or, maybe, trimmer must ha' opened it a while to mak' sure o' leavin' the *Grotkau*. It's a demoralisin' thing to see an engine-room flood up after any accident to the gear—demoralisin' and deceptive both. Aweel, the man got what he wanted, for they went aboard the liner cryin' that the *Grotkau* was sinkin'. But it's curious to think o' the consequences. In a' human probability, he's bein' damned in heaps at the present moment aboard another tramp-freighter; an' here am I, wi' five-an'-twenty thousand pounds invested, resolute to go to sea no more—providential's the preceese word—except as a passenger, ye'll understand, Janet.'

McPhee kept his word. He and Janet went for a voyage as passengers in the first-class saloon. They paid seventy pounds for their berths; and Janet found a very sick woman in the second-class saloon, so that for sixteen days she lived below, and chatted with the stewardesses at the foot of the second-saloon stairs while her patient slept. McPhee was a passenger for exactly twenty-four hours. Then the engineers' mess—where the oil-cloth tables are—joyfully took him to its bosom, and for the rest of the voyage that company was richer by the unpaid services of a highly certificated engineer.

'WIRELESS'

'It's a funny thing, this Marconi business, isn't it?' said Mr. Shaynor, coughing heavily. 'Nothing seems to make any difference, by what they tell me—storms, hills, or anything; but if that's true we shall know before morning.'

'Of course it's true,' I answered, stepping behind the counter. 'Where's old Mr. Cashell?'

'He's had to go to bed on account of his influenza. He said you'd very likely drop in.'

'Where's his nephew?'

'Inside, getting the things ready. He told me that the last time they experimented they put the pole on the roof of one of the big hotels here, and the batteries electrified all the water-supply, and'—he giggled—'the ladies got shocks when they took their baths.'

'I never heard of that.'

'The hotel wouldn't exactly advertise it, would it? Just now, by what Mr. Cashell tells me, they're trying to signal from here to Poole, and they're using stronger batteries than ever. But, you see, he being the guvnor's nephew and all that (and it will be in the papers too), it doesn't matter how they electrify things in this house. Are you going to watch?'

'Very much. I've never seen this game. Aren't you going to bed?'

'We don't close till ten on Saturdays. There's a good deal of influenza in town, too, and there'll be a dozen prescriptions coming in before morning. I generally sleep in the chair here. It's warmer than jumping out of bed every time. Bitter cold, isn't it?'

'Freezing hard. I'm sorry your cough's worse.'

'Thank you. I don't mind cold so much. It's this wind that fair cuts me to pieces.' He coughed again hard and hackingly, as an old lady came in for ammoniated quinine. 'We've just run out of it in bottles, madam,' said Mr. Shaynor, returning to the professional tone, 'but if you will wait two minutes, I'll make it up for you, madam.'

I had used the shop for some time, and my acquaintance with the proprietor had ripened into friendship. It was Mr. Cashell who revealed to me the purpose and power of Apothecaries' Hall that time a fellow-chemist had made an error in a prescription of mine, had lied to cover his sloth, and when error and lie were brought home to him had written vain letters.

'A disgrace to our profession,' said the thin, mild-eyed man, hotly, after studying the evidence. 'You couldn't do a better service to the profession than report him to Apothecaries' Hall.'

I did so, not knowing what djinns I should evoke; and the result was such an apology as one might make who had spent a night on the rack. I conceived great respect for Apothecaries' Hall, and esteem for Mr. Cashell, a zealous craftsman who magnified his calling. Until Mr. Shaynor came down from the North his assistants had by no means agreed with Mr. Cashell. 'They forget,' said he, 'that, first and foremost, the compounder is a medicine-man. On him depends the physician's reputation. He holds it literally in the hollow of his hand, sir.'

Mr. Shaynor's manners had not, perhaps, the polish of the grocery and Italian warehouse next door, but he knew and loved his dispensary work in every detail. For relaxation he seemed to go no farther afield than the romance of drugs—their discovery, preparation, packing, and export—but it led him to the ends of the earth, and on this subject, and the Pharmaceutical Formulary, and Nicholas Culpeper, most confident of physicians, we met.

Little by little I grew to know something of his beginnings and his hopes—of his mother, who had been a school-teacher in one of the northern counties, and of his red-headed father, a small job-master at Kirby Moors, who died when he was a child; of the examinations he had passed and of their exceeding and increasing difficulty; of his dreams of a shop in London; of his hate for the price-cutting Co-operative stores; and, most interesting, of his mental attitude towards customers.

'There's a way you get into,' he told me, 'of serving them carefully, and I hope, politely, without stopping your own thinking. I've been reading Christie's *New Commercial Plants* all this autumn, and that needs keeping your mind on it, I can tell you. So long as it isn't a prescription, of course, I can carry as much as half a page of Christie in my head, and at the same time I could sell out all that window twice over, and not a penny wrong at the end. As to prescriptions, I think I could make up the general run of 'em in my sleep, almost.'

For reasons of my own, I was deeply interested in Marconi experiments at their outset in England; and it was of a piece with Mr. Cashell's unvarying thoughtfulness that, when his nephew the electrician appropriated the house for a long-range installation, he should, as I have said, invite me to see the result.

The old lady went away with her medicine, and Mr. Shaynor and I stamped on the tiled floor behind the counter to keep ourselves warm. The shop, by the light of the many electrics, looked like a Paris-diamond mine, for Mr. Cashell believed in all the ritual of his craft. Three superb glass jars—red, green, and blue—of the sort that led Rosamund to parting with her shoes—blazed in the broad plate-glass windows, and there was a confused smell of orris, Kodak films, vulcanite, tooth-powder, sachets, and almond-cream in the air. Mr. Shaynor fed the dispensary stove, and we sucked cayenne-pepper jujubes and menthol lozenges. The brutal east wind had cleared the streets, and the few passers-by were muffled to their puckered eyes. In the Italian warehouse next door some gay feathered birds and game, hung upon hooks, sagged to the wind across the left edge of our window-frame.

'They ought to take these poultry in—all knocked about like that,' said Mr. Shaynor. 'Doesn't it make you feel fair perishing? See that old hare! The wind's nearly blowing the fur off him.'

I saw the belly-fur of the dead beast blown apart in ridges and streaks as the wind caught it, showing bluish skin underneath. 'Bitter cold,' said Mr. Shaynor, shuddering. 'Fancy going out on a night like this! Oh, here's young Mr. Cashell.'

The door of the inner office behind the dispensary opened, and an energetic, spade-bearded man stepped forth, rubbing his hands.

'I want a bit of tin-foil, Shaynor,' he said. 'Good-evening. My uncle told me you might be coming.' This to me, as I began the first of a hundred questions.

'I've everything in order,' he replied. 'We're only waiting until Poole calls us up. Excuse me a minute. You can come in whenever you like—but I'd better be with the instruments. Give me that tin-foil. Thanks.'

While we were talking, a girl—evidently no customer —had come into the shop, and the face and bearing of Mr. Shaynor changed. She leaned confidently across the counter.

'But I can't,' I heard him whisper uneasily—the flush on his cheek was dull red, and his eyes shone like a drugged moth's. 'I can't. I tell you I'm alone in the place.'

'No, you aren't. Who's *that*? Let him look after it for half an hour. A brisk walk will do you good. Ah, come now, John.'

'But he isn't——'

'I don't care. I want you to; we'll only go round by St. Agnes. If you don't——'

He crossed to where I stood in the shadow of the dispensary counter, and began some sort of broken apology about a lady-friend.

'Yes,' she interrupted. 'You take the shop for half an hour—to oblige *me*, won't you?'

She had a singularly rich and promising voice that well matched her outline.

'All right,' I said. 'I'll do it—but you'd better wrap yourself up, Mr. Shaynor.'

'Oh, a brisk walk ought to help me. We're only going round by the church.' I heard him cough grievously as they went out together.

I refilled the stove, and, after reckless expenditure of Mr. Cashell's coal, drove some warmth into the shop. I explored many of the glass-knobbed drawers that lined the walls, tasted some disconcerting drugs, and, by the aid of a few cardamoms, ground ginger, chloric-ether, and dilute alcohol, manufactured a new and wildish drink, of which I bore a glassful to young Mr. Cashell, busy in the back office. He laughed shortly when I told him that Mr. Shaynor had stepped out—but a frail coil of wire held all his attention, and he had no word for me bewildered among the batteries and rods. The noise of the sea on the beach began to make itself heard as the traffic in the street ceased. Then briefly, but very lucidly, he gave me the names and uses of the mechanism that crowded the tables and the floor.

'When do you expect to get the message from Poole?' I demanded, sipping my liquor out of a graduated glass.

'About midnight, if everything is in order. We've got our installation-pole fixed to the roof of the house. I shouldn't advise you to turn on a tap or anything to-night. We've connected up with the plumbing, and all the water will be electrified.' He repeated to me the history of the agitated ladies at the hotel at the time of the first installation.

'But what *is* it?' I asked. 'Electricity is out of my beat altogether.'

'Ah, if you knew *that* you'd know something nobody knows. It's just It—what we call Electricity, but the magic—the manifestations—the Hertzian waves—are all revealed by *this*. The coherer, we call it.'

He picked up a glass tube not much thicker than a thermometer, in which, almost touching, were two tiny silver plugs, and between them an infinitesimal pinch of metallic dust. 'That's all,' he said, proudly, as though himself responsible for the wonder. 'That is the thing that will reveal to us the Powers—whatever the Powers may be—at work—through space—a long distance away.'

Just then Mr. Shaynor returned alone and stood coughing his heart out on the mat.

'Serves you right for being such a fool,' said young Mr. Cashell, as annoyed as myself at the interruption. 'Never mind—we've all the night before us to see wonders.'

Shaynor clutched the counter, his handkerchief to his lips. When he brought it away I saw two bright red stains.

'I—I've got a bit of a rasped throat from smoking cig-arettes,' he panted. 'I think I'll try a cubeb.'

'Better take some of this. I've been compounding while you've been away.' I handed him the brew.

''Twon't make me drunk, will it? I'm almost a tee-totaller. My word! That's grateful and comforting.'

He set down the empty glass to cough afresh.

'Brr! But it was cold out there! I shouldn't care to be lying in my grave a night like this. Don't *you* ever have a sore throat from smoking?' He pocketed the handkerchief after a furtive peep.

'Oh, yes, sometimes,' I replied, wondering, while I spoke, into what agonies of terror I should fall if ever I saw those bright red danger-signals under my nose. Young Mr. Cashell among the batteries coughed slightly to show that he was quite ready to continue his scientific explanations, but I was thinking still of the girl with the rich voice and the significantly cut mouth, at whose com-mand I had taken charge of the shop. It flashed across me that she distantly resembled the seductive shape on a gold-framed toilet-water advertisement whose charms were unholily heightened by the glare from the red bottle in the window. Turning to make sure, I saw Mr. Shaynor's eyes bent in the same direction, and by instinct recognised that the flamboyant thing was to him a shrine. 'What do you take for your—cough?' I asked.

'Well, I'm the wrong side of the counter to believe much in patent medicines. But there are asthma cigarettes and there are pastilles. To tell you the truth, if you don't object to the smell, which is very like incense, I believe, though I'm not a Roman Catholic, Blaudett's Cathedral Pastilles relieve me as much as anything.'

'Let's try.' I had never raided a chemist's shop before, so I was thorough. We unearthed the pastilles—brown, gummy cones of benzoin—and set them alight under the toilet-water advertisement, where they fumed in thin blue spirals.

'Of course,' said Mr. Shaynor, to my question, 'what one uses in the shop for one's self comes out of one's pocket. Why, stock-taking in our business is nearly the same as with jewellers—and I can't say more than that. But one gets them'—he pointed to the pastille-box—'at trade prices.' Evidently the censing of the gay, seven-tinted wench with the teeth was an established ritual which cost something.

'And when do we shut up shop?'

'We stay like this all night. The guv—old Mr. Cashell —doesn't believe in locks and shutters as compared with electric light. Besides, it brings trade. I'll just sit here in the chair by the stove and write a letter, if you don't mind. Electricity isn't my prescription.'

The energetic young Mr. Cashell snorted within, and

Shaynor settled himself up in his chair over which he had thrown a staring red, black, and yellow Austrian jute blanket, rather like a table-cover. I cast about, amid patent-medicine pamphlets, for something to read, but finding little, returned to the manufacture of the new drink. The Italian warehouse took down its game and went to bed. Across the street blank shutters flung back the gaslight in cold smears; the dried pavement seemed to rough up in goose-flesh under the scouring of the savage wind, and we could hear, long ere he passed, the policeman flapping his arms to keep himself warm. Within, the flavours of cardamoms and chloric-ether disputed those of the pastilles and a score of drugs and perfume and soap scents. Our electric lights, set low down in the windows before the tun-bellied Rosamund jars, flung inward three monstrous daubs of red, blue, and green, that broke into kaleidoscopic lights on the faceted knobs of the drug-drawers, the cut-glass scent flagons, and the bulbs of the sparklet bottles. They flushed the white-tiled floor in gorgeous patches; splashed along the nickel-silver counterrails, and turned the polished mahogany counter-panels to the likeness of intricate grained marbles—slabs of porphyry and malachite. Mr. Shaynor unlocked a drawer, and ere he began to write, took out a meagre bundle of letters. From my place by the stove, I could see the scalloped edges of the paper with a flaring monogram in the corner and could even smell the reek of chypre. At each page he turned toward the toilet-water lady of the advertisement and devoured her with over-luminous eyes. He had drawn the Austrian blanket over his shoulders, and among those warring lights he looked more than ever the incarnation of a drugged moth—a tiger-moth as I thought.

He put his letter into an envelope, stamped it with stiff mechanical movements, and dropped it in the drawer. Then I became aware of the silence of a great city asleep—the silence that underlaid the even voice of the breakers along the sea-front—a thick, tingling quiet of warm life stilled down for its appointed time, and unconsciously I moved about the glittering shop as one moves in a sickroom. Young Mr. Cashell was adjusting some wire that crackled from time to time with the tense, knuckle-stretching sound of the electric spark. Upstairs, where a door shut and opened swiftly, I could hear his uncle coughing abed.

'Here,' I said, when the drink was properly warmed, 'take some of this, Mr. Shaynor.'

He jerked in his chair with a start and a wrench, and held out his hand for the glass. The mixture, of a rich port-wine colour, frothed at the top.

'It looks,' he said, suddenly, 'it looks—those bubbles —like a string of pearls winking at you—rather like the pearls round that young lady's neck.' He turned again to the advertisement where the female in the dove-coloured corset had seen fit to put on all her pearls before she cleaned her teeth.

'Not bad, is it?' I said.

'Eh?'

He rolled his eyes heavily full on me, and, as I stared, I beheld all meaning and consciousness die out of the swiftly dilating pupils. His figure lost its stark rigidity, softened into the chair, and, chin on chest, hands dropped before him, he rested open-eyed, absolutely still.

'I'm afraid I've rather cooked Shaynor's goose,' I said, bearing the fresh drink to young Mr. Cashell. 'Perhaps it was the chloric-ether.'

'Oh, he's all right.' The spade-bearded man glanced at him pityingly. 'Consumptives go off in those sort of doses very often. It's exhaustion . . . I don't wonder. I daresay the liquor will do him good. It's grand stuff,' he finished his share appreciatively. 'Well, as I was saying—before he interrupted—about this little coherer. The pinch of dust, you see, is nickel-filings. The Hertzian waves, you see, come out of space from the station that despatches 'em, and all these little particles are attracted together—cohere, we call it—for just so long as the current passes through them. Now, it's important to remember that the current is an induced current. There are a good many kinds of induction——'

'Yes, but what *is* induction?'

'That's rather hard to explain untechnically. But the long and the short of it is that when a current of electricity passes through a wire there's a lot of magnetism present round that wire; and if you put another wire parallel to, and within what we call its magnetic field—why then, the second wire will also become charged with electricity.'

'On its own account?'

'On its own account.'

'Then let's see if I've got it correctly. Miles off, at Poole, or wherever it is——'

'It will be anywhere in ten years.'

'You've got a charged wire——'

'Charged with Hertzian waves which vibrate, say, two

175

hundred and thirty million times a second.' Mr. Cashell snaked his forefinger rapidly through the air.

'All right—a charged wire at Poole, giving out these waves into space. Then this wire of yours sticking out into space—on the roof of the house—in some mysterious way gets charged with those waves from Poole——'

'Or anywhere—it only happens to be Poole to-night.'

'And those waves set the coherer at work, just like an ordinary telegraph-office ticker?'

'No! That's where so many people make the mistake. The Hertzian waves wouldn't be strong enough to work a great heavy Morse instrument like ours. They can only just make that dust cohere, and while it coheres (a little while for a dot and a longer while for a dash) the current from this battery—the home battery'—he laid his hand on the thing—'can get through to the Morse printing-machine to record the dot or dash. Let me make it clearer. Do you know anything about steam?'

'Very little. But go on.'

'Well, the coherer is like a steam-valve. Any child can open a valve and start a steamer's engines, because a turn of the hand lets in the main steam, doesn't it? Now, this home battery here ready to print is the main steam. The coherer is the valve, always ready to be turned on. The Hertzian wave is the child's hand that turns it.'

'I see. That's marvellous.'

'Marvellous, isn't it? And, remember, we're only at the beginning. There's nothing we shan't be able to do in ten years. I want to live—my God, how I want to live, and see it develop!' He looked through the door at Shaynor breathing lightly in his chair. 'Poor beast! And he wants to keep company with Fanny Brand.'

'Fanny *who*?' I said, for the name struck an obscurely familiar chord in my brain—something connected with a stained handkerchief, and the word 'arterial.'

'Fanny Brand—the girl you kept shop for.' He laughed. 'That's all I know about her, and for the life of me I can't see what Shaynor sees in her, or she in him.'

'*Can't* you see what he sees in her?' I insisted.

'Oh, yes, if *that's* what you mean. She's a great, big, fat lump of a girl, and so on. I suppose that's why he's so crazy after her. She isn't his sort. Well, it doesn't matter. My uncle says he's bound to die before the year's out. Your drink's given him a good sleep, at any rate.' Young Mr. Cashell could not catch Mr. Shaynor's face, which was half turned to the advertisement.

I stoked the stove anew, for the room was growing cold, and lighted another pastille. Mr. Shaynor in his chair, never moving, looked through and over me with eyes as wide and lustreless as those of a dead hare.

'Poole's late,' said young Mr. Cashell, when I stepped back. 'I'll just send them a call.'

He pressed a key in the semi-darkness, and with a rending crackle there leaped between two brass knobs a spark, streams of sparks, and sparks again.

'Grand, isn't it? *That's* the Power—our unknown Power—kicking and fighting to be let loose,' said young Mr. Cashell. 'There she goes—kick—kick—kick into space. I never get over the strangeness of it when I work a sending-machine—waves going into space, you know. T.R. is our call. Poole ought to answer with L. L. L.'

We waited two, three, five minutes. In that silence, of which the boom of the tide was an orderly part, I caught the clear '*kiss—kiss—kiss*' of the halliards on the roof, as they were blown against the installation-pole.

'Poole is not ready. I'll stay here and call you when he is.'

I returned to the shop, and set down my glass on a marble slab with a careless clink. As I did so, Shaynor rose to his feet, his eyes fixed once more on the advertisement, where the young woman bathed in the light from the red jar simpered pinkly over her pearls. His lips moved without cessation. I stepped nearer to listen. 'And threw—and threw—and threw,' he repeated, his face all sharp with some inexplicable agony.

I moved forward astonished. But it was then he found words—delivered roundly and clearly. These:—

And threw warm gules on Madeleine's young breast.

The trouble passed off his countenance, and he returned lightly to his place, rubbing his hands.

It had never occurred to me, though we had many times discussed reading and prize-competitions as a diversion, that Mr. Shaynor ever read Keats, or could quote him at all appositely. There was, after all, a certain stained-glass effect of light on the high bosom of the highly-polished picture which might, by stretch of fancy, suggest, as a vile chromo recalls some incomparable canvas, the line he had spoken. Night, my drink, and solitude were evidently turning Mr. Shaynor into a poet. He sat down again and wrote swiftly on his villainous note-paper, his lips quivering.

I shut the door into the inner office and moved up behind him. He made no sign that he saw or heard. I looked over his shoulder, and read, amid half-formed words, sentences, and wild scratches:—

>   ——Very cold it was. Very cold
>   The hare—the hare—the hare—
>   The birds——

He raised his head sharply, and frowned toward the blank shutters of the poulterer's shop where they jutted out against our window. Then one clear line came:—

>   'The hare, in spite of fur, was very cold.'

The head, moving machine-like, turned right to the advertisement where the Blaudett's Cathedral pastille reeked abominably. He grunted, and went on:—

>   'Incense in a censer—
>   Before her darling picture framed in gold—
>   Maiden's picture—angel's portrait——'

'Hsh!' said Mr. Cashell guardedly from the inner office, as though in the presence of spirits. 'There's something coming through from somewhere; but it isn't Poole.' I heard the crackle of sparks as he depressed the keys of the transmitter. In my own brain, too, something crackled, or it might have been the hair on my head. Then I heard my own voice, in a harsh whisper: 'Mr. Cashell, there is something coming through here, too. Leave me alone till I tell you.'

'But I thought you'd come to see this wonderful thing—sir,' indignantly at the end.

'Leave me alone till I tell you. Be quiet.'

I watched—I waited. Under the blue-veined hand—

the dry hand of the consumptive—came away clear, without erasure:—

> And my weak spirit fails
> To think how the dead must freeze—

he shivered as he wrote—

> Beneath the churchyard mould.

Then he stopped, laid the pen down, and leaned back.

For an instant, that was half an eternity, the shop spun before me in a rainbow-tinted whirl, in and through which my own soul most dispassionately considered my own soul as that fought with an over-mastering fear. Then I smelt the strong smell of cigarettes from Mr. Shaynor's clothing, and heard, as though it had been the rending of trumpets, the rattle of his breathing. I was still in my place of observation, much as one would watch a rifle-shot at the butts, half-bent, hands on my knees, and head within a few inches of the black, red, and yellow blanket of his shoulder. I was whispering encouragement, evidently to my other self, sounding sentences, such as men pronounce in dreams.

'If he has read Keats, it proves nothing. If he hasn't— like causes *must* beget like effects. There is no escape from this law. *You* ought to be grateful that you know "St. Agnes' Eve" without the book; because, given the circumstances, such as Fanny Brand, who is the key of the enigma, and approximately represents the latitude and longitude of Fanny Brawne; allowing also for the bright red colour of the arterial blood upon the handker-chief, which was just what you were puzzling over in the shop just now; and counting the effect of the professional environment, here almost perfectly duplicated—the result is logical and inevitable. As inevitable as induction.'

Still, the other half of my soul refused to be comforted. It was cowering in some minute and inadequate corner—at an immense distance.

Hereafter, I found myself one person again, my hands still gripping my knees, and my eyes glued on the page before Mr. Shaynor. As dreamers accept and explain the upheaval of landscapes and the resurrection of the dead, with excerpts from the evening hymn or the multiplication-table, so I had accepted the facts, whatever they might be, that I should witness, and had devised a theory, sane and plausible to my mind, that explained them all. Nay, I was even in advance of my facts, walking hurriedly before them, assured that they would fit my theory. And all that I now recall of that epoch-making theory are the lofty words: 'If he has read Keats it's the chloric-ether. If he hasn't, it's the identical bacillus, or Hertzian wave of tuberculosis, *plus* Fanny Brand and the professional status which, in conjunction with the main-stream of subconscious thought common to all mankind, has thrown up temporarily an induced Keats.'

Mr. Shaynor returned to his work, erasing and rewriting as before with swiftness. Two or three blank pages he tossed aside. Then he wrote, muttering:—

The little smoke of a candle that goes out.

'No,' he muttered. 'Little smoke—little smoke—little smoke. What else?' He thrust his chin forward toward the advertisement, whereunder the last of the Blaudett's Cathedral pastilles fumed in its holder. 'Ah!' Then with relief:—

The little smoke that dies in moonlight cold.

Evidently he was snared by the rhymes of his first verse, for he wrote and rewrote 'gold—cold—mould' many times. Again he sought inspiration from the advertisement, and set down, without erasure, the line I had overheard:—

And threw warm gules on Madeleine's young breast.

As I remembered the original it is 'fair'—a trite word—instead of 'young,' and I found myself nodding approval, though I admitted that the attempt to reproduce 'its little smoke in pallid moonlight died' was a failure.

Followed without a break ten or fifteen lines of bald prose—the naked soul's confession of its physical yearning for its beloved—unclean as we count uncleanliness; unwholesome, but human exceedingly; the raw material, so it seemed to me in that hour and in that place, whence Keats wove the twenty-sixth, seventh, and eighth stanzas of his poem. Shame I had none in overseeing this revelation; and my fear had gone with the smoke of the pastille.

'That's it,' I murmured. 'That's how it's blocked out. Go on! Ink it in, man. Ink it in!'

Mr. Shaynor returned to broken verse wherein 'loveliness' was made to rhyme with a desire to look upon 'her empty dress.' He picked up a fold of the gay, soft blanket, spread it over one hand, caressed it with infinite tenderness, thought, muttered, traced some snatches which I could not decipher, shut his eyes drowsily, shook his head, and dropped the stuff. Here I found myself at fault, for I could not then see (as I do now) in what manner a red, black, and yellow Austrian blanket coloured his dreams.

In a few minutes he laid aside his pen, and, chin on hand, considered the shop with thoughtful and intelligent eyes. He threw down the blanket, rose, passed along a line of drug-drawers, and read the names on the labels aloud. Returning, he took from his desk Christie's *New Commercial Plants* and the old Culpeper that I had given him, opened and laid them side by side with a clerky air, all trace of passion gone from his face, read first in one and then in the other, and paused with pen behind his ear.

'What wonder of Heaven's coming now?' I thought.

'Manna—manna—manna,' he said at last, under wrinkled brows. 'That's what I wanted. Good! Now then! Now then! Good! Good! Oh, by God, that's good!' His voice rose and he spoke rightly and fully without a falter:—

> Candied apple, quince and plum and gourd,
> And jellies smoother than the creamy curd,
> And lucent syrups tinct with cinnamon,
> Manna and dates in Argosy transferred
> From Fez; and spiced dainties, every one
> From silken Samarcand to cedared Lebanon.

He repeated it once more, using 'blander' for 'smoother' in the second line; then wrote it down without erasure, but this time (my set eyes missed no stroke of any word) he substituted 'smoother' for his atrocious second thought, so that it came away under his hand as it is written in the book—as it is written in the book.

A wind went shouting down the street, and on the heels of the wind followed a spurt and rattle of rain.

After a smiling pause—and good right had he to

smile—he began anew, always tossing the last sheet over his shoulder:—

> The sharp rain falling on the window-pane,
> Rattling sleet—the wind-blown sleet.

Then prose: 'It is very cold of mornings when the wind brings rain and sleet with it. I heard the sleet on the window-pane outside, and thought of you, my darling. I am always thinking of you. I wish we could both run away like two lovers into the storm and get that little cottage by the sea which we are always thinking about, my own dear darling. We could sit and watch the sea beneath our windows. It would be a fairyland all of our own—a fairy sea—a fairy sea. . . .'

He stopped, raised his head, and listened. The steady drone of the Channel along the sea-front that had borne us company so long leaped up a note to the sudden fuller surge that signals the change from ebb to flood. It beat in like the change of step throughout an army—this renewed pulse of the sea—and filled our ears till they, accepting it, marked it no longer.

> A fairyland for you and me
> Across the foam—beyond . . .
> A magic foam, a perilous sea.

He grunted again with effort and bit his underlip. My throat dried, but I dared not gulp to moisten it lest I should break the spell that was drawing him nearer and nearer to the high-water mark but two of the sons of Adam have reached. Remember that in all the millions permitted there are no more than five—five little lines—of which one can say: 'These are the pure Magic. These are the clear Vision. The rest is only poetry.' And Mr. Shaynor was playing hot and cold with two of them!

I vowed no unconscious thought of mine should influence the blindfold soul, and pinned myself desperately to the other three, repeating and re-repeating:—

> A savage spot as holy and enchanted
> As e'er beneath a waning moon was haunted
> By woman wailing for her demon lover.

But though I believed my brain thus occupied, my every sense hung upon the writing under the dry, bony hand, all brown-fingered with chemicals and cigarettesmoke.

> Our windows fronting on the dangerous foam,

(he wrote, after long, irresolute snatches), and then—

> Our open casements facing desolate seas
> Forlorn—forlorn—

Here again his face grew peaked and anxious with that sense of loss I had first seen when the Power snatched him. But this time the agony was tenfold keener. As I watched it mounted like mercury in the tube. It lighted his face from within till I thought the visibly scourged soul must leap forth naked between his jaws, unable to endure. A drop of sweat trickled from my forehead down my nose and splashed on the back of my hand.

> Our windows facing on the desolate seas
> And pearly foam of magic fairyland—

'Not yet—not yet,' he muttered, 'wait a minute. *Please* wait a minute. I shall get it then—

> Our magic windows fronting on the sea,
> The dangerous foam of desolate seas . . .
> > For aye.

Ouh, my God!'

From head to heel he shook—shook from the marrow of his bones outwards—then leaped to his feet with raised arms, and slid the chair screeching across the tiled floor where it struck the drawers behind and fell with a jar. Mechanically, I stooped to recover it.

As I rose, Mr. Shaynor was stretching and yawning at leisure.

'I've had a bit of a doze,' he said. 'How did I come to knock the chair over? You look rather——'

'The chair startled me,' I answered. 'It was so sudden in this quiet.'

Young Mr. Cashell behind his shut door was offendedly silent.

'I suppose I must have been dreaming,' said Mr. Shaynor.

'I suppose you must,' I said. 'Talking of dreams—I—I noticed you writing—before——'

He flushed consciously.

'I meant to ask you if you've ever read anything written by a man called Keats.'

'Oh! I haven't much time to read poetry, and I can't say that I remember the name exactly. Is he a popular writer?'

'Middling. I thought you might know him because he's the only poet who was ever a druggist. And he's rather what's called the lover's poet.'

'Indeed. I must dip into him. What did he write about?'

'A lot of things. Here's a sample that may interest you.'

Then and there, carefully, I repeated the verse he had twice spoken and once written not ten minutes ago.

'Ah! Anybody could see he was a druggist from that line about the tinctures and syrups. It's a fine tribute to our profession.'

'I don't know,' said young Mr. Cashell, with icy politeness, opening the door one half-inch, 'if you still happen to be interested in our trifling experiments. But, should such be the case——'

I drew him aside, whispering, 'Shaynor seemed going off into some sort of fit when I spoke to you just now. I thought, even at the risk of being rude, it wouldn't do to take you off your instruments just as the call was coming through. Don't you see?'

'Granted—granted as soon as asked,' he said, unbending. 'I *did* think it a shade odd at the time. So that was why he knocked the chair down?'

'I hope I haven't missed anything,' I said.

'I'm afraid I can't say that, but you're just in time for the end of a rather curious performance. You can come in too, Mr. Shaynor. Listen, while I read it off.'

The Morse instrument was ticking furiously. Mr. Cashell interpreted: '"*K.K.V. Can make nothing of your signals.*"' A pause. '"*M.M.V. M.M.V. Signals unintelligible. Purpose anchor Sandown Bay. Examine instruments tomorrow.*" Do you know what that means? It's a couple of men-o'-war working Marconi signals off the Isle of Wight. They are trying to talk to each other. Neither can read the other's messages, but all their messages are being taken in by our receiver here. They've been going on for ever so long. I wish you could have heard it.'

'How wonderful!' I said. 'Do you mean we're overhearing Portsmouth ships trying to talk to each other— that we're eavesdropping across half South England?'

'Just that. Their transmitters are all right, but their receivers are out of order, so they only get a dot here and a dash there. Nothing clear.'

'Why is that?'

'God knows—and Science will know to-morrow. Perhaps the induction is faulty; perhaps the receivers aren't tuned to receive just the number of vibrations per second that the transmitter sends. Only a word here and there. Just enough to tantalise.'

Again the Morse sprang to life.

'That's one of 'em complaining now. Listen: "*Disheartening—most disheartening.*" It's quite pathetic. Have you ever seen a spiritualistic séance? It reminds me of that sometimes—odds and ends of messages coming out of nowhere—a word here and there—no good at all.'

'But mediums are all impostors,' said Mr. Shaynor, in the doorway, lighting an asthma-cigarette. 'They only do it for the money they can make. I've seen 'em.'

'Here's Poole, at last—clear as a bell. L.L.L. *Now* we shan't be long.' Mr. Cashell rattled the keys merrily. 'Anything you'd like to tell 'em?'

'No, I don't think so,' I said. 'I'll go home and get to bed. I'm feeling a little tired.'

FAIRY-KIST

The only important society in existence to-day is the E.C.F.—the Eclectic *but* Comprehensive Fraternity for the Perpetuation of Gratitude towards Lesser Lights. Its founders were William Lemming, of Lemming and Orton, print-sellers; Alexander Hay McKnight, of Ellis and McKnight, provision-merchants; Robert Keede, M.R.C.P., physician, surgeon, and accoucheur; Lewis Holroyd Burges, tobacconist and cigar importer—all of the South-eastern postal districts—and its zealous, hard-working, but unappreciated Secretary. The meetings are usually at Mr. Lemming's little place in Berkshire, where he raises pigs.

I had been out of England for a while, missing several dinners, but was able to attend a summer one with none present but ourselves; several red mullets in paper; a few green peas and ducklings; an arrangement of cockscombs with olives, and capers as large as cherries; strawberries and cream; some 1903 Château la Tour; and that locked cabinet of cigars to which only Burges has the key.

It was at the hour when men most gracefully curvet abroad on their hobbies, and after McKnight had been complaining of systematic pilfering in his three big shops, that Burges told us how an illustrious English astrologer called Lily had once erected a horoscope to discover the whereabouts of a parcel of stolen fish. The stars led him straight to it and the thief and, incidentally, into a breeze with a lady over 'seven Portugal onions' also gone adrift, but not included in the horoscope. Then we wondered why detective-story writers so seldom use astrology to help out the local Sherlock Holmes; how many illegitimate children that great original had begotten in magazine form; and so drifted on to murder at large. Keede, whose profession gives him advantages, illustrated the subject.

'I wish I could do a decent detective story,' I said at last. 'I never get further than the corpse.'

'Corpses are foul things,' Lemming mused aloud. 'I wonder what sort of a corpse I shall make.'

'You'll never know,' the gentle, silver-haired Burges replied. 'You won't even know you're dead till you look in the glass and see no reflection. An old woman told me that once at Barnet Horse Fair—and I couldn't have been more than seven at the time.'

We were quiet for a few minutes, while the Altar of the Lesser Lights, which is also our cigar-lighter, came into use. The single burner atop, representing gratitude towards Lesser Lights in general, was of course lit. Whenever gratitude towards a named Lesser Light is put forward and proven, one or more of the nine burners round the base can be thrown into action by pulling its pretty silver draw-chain.

'What will you do for me,' said Keede, puffing, 'if I give you an absolutely true detective yarn?'

'If I can make anything of it,' I replied, 'I'll finish the Millar Gift.'

This meant the cataloguing of a mass of Masonic pamphlets (1831–59), bequeathed by a Brother to Lodge

Faith and Works 5836 E.C.—a job which Keede and I, being on the Library Committee, had together shirked for months.

'Promise you won't doctor it if you use it?' said Keede.

'And for goodness' sake don't bring *me* in any more than you can help,' said Lemming.

No practitioner ever comprehends another practitioner's methods; but a promise was given, a bargain struck; and the tale runs here substantially as it was told.

That past autumn, Lemming's pig-man (who had been sitting up with a delicate lady-Berkshire) discovered, on a wet Sunday dawn in October, the body of a village girl called Ellen Marsh lying on the bank of a deep cutting where the road from the village runs into the London Road. Ellen, it seemed, had many friends with whom she used to make evening appointments, and Channet's Ash, as the cross-roads were called, from the big ash that overhung them, was one of her well-known trysting-places. The body lay face down at the highest point of a sloping footpath which the village children had trodden out up the bank, and just where that path turned the corner under Channet's Ash and dropped into the London Road. The pig-man roused the village constable, an ex-soldier called Nicol, who picked up, close to the corpse, a narrow-bladed fern-trowel, its handle wrapped with twine. There were no signs of a struggle, but it had been raining all night. The pig-man then went off to wake up Keede, who was spending the week-end with Lemming. Keede did not disturb his host, Mrs. Lemming being ill at the time, but he and the policeman commandeered a builder's handcart from some half-built shops down the London Road; wheeled the body to the nearest inn—the Cup o' Grapes—pushed a car out of a lock-up; took the shove-halfpenny board from the Oddfellows' Room, and laid the body on it till the regular doctor should arrive.

'He was out,' Keede said, 'so I made an examination on my own. There was no question of assault. She had been dropped by one scientific little jab, just at the base of the skull, by someone who knew his anatomy. That was all. Then Nicol, the bobby, asked me if I'd care to walk over with him to Jimmy Tigner's house.'

'Who was Jimmy Tigner?' I asked.

'Ellen's latest young man—a believing soul. He was assistant at the local tinsmith's, living with his mother in a cottage down the street. It was seven o'clock then, and not a soul about. Jimmy had to be waked up. He stuck his head out of the window, and Nicol stood in the garden among the cabbages—friendly as all sin—and asked him what he'd been doing the night before, because someone had been knocking Ellen about. Well, there wasn't much doubt what Jimmy had been up to. He was altogether "the morning after." He began dressing and talking out of the window at the same time, and said he'd kill any man who touched Ellen.'

'Hadn't the policeman cautioned him?' McKnight demanded.

'What for? They're all friends in this village. Then Jimmy said that, on general principles, Ellen deserved anything she might have got. He'd done with her. He told us a few details (some girl must have given her away), but the point he kept coming back to was that they had parted in "high dungeon." He repeated that a dozen times. Nicol let him run on, and when the boy was quite dressed, he said: "Well, you may as well come on up-street an' look at her. She don't bear you any malice now." (Oh, I tell you the War has put an edge on things all round!) Jimmy came down, jumpy as a cat, and, when we were going through the Cup o' Grapes yard, Nicol unlocked the garage and pushed him in. The face hadn't been covered either.'

'Drastic,' said Burges, shivering.

'It was. Jimmy went off the handle at once; and Nicol kept patting him on the back and saying: "That's all right! I'll go bail *you* didn't do it." Then Jimmy wanted to know why the deuce he'd been dragged into it. Nicol said: "Oh, that's what the French call a confrontation. But you're all right." Then Jimmy went for Nicol. So we got him out of the garage, and gave him a drink, and took him back to his mother. But at the inquest he accounted for every minute of his time. He'd left Ellen under Channet's Ash, telling her what he thought of her over his shoulder for a quarter of a mile down the lane (that's what "high dungeon" meant in their language). Luckily two or three of the girls and the bloods of the village had heard 'em. After that, he'd gone to the Cup o' Grapes, filled himself up, and told everybody his grievances against Ellen till closing-time. The interestin' thing was that he seemed to be about the only decent boy of the lot.'

'Then,' Lemming interrupted, 'the reporters began looking for clues. They—they behaved like nothing I've ever imagined! I was afraid we'd be dragged into it. You see, that wretched Ellen had been our scullery-maid a few months before, and—my wife—as ill as she was . . . But mercifully that didn't come out at the inquest.'

'No,' Keede went on. 'Nicol steered the thing. He's

related to Ellen. And by the time Jimmy had broken down and wept, and the reporters had got their sensation, it was brought in "person or persons unknown."'

'What about the trowel?' said McKnight, who is a notable gardener.

'It was a most valuable clue, of course, because it explained the *modus operandi*. The punch—with the handle, the local doctor said—had been delivered through her back hair, with just enough strength to do the job and no more. I couldn't have operated more neatly myself. The Police took the trowel, but they couldn't trace it to anyone, somehow. The main point in the village was that no one who knew her wanted to go into Ellen's character. She was rather popular, you see. Of course the village was a bit disappointed about Jimmy's getting off; and when he broke down again at her funeral, it revived suspicion. Then the Huish poisoning case happened up in the North; and the reporters had to run off and take charge of it. What did your pig-man say about 'em, Will?'

'Oh, Griffiths said: "'Twas Gawd's own Mercy those young gen'lemen didn't 'ave 'alf of us 'ung before they left. They were that energetic!"'

'They were,' said Keede. 'That's why I kept back my evidence.'

'There was the wife to be considered too,' said Lemming. 'She'd never have stood being connected with the thing, even remotely.'

'I took it upon myself to act upon that belief,' Keede replied gravely. 'Well—now for *my* little bit. I'd come down that Saturday night to spend the week-end with Will here; and I couldn't get here till late. It was raining hard, and the car skidded badly. Just as I turned off the

London Road into the lane under Channet's Ash, my lights picked up a motor-bike lying against the bank where they found Ellen; and I saw a man bending over a woman up the bank. Naturally one don't interfere with these little things as a rule; but it occurred to me there might have been a smash. So I called out: "Anything wrong? Can I help?" The man said: "No, thanks. We're all right," or words to that effect, and I went on. *But* the bike's letters happened to be my own initials, and its number was the year I was born in. I wasn't likely to forget 'em, you see.'

'You told the Police?' said McKnight severely.

'Took 'em into my confidence at once, Sandy,' Keede replied. 'There was a Sergeant, Sydenham way, that I'd been treating for Salonika fever. I told him I was afraid I'd brushed a motor-bike at night coming up into West Wickham, on one of those blind bends up the hill, and I'd be glad to know I hadn't hurt him. He gave me what I wanted in twenty-four hours. The bike belonged to one Henry Wollin—of independent means—livin' near Mitcham.'

'But West Wickham isn't in Berkshire—nor is Mitcham,' McKnight began.

'Here's a funny thing,' Keede went on, without noticing. 'Most men and nearly all women commit murder single-handed; but no man likes to go man-hunting alone. Primitive instinct, I suppose. That's why I lugged Will into the Sherlock Holmes business. You hated it too.'

'I hadn't recovered from those reporters,' said Lemming.

'They *were* rather energetic. But I persuaded Will that

we'd call upon Master Wollin and apologise—as penitent motorists—and we went off to Mitcham in my two-seater. Wollin had a very nice little detached villa down there. The old woman—his housekeeper—who let us in, was West Country, talkin' as broad as a pat o' butter. She took us through the hall to Wollin, planting things in his back-garden.'

'A wonderful little garden for that soil,' said Lemming, who considers himself an even greater gardener than McKnight, although he keeps two men less.

'He was a big, strong, darkish chap—middle-aged—wide as a bull between the eyes—no beauty, and evidently had been a very sick man. Will and I apologised to him, and he began to lie at once. He said he'd been at West Wickham at the time (on the night of the murder, you know), and he remembered dodging out of the way of a car. He didn't seem pleased that we should have picked up his number so promptly. Seeing we were helping him to establish an *alibi*, he ought to have been, oughtn't he?'

'Ye mean,' said McKnight, suddenly enlightened, 'that he was committing the murder here in Berkshire on the night that he told you he was in West Wickham, which is in Kent.'

'Which is in Kent. Thank you. It is. And we went on talking about that West Wickham hill till he mentioned he'd been in the War, and that gave me *my* chance to talk. And he was an enthusiastic gardener, he said, and that let Will in. It struck us both that he was nervous in a carneying way that didn't match his build and voice at all. Then we had a drink in his study. Then the fun began. There were four pictures on the wall.'

'Prints—prints,' Lemming corrected professionally.

'Same thing, aren't they, Will? Anyhow, *you* got excited enough over them. At first I thought Will was only playing up. But he was genuine.'

'So were they,' Lemming said. 'Sandy, you remember those four "Apostles" I sold you last Christmas?'

'I have my counterfoil yet,' was the dry answer.

'What sort of prints were they?' Burges demanded.

The moonlike face of Alexander McKnight, who collects prints along certain lines, lit with devout rapture. He began checking off on his fingers.

'The firrst,' said he, 'was the draped one of Ray—the greatest o' them all. Next, yon French print o' Morrison, when he was with the Duke of Orleans at Blois; third, the Leyden print of Grew in his youth; and, fourth, that wreathed Oxford print of Hales. The whole aapostolic succession of them.'

'I never knew Morrison laid out links in France,' I said.

'Morrison? Links? Links? Did you think those four were gowfers then?'

'Wasn't old Tom Morrison a great golfer?' I ventured.

McKnight turned on me with utter scorn. 'Those prints—' he began. 'But ye'd not understand. They were —we'll say they were just pictures of some garrdeners I happened to be interested in.'

This was rude of McKnight, but I forgave him because of the excellence of his imported groceries. Keede went on.

'After Will had talked the usual buyer's talk, Wollin seemed willin' to part with 'em, and we arranged we'd call again and complete the deal. Will 'ud do business with a criminal on the drop o' course. He gave Wollin his card, and we left; Wollin carneying and suckin' up to us right to the front door. We hadn't gone a couple of miles when Will found he'd given Wollin his personal card—*not* his business one—with his private address in Berkshire! The murder about ten days old, and the papers still stinkin' with it! I think I told you at the time you were a fool, Will?'

'You did. I never saw how I came to make the mistake. These cards are different sizes too,' poor Lemming said.

'No, we were not a success as man-hunters,' Keede laughed. 'But Will and I had to call again, of course, to settle the sale. That was a week after. And this time, of course, Wollin—not being as big a fool as Will—had hopped it and left no address. The old lady said he was given to going off for weeks at a time. That hung us up; but to do Will justice, which I don't often, he saved the situation by his damned commercial instincts. He said he wanted to look at the prints again. The old lady was agreeable—rather forthcomin' in fact. She let us into the study, had the prints down, and asked if we'd like some tea. While she was getting it, and Will was hanging over the prints, I looked round the room. There was a cupboard, half opened, full of tools, and on top of 'em a new—what did you say it was, Will?—fern-trowel. Same pattern as the one Nicol found by Ellen's head. That gave me a bit of a turn. I'd never done any Sherlockin' outside my own profession. Then the old lady came back and I made up to her. When I was a sixpenny doctor at Lambeth, half my great success——'

'Ye can hold that over,' McKnight observed. 'The murrder's what's interestin' me.'

'Wait till your next go of gout. *I'll* interest you, Sandy.

Well, she expanded (they all do with me), and, like patients, she wanted advice gratis. So I gave it. Then she began talking about Wollin. She'd been his nurse, I fancy. Anyhow, she'd known him all his life, and she said he was full of virtue and sickness. She said he'd been wounded and gassed and gangrened in the War, and after that—oh, she worked up to it beautifully—he'd been practically off his head. She called it "fairy-kist."'

'That's pretty—very pretty,' said Burges.

'Meanin' he'd been kissed by the fairies?' McKnight inquired.

'It would appear so, Sandy. I'd never heard the word before. West Country, I suppose. And she had one of those slow, hypnotic voices, like cream from a jug. Everything she said squared with my own theories up to date. Wollin was on the break of life, and, given wounds, gas, and gangrene just at that crisis, why, anything—Jack the Ripperism or religious mania—might come uppermost. I knew that, and the old lady was as good as telling it me over again, and putting up a defence for him in advance. Wonderful bit of work. Patients' relatives *are* like that sometimes—specially wives.'

'Yes, but what about Wollin?' I said.

'Wait a bit. Will and I went away, and we talked over the fern-trowel and so forth, and we both agreed we ought to release our evidence. There, somehow, we stuck. Man-hunting's a dirty job. So we compromised. I knew a fellow in the C.I.D., who thought he had a floating kidney, and we decided to put the matter before him and let him take charge. He had to go North, however, and he wrote he could not see us before the Tuesday of next week. This would be four or five weeks after the murder. I came down here again that week-end to stay with Will, and on Saturday night Will and I went to his study to put the finishing touches to our evidence. I was trying to keep my own theory out of it as much as I could. Yes, if you want to know, Jack the Ripper *was* my notion, and my theory was that my car had frightened the brute off before he could do anything in that line. And *then*, Will's housemaid shot into the study with Nicol after her, and Jimmy Tigner after him!'

'Luckily my wife was up in town at the time,' said Lemming. 'They all shouted at once too.'

'They did!' said Keede. 'Nicol shouted loudest, though. He was plastered with mud, waving what was left of his helmet, and Jimmy was in hysterics. Nicol yelled:— "Look at me! Look at this! It's all right! Look at me! I've got it!" He *had* got it too! It came out, when they quieted down, that he had been walking with Jimmy in the lane by Channet's Ash. Hearing a lorry behind 'em—you know what a narrow lane it is—they stepped up on to that path on the bank (I told you about it) that the school-children had made. It was a contractor's lorry—Higbee and Norton, a local firm—with two girders for some new shops on the London Road. They were deliverin' late on Saturday evening, so's the men could start on Monday. Well, these girders had been chucked in anyhow on to a brick lorry with a tail-board. Instead of slopin' forward they cocked up backwards like a pheasant's tail, sticking up high and overhanging. They were tied together with a few turns of rope at the far ends. Do you see?'

So far we could see nothing. Keede made it plainer.

'Nicol said he went up the bank first—Jimmy behind him—and after a few steps he found his helmet knocked off. If he'd been a foot higher up the bank his head 'ud have gone. The lorry had skidded on the tar of the London Road, as it turned into it left-handed—her tail swung to the right, and the girders swung with it, just missing braining Nicol up on the bank. The lorry was well in the left-hand gutter when he got his breath again. He went for the driver at once. The man said all the lorries always skidded under Channet's Ash, when it was wet, because of the camber of the road, and they allowed for it as a regular stunt. And he damned the road authorities, and Nicol for being in the light. Then Jimmy Tigner, Nicol told us, caught on to what it meant, and he climbed into the lorry shouting:—"*You* killed Ellen!" It was all Nicol could do to prevent him choking the fellow there and then; but Nicol didn't pull him off till Jimmy got it out of the driver that he had been delivering girders the night Ellen was killed. Of course, he hadn't noticed anything.

'Then Nicol came over to Lemming and me to talk it over. I gave Jimmy a bromide and sent him off to his mother. He wasn't any particular use, except as a witness—and no good after. Then Nicol went over the whole thing again several times, to fix it in our minds. Next morning he and I and Will called on old Higbee before he could get to church. We made him take out the particular lorry implicated, with the same driver, and a duplicate load packed the same way, and demonstrate for us. We kept her stunting half Sunday morning in the rain, and the skid delivered her into the left-hand gutter of the London Road every time she took that corner; and *every* time her tail with the girders swiped along the bank of that lane like a man topping a golf-ball. And when she did that, there were half a dozen paces—not more—along that school-children's path, that meant sure death to anyone on it at the time. Nicol was just climbing into the danger-zone when he stepped up, but he was a foot too low. The girders only brushed through his hair. We got some laths and stuck 'em in along the path (Jimmy Tigner told us Ellen was five foot three) to test our theory. The last lath was as near as could be to where the pig-man had found the body; and that happened to be the extreme end of the lorry's skid. See what happened? *We* did. At the end of her skid the lorry's rear wheels 'ud fetch up every time with a bit of a jar against the bank, and the girders 'ud quiver and lash out a few inches—like a golf-club wigglin', Ellen must have caught just enough of that little sideway flick, at the base of her skull, to drop her like a pithed ox. We worked it all out on the last lath. The rope wrappings on the end of the damned things saved the skin being broken. Hellish, isn't it? And then Jimmy Tigner realised that if she had only gone two paces further she'd have been round the corner of the bank and safe. Then it came back to him that she'd stopped talkin' "in dungeon" rather suddenly, and he hadn't gone back to see! I spent most of the afternoon sitting with him. He'd been tried too high—too high. I had to sign his certificate a few weeks later. No! He won't get better.'

We commented according to our natures, and then McKnight said:—'But—if so—why did Wollin disappear?'

'That comes next on the agenda, Worshipful Sir. Brother Lemming has *not* the instincts of the real man-hunter. He felt shy. I had to remind him of the prints before he'd call on Wollin again. We'd allowed our prey ten days to get the news, while the papers were busy explainin' Ellen's death, and people were writin' to 'em and saying they'd nearly been killed by lorries in the same way in other places. Then old Higbee gave Ellen's people a couple of hundred without prejudice (he wanted to get a higher seat in the Synagogue—the Squire's pew, I think), and everyone felt that her character had been cleared.'

'But Wollin?' McKnight insisted.

'When Will and I went to call on him he'd come home again. I hadn't seen him for—let's see, it must have been going on for a month—but I hardly recognised him. He was burned out—all his wrinkles gashes, and his eyes readjustin' 'emselves after looking into Hell. One gets to know that kind of glare nowadays. But he was immensely relieved to see us. So was the old lady. If he'd been a dog, he'd have been wagging his tail from the nose down. That was rather embarrassing too, because it wasn't our fault we hadn't had him tried for his life. And while we were talking over the prints, he said, quite suddenly: "*I* don't blame you! I'd have believed it against myself on the evidence!" That broke the ice with a brick. He told us he'd almost stepped on Ellen's body that night—dead and stiffening. Then I'd come round the corner and hailed him, and that panicked him. He jumped on his bike and fled, forgetting the trowel. So he'd bought another with some crazy notion of putting the Law off the track. That's what hangs murderers.

'When Will and I first called on him, with our fairy-tales about West Wickham, he had fancied he might be under observation, and Will's mixing up the cards clinched it. . . . So he disappeared. He went down into his own cellar, he said, and waited there, with his revolver, ready to blow his brains out when the warrant came. What a month! Think of it! A cellar and a candle, a file of gardening papers, and a loaded revolver for company! Then I asked why. He said no jury on earth would have believed his explanation of his movements. "Look at it from the prosecution's point of view," he said. "Here's a middle-aged man with a medical record that 'ud account for any loss of controls—and that would mean Broadmoor—fifty or sixty miles from his home in a rainstorm, on the top of a fifteen-foot cutting, at night. He leaves behind him, with the girl's body, the very sort of weapon that might have caused her death. I read about the trowel in the papers. Can't you see how the thing 'ud be handled?" he said.

'I asked him then what in the world he really *was* doing that had to be covered up by suicide. He said he was planting things. I asked if he meant stolen goods. After the trouble we'd given him, Will and I wouldn't have peached on him for that, would we, Will?'

'No,' said Lemming. 'His face was enough. It was like—' and he named a picture by an artist called Goya.

'"Stolen goods be damned," Wollin said to me. "If you *must* have it, I was planting out plants from my garden." What did you say to him then, Will?'

'I asked him what the plants were, of course,' said Lemming, and turned to McKnight. 'They were daffodils, and a sort of red honeysuckle, and a special loosestrife—a hybrid.' McKnight nodded judicially while Lemming talked incomprehensible horticulture for a minute or two.

'Gardening isn't my line,' Keede broke in, 'but Will's

questions acted on Master Wollin like a charm. He dropped his suicide talk, and began on gardening. After that it was Will's operation. I hadn't a look-in for ten minutes. Then I said: "What's there to make a fuss about in all this?" Then he turned away from Will and spoke to me, carneying again—like patients do. He began with his medical record—one shrapnel peppering, and one gassing, with gangrene. He had put in about fourteen months in various hospitals, and he was full of medical talkee-talkee. Just like *you*, Sandy, when you've been seeing your damned specialists. And he'd been doped for pain and pinched nerves, till the wonder was he'd ever pulled straight again. He told us that the only thing that had helped him through the War was his love of gardening. He'd been mad keen on it all his life—and even in the worst of the Somme he used to get comfort out of plants and bot'ny, and that sort of stuff. I never did. Well, I saw he was speaking the truth; but next minute he began to hedge. I noticed it, and said something, and then he sweated in rivers. He hadn't turned a hair over his proposed suicide, but now he sweated till he had to wipe it off his forehead.

'Then I told him I was something else besides a G.P., and Will was too, if that 'ud make things easier for him. And it did. From then on he told the tale on the square, in grave distress, you know. At his last hospital he'd been particularly doped, and he fancied that that was where his mind had gone. He told me that he was insane, and had been for more than a year. I asked him not to start on his theories till he'd finished with his symptoms. (You patients are all the same.) He said there were Gotha raids round his hospital, which used to upset the wards. And there was a V.A.D.—she must have been something of a woman, too—who used to read to him and tell him stories to keep him quiet. He liked 'em because, as far as he remembered, they were all about gardening. *But*, when he grew better, he began to hear Voices—little whispers at first, growing louder and ending in regular uproars—ordering him to do certain things. He used to lie there shaking with horror, because he funked going mad. He wanted to live and be happy again, in his garden—like the rest of us.

'When he was discharged, he said, he left hospital with a whole Army Corps shouting into his ears. The sum and substance of their orders was that he must go out and plant roots and things at large up and down the country-side. Naturally, he suffered a bit, but, after a while, he went back to his house at Mitcham and obeyed orders, because, he said, as long as he was carrying 'em out the Voices stopped. If he knocked off even for a week, he said, they helled him on again. Being a methodical bird, he'd bought a motor-bike and a basket lined with oil-cloth, and he used to skirmish out planting his silly stuff by the wayside, and in coppices and on commons. He'd spy out likely spots by day and attend to 'em after dark. He was working round Channet's Ash that night, and he'd come out of the meadow, and down the school-children path, right on to Ellen's body. That upset him. I wasn't worryin' about Ellen for the moment. I headed him back to his own symptoms. The devil of it was that, left to himself, there was nothing he'd have liked better than this planting job; but the Voices ordering him to do it, scared the soul out of him. Then I asked him if the Voices had worried him much when he was in the cellar with his revolver. He said, comin' to think of it, that they had not; and I reminded him that there was very little seasickness in the boats when submarines were around.'

'You've forgotten,' said Lemming, 'that he stopped fawning as soon as he found out we were on the square.'

'He did so,' Keede assented. '*And* he insisted on our staying to supper, so's he could tell his symptoms properly. (Might have been you again, Sandy.) The old lady backed him up. She was clinging to us too, as though we'd done her a favour. And Wollin told us that if he'd been in the dock, he *knew* he'd have come out with his tale of his Voices and night-plantings, just like the Ancient Mariner; and that would have sent him to Broadmoor. It was Broadmoor, not hanging, that he funked. And so he went on and on about his Voices, and I cross-examined. He said they used to begin with noises in his head like rotten walnuts being smashed; but he fancied that must have been due to the bombs in the raid. I reminded him again that I didn't want his theories. The Voices were sometimes like his V.A.D.'s, but louder, and they were all mixed up with horrible dope-dreams. For instance, he said, there was a smiling dog that ran after him and licked his face, and the dog had something to do with being able to read gardening books, and that gave him the notion, as he lay abed in hospital, that he had water on the brain, and that that 'ud prevent him from root-gatherin' an' obeying his orders.'

'He used the words "root-gathering." It's an unusual combination nowadays,' said Lemming suddenly. 'That made me take notice, Sandy.'

Keede held up his hand. 'No, you don't, Will! I tell this tale much better than you. Well, then Will cut in, and asked Wollin if he could remember exactly what sort of stuff his V.A.D. had read to him during the raids. He couldn't; except that it was all about gardening, and it made him feel as if he were in Paradise. Yes, Sandy, he used the word "Paradise." Then Will asked him if he could give us the precise wording of his orders to plant things. He couldn't do that either. Then Will said, like a barrister: "I put it to you, that the Voices ordered you to plant things by the wayside *for such as have no gardens.*" And Will went over it slowly twice. "My God!" said Wollin. "That's the *ipsissima verba.*" "Good," said Will. "Now for your dog. I put it to you that the smiling dog was really a secret friend of yours. What was his colour?" "Dunno," said Wollin. "It was yellow," says Will. "A big yellow bull-terrier." Wollin thought a bit and agreed. "When he ran after you," says Will, "did you ever hear anyone trying to call him off, in a very loud voice?" "Sometimes," said Wollin. "Better still," says Will. "Now, I put it to you that that yellow bull-terrier came into a library with a Scotch gardener who said it was a great privilege to be able to consult botanical books." Wollin thought a bit, and said that those were some of the exact words that were mixed up with his Voices, and his trouble about not being able to read. I shan't forget his face when he said it, either. My word, he sweated.'

Here Sandy McKnight smiled and nodded across to Lemming, who nodded back as mysteriously as a Freemason or a gardener.

'All this time,' Keede continued, 'Will looked more important than ever I've seen him outside of his shop; and he said to Wollin: "Now I'll tell you the story, Mr. Wollin, that your V.A.D. read or told you. Check me where your memory fails, and I'll refresh it." That's what you said, wasn't it, Will? And Will began to spin him a long nursery-yarn about some children who planted flowers out in a meadow that wasn't theirs, so that such as had no gardens might enjoy them; and one of the children called himself an Honest Root-gatherer, and one of 'em had something like water on the brain; and there was an old Squire who owned a smiling yellow bull-terrier that was fond of the children, and he kept his walnuts till they were rotten, and then he smashed 'em all. You ought to have heard Will! He can talk—even when there isn't money in it.'

'*Mary's Meadow!*' Sandy's hand banged the table.

'Hsh!' said Burges, enthralled. 'Go on, Robin.'

'And Wollin checked it all, with the sweat drying on him—remember, Will?—and he put in his own reminiscences—one about a lilac sun-bonnet, I remember.'

'Not lilac—marigold. One string of it was canary colour and one was white.' McKnight corrected as though this were a matter of life and death.

'Maybe. And there was a nightingale singing to the Man in the Moon, and an old Herbal—not Gerard's, or I'd have known it—"Paradise" something. Wollin contributed that sort of stuff all the time, with ten years knocked off his shoulders and a voice like the Town Crier's. Yes, Sandy, the story *was* called *Mary's Meadow*. It all came back to him—*via* Will.'

'And that helped?' I asked.

'Well,' Keede said slowly, 'a General Practitioner can't much believe in the remission of sins, can he? But if that's possible, I know how a redeemed soul looks. The old lady had pretended to get supper, but she stopped when Will began his yarn, and listened all through. Then Wollin put up his hand, as though he were hearing his dam' Voices. Then he brushed 'em away, and he dropped his head on the table and wept. My God, how he wept! And then she kissed him, *and* me. Did she kiss you, Will?'

'She certainly did not,' said the scandalised Lemming, who has been completely married for a long while.

'You missed something. She has a seductive old mouth still. And Wollin wouldn't let us go—hung on to us like a child. So, after supper, we went over the affair in detail, till all hours. The pain and the dope had made that nursery story stick in one corner of his mind till it took charge—it does sometimes—but all mixed up with bombings and nightmares. As soon as he got the explanation it evaporated like ether and didn't leave a stink. I sent him to bed full of his own beer, and growing a shade dictatorial. He was a not uncommon cross between a brave bully and an old maid; but a man, right enough, when the pressures were off. The old lady let us out— she didn't kiss me again, worse luck! She was primitive Stone Age—bless her! She looked on us as a couple of magicians who'd broken the spell on him, she said.'

'Well, you had,' said Burges. 'What did he do afterwards?'

'Bought a side-car to his bike, to hold more vegetables—he'll be had up for poaching or trespassing, some day—and he cuts about the Home Counties planting his stuff as happy as—oh my soul! *What* wouldn't I give to be even one fraction as happy as he is! *But*, mind you, he'd have committed suicide on the nod if Will and I had had him arrested. We aren't exactly first-class Sherlocks.'

McKnight was grumbling to himself. 'Juliaana Horratia Ewing,' said he. 'The best, the kindest, the sweetest, the most eenocent tale ever the soul of a woman gied birth to. I may sell tapioca for a living in the suburbs, but I know *that*. An' as for those prints o' mine,' he turned to me, 'they were not garrdeners. They were the Four Great British Botanists, an'—an'—I ask your pardon.'

He pulled the draw-chains of all the nine burners round the Altar of the Lesser Lights before we had time to put it to the vote.

THE STORY OF MUHAMMAD DIN

> Who is the happy man? He that sees in his own
> house at home, little children crowned with
> dust, leaping and falling and crying.
>
> —*Munichandra*,
> translated by Professor Peterson

The polo-ball was an old one, scarred, chipped, and
dinted. It stood on the mantelpiece among the pipe-stems
which Imam Din, *khitmatgar*, was cleaning for me.

'Does the Heaven-born want this ball?' said Imam Din
deferentially.

The Heaven-born set no particular store by it; but of
what use was a polo-ball to a *khitmatgar*?

'By Your Honour's favour, I have a little son. He has
seen this ball, and desires it to play with. I do not want it
for myself.'

No one would for an instant accuse portly old Imam
Din of wanting to play with polo-balls. He carried out the
battered thing into the verandah; and there followed a
hurricane of joyful squeaks, a patter of small feet, and
the *thud-thud-thud* of the ball rolling along the ground.
Evidently the little son had been waiting outside the
door to secure his treasure. But how had he managed to
see that polo-ball?

Next day, coming back from office half an hour earlier

than usual, I was aware of a small figure in the dining-room—a tiny, plump figure in a ridiculously inadequate shirt which came, perhaps, half-way down the tubby stomach. It wandered round the room, thumb in mouth, crooning to itself as it took stock of the pictures. Undoubtedly this was the 'little son.'

He had no business in my room, of course; but was so deeply absorbed in his discoveries that he never noticed me in the doorway. I stepped into the room and startled him nearly into a fit. He sat down on the ground with a gasp. His eyes opened, and his mouth followed suit. I knew what was coming, and fled, followed by a long, dry howl which reached the servants' quarters far more quickly than any command of mine had ever done. In ten seconds Imam Din was in the dining-room. Then despairing sobs arose, and I returned to find Imam Din admonishing the small sinner, who was using most of his shirt as a handkerchief.

'This boy,' said Imam Din judicially, 'is a *budmash*—a big *budmash*. He will, without doubt, go to the *jail-khana* for his behaviour.' Renewed yells from the penitent, and an elaborate apology to myself from Imam Din.

'Tell the baby,' said I, 'that the Sahib is not angry, and take him away.' Imam Din conveyed my forgiveness to the offender, who had now gathered all his shirt round his neck, stringwise, and the yell subsided into a sob. The two set off for the door. 'His name,' said Imam Din, as though the name were part of the crime, 'is Muhammad Din, and he is a *budmash*.' Freed from present danger, Muhammad Din turned round in his father's arms, and said gravely, 'It is true that my name is Muhammad Din, Tahib, but I am not a *budmash*. I am a *man*!'

From that day dated my acquaintance with Muhammad Din. Never again did he come into my dining-room, but on the neutral ground of the garden we greeted each other with much state, though our conversation was confined to '*Talaam, Tahib*' from his side, and '*Salaam, Muhammad Din*' from mine. Daily on my return from office, the little white shirt and the fat little body used to rise from the shade of the creeper-covered trellis where they had been hid; and daily I checked my horse here, that my salutation might not be slurred over or given unseemly.

Muhammad Din never had any companions. He used to trot about the compound, in and out of the castor-oil bushes, on mysterious errands of his own. One day I stumbled upon some of his handiwork far down the grounds. He had half buried the polo-ball in dust, and stuck six shrivelled old marigold flowers in a circle round it. Outside that circle again was a rude square, traced out in bits of red brick alternating with fragments of broken china; the whole bounded by a little bank of dust. The water-man from the well-curb put in a plea for the small architect, saying that it was only the play of a baby and did not much disfigure my garden.

Heaven knows that I had no intention of touching the child's work then or later; but, that evening, a stroll through the garden brought me unawares full on it; so that I trampled, before I knew, marigold-heads, dust-bank, and fragments of broken soap-dish into confusion past all hope of mending. Next morning, I came upon Muhammad Din crying softly to himself over the ruin I had wrought. Some one had cruelly told him that the Sahib was very angry with him for spoiling the garden, and had scattered his rubbish, using bad language the while. Muhammad Din laboured for an hour at effacing every trace of the dust-bank and pottery fragments, and it was with a tearful and apologetic face that he said, '*Talaam, Tahib*,' when I came home from office. A hasty inquiry resulted in Imam Din informing Muhammad Din that, by my singular favour, he was permitted to disport himself as he pleased. Whereat the child took heart and fell to tracing the ground-plan of an edifice which was to eclipse the marigold-polo-ball creation.

For some months the chubby little eccentricity revolved in his humble orbit among the castor-oil bushes and in the dust; always fashioning magnificent palaces from stale flowers thrown away by the bearer, smooth water-worn pebbles, bits of broken glass, and feathers pulled, I fancy, from my fowls—always alone, and always crooning to himself.

A gaily-spotted sea-shell was dropped one day close to the last of his little buildings; and I looked that Muhammad Din should build something more than ordinarily splendid on the strength of it. Nor was I disappointed. He meditated for the better part of an hour, and his crooning rose to a jubilant song. Then he began tracing in the dust. It would certainly be a wondrous palace, this one, for it was two yards long and a yard broad in ground-plan. But the palace was never completed.

Next day there was no Muhammad Din at the head of the carriage-drive, and no '*Talaam, Tahib*' to welcome my return. I had grown accustomed to the greeting, and its omission troubled me. Next day Imam Din told me that the child was suffering slightly from fever and needed quinine. He got the medicine, and an English doctor.

'They have no stamina, these brats,' said the Doctor, as he left Imam Din's quarters.

A week later, though I would have given much to have avoided it, I met on the road to the Musulman burying-ground Imam Din, accompanied by one other friend, carrying in his arms, wrapped in a white cloth, all that was left of little Muhammad Din.

'MY SON'S WIFE'

He had suffered from the disease of the century since his early youth, and before he was thirty he was heavily marked with it. He and a few friends had rearranged Heaven very comfortably, but the reorganisation of Earth, which they called Society, was even greater fun. It demanded Work in the shape of many taxi-rides daily; hours of brilliant talk with brilliant talkers; some sparkling correspondence; a few silences (but on the understanding that their own turn should come soon) while other people expounded philosophies; and a fair number of picture-galleries, tea-fights, concerts, theatres, music-halls, and cinema shows; the whole trimmed with love-making to women whose hair smelt of cigarette-smoke. Such strong days sent Frankwell Midmore back to his flat assured that he and his friends had helped the World a step nearer the Truth, the Dawn, and the New Order.

His temperament, he said, led him more towards con-crete data than abstract ideas. People who investigate detail are apt to be tired at the day's end. The same temperament, or it may have been a woman, made him early attach himself to the Immoderate Left of his Cause in the capacity of an experimenter in Social Relations. And since the Immoderate Left contains plenty of women anxious to help earnest inquirers with large independent incomes to arrive at evaluations of essentials, Frankwell Midmore's lot was far from contemptible.

At that hour Fate chose to play with him. A widowed aunt, widely separated by nature, and more widely by marriage, from all that Midmore's mother had ever been or desired to be, died and left him possessions. Mrs. Midmore, having that summer embraced a creed which denied the existence of death, naturally could not stoop to burial; but Midmore had to leave London for the dank country at a season when Social Regeneration works best through long, cushioned conferences, two by two, after tea. There he faced the bracing ritual of the British funeral, and was wept at across the raw grave by an elderly coffin-shaped female with a long nose, who called him 'Master Frankie'; and there he was congratulated behind an echoing top-hat by a man he mistook for a mute, who turned out to be his aunt's lawyer. He wrote his mother next day, after a bright account of the funeral:

'So far as I can understand, she has left me between four and five hundred a year. It all comes from Ther Land, as they call it down here. The unspeakable attorney, Sperrit, and a green-eyed daughter, who hums to herself as she tramps but is silent on all subjects except "huntin'," insisted on taking me to see it. Ther Land is brown and green in alternate slabs like chocolate and pistachio cakes, speckled with occasional peasants who do not utter. In case it should not be wet enough there is a wet brook in the middle of it. Ther House is by the brook. I shall look into it later. If there should be any little memento of Jenny that you care for, let me know. Didn't you tell me that mid-Victorian furniture is coming into the market again? Jenny's old maid—it is called Rhoda

Dolbie—tells me that Jenny promised it thirty pounds a year. The will does not. Hence, I suppose, the tears at the funeral. But that is close on ten per cent of the income. I fancy Jenny has destroyed all her private papers and records of her *vie intime*, if, indeed, life be possible in such a place. The Sperrit man told me that if I had means of my own I might come and live on Ther Land. I didn't tell him how much I would pay not to! I cannot think it right that any human being should exercise mastery over others in the merciless fashion our tom-fool social system permits; so, as it is all mine, I intend to sell it whenever the unholy Sperrit can find a purchaser.'

And he went to Mr. Sperrit with the idea next day, just before returning to town.

'Quite so,' said the lawyer. 'I see your point, of course. But the house itself is rather old-fashioned—hardly the type purchasers demand nowadays. There's no park, of course, and the bulk of the land is let to a life-tenant, a Mr. Sidney. As long as he pays his rent, he can't be turned out, and even if he didn't'—Mr. Sperrit's face relaxed a shade—'you might have a difficulty.'

'The property brings four hundred a year, I understand,' said Midmore.

'Well, hardly—ha-ardly. Deducting land and income tax, tithes, fire insurance, cost of collection and repairs of course, it returned two hundred and eighty-four pounds last year. The repairs are rather a large item—owing to the brook. I call it Liris—out of Horace, you know.'

Midmore looked at his watch impatiently.

'I suppose you can find somebody to buy it?' he repeated.

'We will do our best, of course, if those are your

instructions. Then, that is all except'—here Midmore half rose, but Mr. Sperrit's little grey eyes held his large brown ones firmly—'except about Rhoda Dolbie, Mrs. Werf's maid. I may tell you that we did not draw up your aunt's last will. She grew secretive towards the last—elderly people often do—and had it done in London. I expect her memory failed her, or she mislaid her notes. She used to put them in her spectacle-case. . . . My motor only takes eight minutes to get to the station, Mr. Midmore . . . but, as I was saying, whenever she made her will with *us*, Mrs. Werf always left Rhoda thirty pounds per annum. Charlie, the wills!' A clerk with a baldish head and a long nose dealt documents on to the table like cards, and breathed heavily behind Midmore. 'It's in no sense a legal obligation, of course,' said Mr. Sperrit, 'Ah, that one is dated January the 11th, eighteen eighty-nine.'

Midmore looked at his watch again and found himself saying with no good grace: 'Well, I suppose she'd better have it—for the present at any rate.'

He escaped with an uneasy feeling that two hundred and fifty-four pounds a year was not exactly four hundred, and that Charlie's long nose annoyed him. Then he returned, first-class, to his own affairs.

Of the two, perhaps three, experiments in Social Relations which he had then in hand, one interested him acutely. It had run for some months and promised most variegated and interesting developments, on which he dwelt luxuriously all the way to town. When he reached his flat he was not well prepared for a twelve-page letter explaining, in the diction of the Immoderate Left which rubricates its I's and illuminates its T's, that the lady had realised greater attractions in another Soul. She re-stated, rather than pleaded, the gospel of the Immoderate Left as her justification, and ended in an impassioned demand for her right to express herself in and on her own life, through which, she pointed out, she could pass but once. She added that if, later, she should discover Midmore was 'essentially complementary to her needs,' she would tell him so. That Midmore had himself written much the same sort of epistle—barring the hint of return—to a woman of whom his needs for self-expression had caused him to weary three years before, did not assist him in the least. He expressed himself to the gas-fire in terms essential but not complimentary. Then he reflected on the detached criticism of his best friends and her best friends, male and female, with whom he and she and others had talked so openly while their gay adventure was in flower. He recalled, too—this must have been about midnight— her analysis from every angle, remote and most intimate, of the mate to whom she had been adjudged under the base convention which is styled marriage. Later, at that bad hour when the cattle wake for a little, he remembered her in other aspects and went down into the hell appointed; desolate, desiring, with no God to call upon. About eleven o'clock next morning Eliphaz the Temanite, Bildad the Shuhite, and Zophar the Naamathite called upon him 'for they had made appointment together' to see how he took it; but the janitor told them that Job had gone—into the country, he believed.

Midmore's relief when he found his story was not written across his aching temples for Mr. Sperrit to read—the defeated lover, like the successful one, believes all earth privy to his soul—was put down by Mr. Sperrit to quite different causes. He led him into a morning-room. The rest of the house seemed to be full of people, singing to a loud piano idiotic songs about cows, and the hall smelt of damp cloaks.

'It's our evening to take the winter cantata,' Mr. Sperrit explained. 'It's "High Tide on the Coast of Lincolnshire." I hoped you'd come back. There are scores of little things to settle. As for the house, of course, it stands ready for you at any time. I couldn't get Rhoda out of it—nor could Charlie for that matter. She's the sister, isn't she, of the nurse who brought you down here when you were four, she says, to recover from measles?'

'Is she? Was I?' said Midmore through the bad tastes in his mouth. 'D'you suppose I could stay there the night?'

Thirty joyous young voices shouted appeal to some one to leave their 'pipes of parsley 'ollow—'ollow—'ollow!' Mr. Sperrit had to raise his voice above the din.

'Well, if I asked you to stay *here*, I should never hear the last of it from Rhoda. She's a little cracked, of course, but the soul of devotion and capable of anything. *Ne sit ancillae*, you know.'

'Thank you. Then I'll go. I'll walk.' He stumbled out dazed and sick into the winter twilight, and sought the square house by the brook.

It was not a dignified entry, because when the door was unchained and Rhoda exclaimed, he took two valiant steps into the hall and then fainted—as men sometimes will after twenty-two hours of strong emotion and little food.

'I'm sorry,' he said when he could speak. He was lying at the foot of the stairs, his head on Rhoda's lap.

'Your 'ome is your castle, sir,' was the reply in his hair.

'I smelt it wasn't drink. You lay on the sofa till I get your supper.'

She settled him in a drawing-room hung with yellow silk, heavy with the smell of dead leaves and oil lamp. Something murmured soothingly in the background and overcame the noises in his head. He thought he heard horses' feet on wet gravel and a voice singing about ships and flocks and grass. It passed close to the shuttered bay window.

> But each will mourn his own, she saith,
> And sweeter woman ne'er drew breath
> Than my son's wife, Elizabeth . . .
> Cusha—cusha—cusha—calling.

The hoofs broke into a canter as Rhoda entered with the tray. 'And then I'll put you to bed,' she said. 'Sidney's coming in the morning.' Midmore asked no questions. He dragged his poor bruised soul to bed and would have pitied it all over again, but the food and warm sherry and water drugged him to instant sleep.

Rhoda's voice wakened him, asking whether he would have "ip, foot, or sitz,' which he understood were the baths of the establishment. 'Suppose you try all three,' she suggested. 'They're all yours, you know, sir.'

He would have renewed his sorrows with the daylight, but her words struck him pleasantly. Everything his eyes opened upon was his very own to keep for ever. The carved four-post Chippendale bed, obviously worth hundreds; the wavy walnut William and Mary chairs—he had seen worse ones labelled twenty guineas apiece; the oval medallion mirror; the delicate eighteenth-century wire fireguard; the heavy brocaded curtains were his—all his. So, too, a great garden full of birds that faced him when he shaved; a mulberry tree, a sun-dial, and a dull, steel-coloured brook that murmured level with the edge of a lawn a hundred yards away. Peculiarly and privately his own was the smell of sausages and coffee that he sniffed at the head of the wide square landing, all set round with mysterious doors and Bartolozzi prints. He spent two hours after breakfast in exploring his new possessions. His heart leaped up at such things as sewing-machines, a rubber-tyred bath-chair in a tiled passage, a malachite-headed Malacca cane, boxes and boxes of unopened stationery, seal-rings, bunches of keys, and at the bottom of a steel-net reticule a little leather purse with seven pounds ten shillings in gold and eleven shillings in silver.

'You used to play with that when my sister brought you down here after your measles,' said Rhoda as he slipped the money into his pocket. 'Now, this was your pore dear auntie's business-room.' She opened a low door. 'Oh, I forgot about Mr. Sidney! There he is.' An enormous old man with rheumy red eyes that blinked under downy white eyebrows sat in an Empire chair, his cap in his hands. Rhoda withdrew sniffing. The man looked Midmore over in silence, then jerked a thumb towards the door. 'I reckon she told you who I be,' he began. 'I'm the only farmer you've got. Nothin' goes off my place 'thout it walks on its own feet. What about my pig-pound?'

'Well, what about it?' said Midmore.

'That's just what I be come about. The County Councils are getting more particular. Did ye know there was swine fever at Pashell's? There *be*. It'll 'ave to be in brick.'

'Yes,' said Midmore politely.

'I've bin at your aunt that was, plenty times about it. I don't say she wasn't a just woman, but she didn't read the lease same way I did. I be used to bein' put upon, but there's no doing any longer 'thout that pig-pound.'

'When would you like it?' Midmore asked. It seemed the easiest road to take.

'Any time or other suits me, I reckon. He ain't thrivin' where he is, an' I paid eighteen shillin' for him.' He crossed his hands on his stick and gave no further sign of life.

'Is that all?' Midmore stammered.

'All now—excep''—he glanced fretfully at the table beside him—'excep' my usuals. Where's that Rhoda?'

Midmore rang the bell. Rhoda came in with a bottle and a glass. The old man helped himself to four stiff fingers, rose in one piece, and stumped out. At the door he cried ferociously: 'Don't suppose it's any odds to you whether I'm drowned or not, but them flood-gates want a wheel and winch, they do. I be too old for liftin' 'em with the bar—my time o' life.'

'Good riddance if 'e was drowned,' said Rhoda. 'But don't you mind him. He's only amusin' himself. Your pore dear auntie used to give 'im 'is usual—'tisn't the whisky *you* drink—an' send 'im about 'is business.'

'I see. Now, is a pig-pound the same thing as a pigsty?'

Rhoda nodded. ''E needs one, too, but 'e ain't entitled to it. You look at 'is lease—third drawer on the left in that Bombay cab'net—an' next time 'e comes you ask 'im to read it. That'll choke 'im off, because 'e can't!'

There was nothing in Midmore's past to teach him the

message and significance of a hand-written lease of the late 'eighties, but Rhoda interpreted.

'It don't mean anything reelly,' was her cheerful conclusion, 'excep' you mustn't get rid of him anyhow, an' 'e can do what 'e likes always. Lucky for us 'e *do* farm; and if it wasn't for 'is woman—'

'Oh, there's a Mrs. Sidney, is there?'

'Lor, *no*! The Sidneys don't marry. They keep. That's his fourth since—to my knowledge. He was a takin' man from the first.'

'Any families?'

'They'd be grown up by now if there was, wouldn't they? But you can't spend all your days considerin' 'is interests. That's what gave your pore aunt 'er indigestion. 'Ave you seen the gun-room?'

Midmore held strong views on the immorality of taking life for pleasure. But there was no denying that the late Colonel Werf's seventy-guinea breechloaders were good at their filthy job. He loaded one, took it out and pointed—merely pointed—it at a cock-pheasant which rose out of a shrubbery behind the kitchen, and the flaming bird came down in a long slant on the lawn, stone dead. Rhoda from the scullery said it was a lovely shot, and told him lunch was ready.

He spent the afternoon gun in one hand, a map in the other, beating the bounds of his lands. They lay altogether in a shallow, uninteresting valley, flanked with woods and bisected by a brook. Up stream was his own house; down stream, less than half a mile, a low red farmhouse squatted in an old orchard, beside what looked like small lock-gates on the Thames. There was no doubt as to ownership. Mr. Sidney saw him while yet far off, and bellowed at him about pig-pounds and flood-gates. These last were two great sliding shutters of weedy oak across the brook, which were prised up inch by inch with a crowbar along a notched strip of iron, and when Sidney opened them they at once let out half the water. Midmore watched it shrink between its aldered banks like some conjuring trick. This, too, was his very own.

'I see,' he said. 'How interesting! Now, what's that bell for?' he went on, pointing to an old ship's bell in a rude belfry at the end of an outhouse. 'Was that a chapel once?' The red-eyed giant seemed to have difficulty in expressing himself for the moment and blinked savagely.

'Yes,' he said at last. 'My chapel. When you 'ear that bell ring you'll 'ear something. Nobody but me 'ud put up with it—but I reckon it don't make any odds to you.' He slammed the gates down again, and the brook rose behind them with a suck and a grunt.

Midmore moved off, conscious that he might be safer with Rhoda to hold his conversational hand. As he passed the front of the farm-house a smooth fat woman, with neatly parted grey hair under a widow's cap, curtsied to him deferentially through the window. By every teaching of the Immoderate Left she had a perfect right to express herself in any way she pleased, but the curtsey revolted him. And on his way home he was hailed from behind a hedge by a manifest idiot with no roof to his mouth, who hallooed and danced round him.

'What did that beast want?' he demanded of Rhoda at tea.

'Jimmy? He only wanted to know if you 'ad any telegrams to send. 'E'll go anywhere so long as 'tisn't across running water. That gives 'im 'is seizures. Even talkin' about it for fun like makes 'im shake.'

'But why isn't he where he can be properly looked after?'

'What 'arm's 'e doing? 'E's a love-child, but 'is family can pay for 'im. If 'e was locked up 'e'd die all off at once, like a wild rabbit. Won't you, please, look at the drive, sir?'

Midmore looked in the fading light. The neat gravel was pitted with large roundish holes, and there was a punch or two of the same sort on the lawn.

'That's the 'unt comin' 'ome,' Rhoda explained. 'Your pore dear auntie always let 'em use our drive for a short cut after the Colonel died. The Colonel wouldn't so much because he preserved; but your auntie was always an 'orsewoman till'er sciatica.'

'Isn't there some one who can rake it over or—or something?' said Midmore vaguely.

'Oh, yes. You'll never see it in the morning, but—you was out when they came 'ome an' Mister Fisher—he's the Master—told me to tell you with 'is compliments that if you wasn't preservin' and cared to 'old to the old under-standin', 'is gravel-pit is at your service same as before. 'E thought, perhaps, you mightn't know, and it 'ad slipped my mind to tell you. It's good gravel, Mister Fisher's, and it binds beautiful on the drive. We'ave to draw it, o' course, from the pit, but——'

Midmore looked at her helplessly.

'Rhoda,' said he, 'what am I supposed to do?'

'Oh, let 'em come through,' she replied. 'You never know. You may want to 'unt yourself some day.'

That evening it rained and his misery returned on him,

the worse for having been diverted. At last he was driven to paw over a few score books in a panelled room called the library, and realised with horror what the late Colonel Werf's mind must have been in its prime. The volumes smelt of a dead world as strongly as they did of mildew. He opened and thrust them back, one after another, till crude coloured illustrations of men on horses held his eye. He began at random and read a little, moved into the drawing-room with the volume, and settled down by the fire still reading. It was a foul world into which he peeped for the first time—a heavy-eating, hard-drinking hell of horse-copers, swindlers, matchmaking mothers, economically dependent virgins selling themselves blushingly for cash and lands, tradesmen, and an ill-considered spawn of Dickens-and-horsedung characters (I give Midmore's own criticism), but he read on, fascinated, and behold, from the pages leaped, as it were, the brother of the red-eyed man of the brook, bellowing at a landlord (here Midmore realised that *he* was that very animal) for new barns; and another man who, like himself again, objected to hoof-marks on gravel. Outrageous as thought and conception were, the stuff seemed to have the rudiments of observation. He dug out other volumes by the same author, till Rhoda came in with a silver candlestick.

'Rhoda,' said he, 'did you ever hear about a character called James Pigg—and Batsey?'

'Why, o' course,' said she. 'The Colonel used to come into the kitchen in 'is dressin'-gown an' read us all those Jorrockses.'

'Oh, Lord!' said Midmore, and went to bed with a book called *Handley Cross* under his arm, and a lonelier

Columbus into a stranger world the wet-ringed moon never looked upon.

Here we omit much. But Midmore never denied that for the epicure in sensation the urgent needs of an ancient house, as interpreted by Rhoda pointing to daylight through attic-tiles held in place by moss, gives an edge to the pleasure of Social Research elsewhere. Equally he found that the reaction following prolonged research loses much of its grey terror if one knows one can at will bathe the soul in the society of plumbers (all the water-pipes had chronic appendicitis), village idiots (Jimmy had taken Midmore under his weak wing and camped daily at the drive-gates), and a giant with red eyelids whose every action is an unpredictable outrage.

Towards spring Midmore filled his house with a few friends of the Immoderate Left. It happened to be the day when, all things and Rhoda working together, a cartload of bricks, another of sand, and some bags of lime had been despatched to build Sidney his almost daily-demanded pig-pound. Midmore took his friends across the flat fields with some idea of showing them Sidney as a type of 'the peasantry.' They hit the minute when Sidney, hoarse with rage, was ordering bricklayer, mate, carts and all off his premises. The visitors disposed themselves to listen.

'You never give me no notice about changin' the pig,' Sidney shouted. The pig—at least eighteen inches long—reared on end in the old sty and smiled at the company.

'But, my good man——' Midmore opened.

'I ain't! For aught you know I be a dam' sight worse than you be. You can't come and be'ave arbit'ry with me.

You *are* be'avin' arbit'ry! All you men go clean away an' don't set foot on my land till I bid ye.'

'But you asked'—Midmore felt his voice jump up— 'to have the pig-pound built.'

'S'pose I did. That's no reason you shouldn't send me notice to change the pig. Comin' down on me like this 'thout warnin'! That pig's got to be got into the cowshed an' all.'

'Then open the door and let him run in,' said Midmore.

'Don't you be'ave arbit'ry with *me*! Take all your dam' men 'ome off my land. I won't be treated arbit'ry.'

The carts moved off without a word, and Sidney went into the house and slammed the door.

'Now, I hold that is enormously significant,' said a visitor. 'Here you have the logical outcome of centuries of feudal oppression—the frenzy of fear.' The company looked at Midmore with grave pain.

'But he *did* worry my life out about his pig-sty,' was all Midmore found to say.

Others took up the parable and proved to him if he only held true to the gospels of the Immoderate Left the earth would soon be covered with 'jolly little' pig-sties, built in the intervals of morris-dancing by 'the peasant' himself.

Midmore felt grateful when the door opened again and Mr. Sidney invited them all to retire to the road, which, he pointed out, was public. As they turned the corner of the house, a smooth-faced woman in a widow's cap curtsied to each of them through the window.

Instantly they drew pictures of that woman's lot, deprived of all vehicle for self-expression—'the set grey life and apathetic end,' one quoted—and they discussed the tremendous significance of village theatricals. Even a month ago Midmore would have told them all that he knew and Rhoda had dropped about Sidney's forms of self-expression. Now, for some strange reason, he was content to let the talk run on from village to metropolitan and world drama.

Rhoda advised him after the visitors left that 'if he wanted to do that again' he had better go up to town.

'But we only sat on cushions on the floor,' said her master.

'They're too old for romps,' she retorted, 'an' it's only the beginning of things. I've seen what *I've* seen. Besides, they talked and laughed in the passage going to their baths—such as took 'em.'

'Don't be a fool, Rhoda,' said Midmore. No man—unless he has loved her—will casually dismiss a woman on whose lap he has laid his head.

'Very good,' she snorted, 'but that cuts both ways. An' now, you go down to Sidney's this evenin' and put him where he ought to be. He was in his right about you givin' 'im notice about changin' the pig, but he 'adn't any right to turn it up before your company. No manners, no pig-pound. He'll understand.'

Midmore did his best to make him. He found himself reviling the old man in speech and with a joy quite new in all his experience. He wound up—it was a plagiarism from a plumber—by telling Mr. Sidney that he looked like a turkey-cock, had the morals of a parish bull, and need never hope for a new pig-pound as long as he or Midmore lived.

'Very good,' said the giant. 'I reckon you thought you

'ad something against me, and now you've come down an' told it me like man to man. Quite right. I don't bear malice. Now, you send along those bricks an' sand, an' I'll make a do to build the pig-pound myself. If you look at my lease you'll find out you're bound to provide me materials for the repairs. Only—only I thought there'd be no 'arm in my askin' you to do it throughout like.'

Midmore fairly gasped. 'Then, why the devil did you turn my carts back when—when I sent them up here to do it throughout for you?'

Mr. Sidney sat down on the floodgates, his eyebrows knitted in thought.

'I'll tell you,' he said slowly. ''Twas too dam' like cheatin' a suckin' baby. My woman, she said so too.'

For a few seconds the teachings of the Immoderate Left, whose humour is all their own, wrestled with those of Mother Earth, who has her own humours. Then Midmore laughed till he could scarcely stand. In due time Mr. Sidney laughed too—crowing and wheezing crescendo till it broke from him in roars. They shook hands, and Midmore went home grateful that he had held his tongue among his companions.

When he reached his house he met three or four men and women on horseback, very muddy indeed, coming down the drive. Feeling hungry himself, he asked them if they were hungry. They said they were, and he bade them enter. Jimmy took their horses, who seemed to know him. Rhoda took their battered hats, led the women upstairs for hairpins, and presently fed them all with teacakes, poached eggs, anchovy toast, and drinks from a coromandel-wood liqueur case which Midmore had never known that he possessed.

'And I *will* say,' said Miss Connie Sperrit, her spurred foot on the fender and a smoking muffin in her whip hand, 'Rhoda does one top-hole. She always did since I was eight.'

'Seven, miss, was when you began to 'unt,' said Rhoda, setting down more buttered toast.

'And so,' the M.F.H. was saying to Midmore, 'when he got to your brute Sidney's land, we had to whip 'em off. It's a regular Alsatia for 'em. They know it. Why'—he dropped his voice—'I don't want to say anything against Sidney as your tenant, of course, but I do believe the old scoundrel's perfectly capable of putting down poison.'

'Sidney's capable of anything,' said Midmore with immense feeling; but once again he held his tongue. They were a queer community; yet when they had stamped and jingled out to their horses again, the house felt hugely big and disconcerting.

This may be reckoned the conscious beginning of his double life. It ran in odd channels that summer—a riding school, for instance, near Hayes Common and a shooting ground near Wormwood Scrubs. A man who has been saddle-galled or shoulder-bruised for half the day is not at his London best of evenings; and when the bills for his amusements come in he curtails his expenses in other directions. So a cloud settled on Midmore's name. His London world talked of a hardening of heart and a tightening of purse-strings which signified disloyalty to the Cause. One man, a confidant of the old expressive days, attacked him robustiously and demanded account of his soul's progress. It was not furnished, for Midmore was calculating how much it would cost to repave stables so dilapidated that even the village idiot apologised for putting visitors' horses into them. The man went away, and served up what he had heard of the pig-pound episode as a little newspaper sketch, calculated to annoy. Midmore read it with an eye as practical as a woman's, and since most of his experiences had been among women, at once sought out a woman to whom he might tell his sorrow at the disloyalty of his own familiar friend. She was so sympathetic that he went on to confide how his bruised heart—she knew all about it—had found so-lace, with a long O, in another quarter which he indicated rather carefully in case it might be betrayed to other loyal friends. As his hints pointed directly towards facile Hampstead, and as his urgent business was the purchase of a horse from a dealer, Beckenham way, he felt he had done good work. Later, when his friend, the scribe, talked to him alluringly of 'secret gardens' and those so-laces to which every man who follows the Wider Morality is entitled, Midmore lent him a five-pound note which he had got back on the price of a ninety-guinea bay gelding. So true it is, as he read in one of the late Colonel Werf's books, that 'the young man of the present day would sooner lie under an imputation against his morals than against his knowledge of horseflesh.'

Midmore desired more than he desired anything else at that moment to ride and, above all, to jump on a ninety-guinea bay gelding with black points and a slovenly habit of hitting his fences. He did not wish many people except Mr. Sidney, who very kindly lent his soft meadow behind the flood-gates, to be privy to the matter, which he rightly foresaw would take him to the autumn. So he told such friends as hinted at country week-end visits that he had practically let his newly inherited house.

The rent, he said, was an object to him, for he had lately lost large sums through ill-considered benevolences. He would name no names, but they could guess. And they guessed loyally all round the circle of his acquaintance as they spread the news that explained so much.

There remained only one couple of his once intimate associates to pacify. They were deeply sympathetic and utterly loyal, of course, but as curious as any of the apes whose diet they had adopted. Midmore met them in a suburban train, coming up to town, not twenty minutes after he had come off two hours' advanced tuition (one guinea an hour) over hurdles in a hall. He had, of course, changed his kit, but his too heavy bridle-hand shook a little among the newspapers. On the inspiration of the moment, which is your natural liar's best hold, he told them that he was condemned to a rest-cure. He would lie in semi-darkness drinking milk, for weeks and weeks, cut off even from letters. He was astonished and delighted at the ease with which the usual lie confounds the unusual intellect. They swallowed it as swiftly as they recommended him to live on nuts and fruit; but he saw in the woman's eyes the exact reason she would set forth for his retirement. After all, she had as much right to express herself as he purposed to take for himself; and Midmore believed strongly in the fullest equality of the sexes.

That retirement made one small ripple in the strenuous world. The lady who had written the twelve-page letter ten months before sent him another of eight pages, analysing all the motives that were leading her back to him—should she come?—now that he was ill and alone. Much might yet be retrieved, she said, out of the waste of jarring lives and piteous misunderstandings. It needed only a hand.

But Midmore needed two, next morning very early, for a devil's diversion, among wet coppices, called 'cubbing.'

'You haven't a bad seat,' said Miss Sperrit through the morning-mists. 'But you're worrying him.'

'He pulls so,' Midmore grunted.

'Let him alone, then. Look out for the branches,' she shouted, as they whirled up a splashy ride. Cubs were plentiful. Most of the hounds attached themselves to a straight-necked youngster of education who scuttled out of the woods into the open fields below.

'Hold on!' some one shouted. 'Turn 'em, Midmore. That's your brute Sidney's land. It's all wire.'

'Oh, Connie, stop!' Mrs. Sperrit shrieked as her daughter charged at a boundary-hedge.

'Wire be damned! I had it all out a fortnight ago. Come on!' This was Midmore, buffeting into it a little lower down.

'*I* knew that!' Connie cried over her shoulder, and she flitted across the open pasture, humming to herself.

'Oh, of course! If some people have private information, they can afford to thrust.' This was a snuff-coloured habit into which Miss Sperrit had cannoned down the ride.

'What! Midmore got Sidney to heel? *You* never did that, Sperrit.' This was Mr. Fisher, M.F.H., enlarging the breach Midmore had made.

'No, confound him!' said the father testily. 'Go on, sir! *Injecto ter pulvere*—you've kicked half the ditch into my eye already.'

They killed that cub a little short of the haven his mother had told him to make for—a two-acre Alsatia of a gorse-patch to which the M.F.H. had been denied access for the last fifteen seasons. He expressed his gratitude before all the field and Mr. Sidney, at Mr. Sidney's farmhouse door.

'And if there should be any poultry claims——' he went on.

'There won't be,' said Midmore. 'It's too like cheating a sucking child, isn't it, Mr. Sidney?'

'You've got me!' was all the reply. 'I be used to bein' put upon, but you've got me, Mus' Midmore.'

Midmore pointed to a new brick pig-pound built in strict disregard of the terms of the life-tenant's lease. The gesture told the tale to the few who did not know, and they shouted.

Such pagan delights as these were followed by pagan sloth of evenings when men and women elsewhere are at their brightest. But Midmore preferred to lie out on a yellow silk couch, reading works of a debasing vulgarity; or, by invitation, to dine with the Sperrits and savages of their kidney. These did not expect flights of fancy or phrasing. They lied, except about horses, grudgingly and of necessity, not for art's sake; and, men and women alike, they expressed themselves along their chosen lines with the serene indifference of the larger animals. Then Midmore would go home and identify them, one by one, out of the natural-history books by Mr. Surtees, on the table beside the sofa. At first they looked upon him coolly, but when the tale of the removed wire and the recaptured gorse had gone the rounds, they accepted him for a person willing to play their games. True, a faction suspended judgment for a while, because they shot, and hoped that Midmore would serve the glorious mammon of pheasant-raising rather than the unkempt god of fox-hunting. But after he had shown his choice, they did not ask by what intellectual process he had arrived at it. He hunted three, sometimes four, times a week, which necessitated not only one bay gelding (£94: 10s.), but a mannerly white-stockinged chestnut (£114), and a black mare, rather long in the back but with a mouth of silk (£150), who so evidently preferred to carry a lady that it would have been cruel to have baulked her. Besides, with that handling she could be sold at a profit. And besides, the hunt was a quiet, intimate, kindly little hunt, not anxious for strangers, of good report in the *Field*, the servant of one M.F.H., given to hospitality, riding well its own horses, and, with the exception of Midmore, not novices. But as Miss Sperrit observed, after the M.F.H. had said some things to him at a gate: 'It *is* a pity you don't know as much as your horse, but you will in time. It takes years and yee-ars. I've been at it for fifteen and I'm only just learning. But you've made a decent kick-off.'

So he kicked off in wind and wet and mud, wondering quite sincerely why the bubbling ditches and sucking pastures held him from day to day, or what so-lace he could find on off days in chasing grooms and bricklayers round outhouses.

To make sure he uprooted himself one week-end of heavy midwinter rain, and re-entered his lost world in the character of Galahad fresh from a rest-cure. They all agreed, with an eye over his shoulder for the next comer, that he was a different man; but when they asked him for the symptoms of nervous strain, and led him all through their own, he realised he had lost much of his old skill in lying. His three months' absence, too, had put him hopelessly behind the London field. The movements, the allusions, the slang of the game had changed. The couples had rearranged themselves or were re-crystallizing in fresh triangles, whereby he put his foot in it badly. Only one great soul (he who had written the account of the pig-pound episode) stood untouched by the vast flux of time, and Midmore lent him another fiver for his integrity. A woman took him, in the wet forenoon, to a pronouncement on the Oneness of Impulse in Humanity, which struck him as a polysyllabic *résumé* of Mr. Sidney's domestic arrangements, plus a clarion call to 'shock civilisation into common-sense.'

'And you'll come to tea with me to-morrow?' she asked, after lunch, nibbling cashew nuts from a saucer. Midmore replied that there were great arrears of work to overtake when a man had been put away for so long.

'But you've come back like a giant refreshed . . . I hope that Daphne'—this was the lady of the twelve- and the eight-page letter—'will be with us too. She has misunderstood herself, like so many of us,' the woman-murmured, 'but I think eventually . . .' she flung out her thin little hands. 'However, these are things that each lonely soul must adjust for itself.'

'Indeed, yes,' said Midmore with a deep sigh. The old tricks were sprouting in the old atmosphere like mushrooms in a dung-pit. He passed into an abrupt reverie, shook his head, as though stung by tumultuous memories, and departed without any ceremony of farewell to—catch a mid-afternoon express where a man meets associates who talk horse, and weather as it affects the horse, all the way down. What worried him most was that he had missed a day with the hounds.

He met Rhoda's keen old eyes without flinching; and the drawing-room looked very comfortable that wet evening at tea. After all, his visit to town had not been wholly a failure. He had burned quite a bushel of letters at his flat. A flat—here he reached mechanically toward the worn volumes near the sofa—a flat was a consuming animal. As for Daphne . . . he opened at random on the words: 'His lordship then did as desired and disclosed a *tableau* of considerable strength and variety.' Midmore reflected: 'And I used to think . . . But she wasn't . . . We were all babblers and skirters together . . . I didn't babble much—thank goodness—but I skirted.' He turned the pages backward for more *Sortes Surteesianae*, and read: 'When at length they rose to go to bed it struck each man as he followed his neighbour upstairs, that the man before him walked very crookedly.' He laughed aloud at the fire.

'What about to-morrow?' Rhoda asked, entering with garments over her shoulder. 'It's never stopped raining since you left. You'll be plastered out of sight an' all in five minutes. You'd better wear your next best, 'adn't you? I'm afraid they've shrank. 'Adn't you best try 'em on?'

'Here?' said Midmore.

'Suit yourself. I bathed you when you wasn't larger than a leg o' lamb,' said the ex-ladies'-maid.

'Rhoda, one of these days I shall get a valet, and a married butler.'

'There's many a true word spoke in jest. But nobody's huntin' to-morrow.'

'Why? Have they cancelled the meet?'

'They say it only means slipping and over-reaching in the mud, and they all 'ad enough of that to-day. Charlie told me so just now.'

'Oh!' It seemed that the word of Mr. Sperrit's confidential clerk had weight.

'Charles came down to help Mr. Sidney lift the gates,' Rhoda continued.

'The flood-gates? They are perfectly easy to handle now. I've put in a wheel and a winch.'

'When the brook's really up they must be took clean out on account of the rubbish blockin' 'em. That's why Charlie came down.'

Midmore grunted impatiently. 'Everybody has talked to me about that brook ever since I came here. It's never done anything yet.'

'This 'as been a dry summer. If you care to look now, sir, I'll get you a lantern.'

She paddled out with him into a large wet night. Half-way down the lawn her light was reflected on shallow brown water, pricked through with grass blades at the edges. Beyond that light, the brook was strangling and kicking among hedges and tree-trunks.

'What on earth will happen to the big rose-bed?' was Midmore's first word.

'It generally 'as to be restocked after a flood. Ah!' she raised her lantern. 'There's two garden-seats knockin' against the sun-dial. Now, that won't do the roses any good.'

'This is too absurd. There ought to be some decently thought-out system—for—for dealing with this sort of thing.' He peered into the rushing gloom. There seemed to be no end to the moisture and the racket. In town he had noticed nothing.

'It can't be 'elped,' said Rhoda. 'It's just what it does do once in just so often. We'd better go back.'

All earth under foot was sliding in a thousand liquid noises towards the hoarse brook. Somebody wailed from the house: ''Fraid o' the water! Come 'ere! 'Fraid o' the water!'

'That's Jimmy. Wet always takes 'im that way,' she explained. The idiot charged into them, shaking with terror.

'Brave Jimmy! How brave of Jimmy! Come into the hall. What Jimmy got now?' she crooned. It was a sodden note which ran: 'Dear Rhoda—Mr. Lotten, with whom I rode home this afternoon, told me that if this wet keeps up, he's afraid the fish-pond he built last year, where Coxen's old mill-dam was, will go, as the dam did once before, he says. If it does it's bound to come down the brook. It may be all right, but perhaps you had better look out. C. S.'

'If Coxen's dam goes, that means . . . I'll 'ave the drawing-room carpet up at once to be on the safe side. The claw-'ammer is in the libery.'

'Wait a minute. Sidney's gates are out, you said?'

'Both. He'll need it if Coxen's pond goes . . . I've seen it once.'

'I'll just slip down and have a look at Sidney. Light the lantern again, please, Rhoda.'

'You won't get *him* to stir. He's been there since he was born. But *she* don't know anything. I'll fetch your waterproof and some top-boots.'

''Fraid o' the water! 'Fraid o' the water!' Jimmy

sobbed, pressed against a corner of the hall, his hands to his eyes.

'All right, Jimmy. Jimmy can help play with the carpet,' Rhoda answered, as Midmore went forth into the darkness and the roarings all round. He had never seen such an utterly unregulated state of affairs. There was another lantern reflected on the streaming drive.

'Hi! Rhoda! Did you get my note? I came down to make sure. I thought, afterwards, Jimmy might funk the water!'

'It's me—Miss Sperrit,' Midmore cried. 'Yes, we got it, thanks.'

'You're back, then. Oh, good! . . . Is it bad down with you?'

'I'm going to Sidney's to have a look.'

'You won't get *him* out. Lucky I met Bob Lotten. I told him he hadn't any business impounding water for his idiotic trout without rebuilding the dam.'

'How far up is it? I've only been there once.'

'Not more than four miles as the water will come. He says he's opened all the sluices.'

She had turned and fallen into step beside him, her hooded head bowed against the thinning rain. As usual she was humming to herself.

'Why on earth did you come out in this weather?' Midmore asked.

'It was worse when you were in town. The rain's taking off now. If it wasn't for that pond, I wouldn't worry so much. There's Sidney's bell. Come on!' She broke into a run. A cracked bell was jangling feebly down the valley.

'Keep on the road!' Midmore shouted. The ditches were snorting bank-full on either side, and towards the brook-side the fields were afloat and beginning to move in the darkness.

'Catch me going off it! There's his light burning all right.' She halted undistressed at a little rise. 'But the flood's in the orchard. Look!' She swung her lantern to show a front rank of old apple-trees reflected in still, outlying waters beyond the half-drowned hedge. They could hear above the thud-thud of the gorged flood-gates, shrieks in two keys as monotonous as a steam-organ.

'The high one's the pig.' Miss Sperrit laughed.

'All right! I'll get *her* out. You stay where you are, and I'll see you home afterwards.'

'But the water's only just over the road,' she objected.

'Never mind. Don't you move. Promise?'

'All right. You take my stick, then, and feel for holes in case anything's washed out anywhere. This *is* a lark!'

Midmore took it, and stepped into the water that moved sluggishly as yet across the farm road which ran to Sidney's front door from the raised and metalled public road. It was half way up to his knees when he knocked. As he looked back Miss Sperrit's lantern seemed to float in mid-ocean.

'You can't come in or the water'll come with you. I've bunged up all the cracks,' Mr. Sidney shouted from within. 'Who be ye?'

'Take me out! Take me out!' the woman shrieked, and the pig from his sty behind the house urgently seconded the motion.

'I'm Midmore! Coxen's old mill-dam is likely to go, they say. Come out!'

'I told 'em it would when they made a fish-pond of it. 'Twasn't ever puddled proper. But it's a middlin' wide

247

valley. She's got room to spread. . . . Keep still, or I'll take and duck you in the cellar! . . . You go 'ome, Mus' Midmore, an' take the law o' Mus' Lotten soon's you've changed your socks.'

'Confound you, aren't you coming out?'

'To catch my death o' cold? I'm all right where I be. I've seen it before. But you can take *her*. She's no sort o' use or sense. . . . Climb out through the window. Didn't I tell you I'd plugged the door-cracks, you fool's daughter?' The parlour window opened, and the woman flung herself into Midmore's arms, nearly knocking him down. Mr. Sidney leaned out of the window, pipe in mouth.

'Take her 'ome,' he said, and added oracularly:

> 'Two women in one house,
> Two cats an' one mouse,
> Two dogs an' one bone—
> Which I will leave alone.

I've seen it before.' Then he shut and fastened the window.

'A trap! A trap! You had ought to have brought a trap for me. I'll be drowned in this wet,' the woman cried.

'Hold up! You can't be any wetter than you are. Come along!' Midmore did not at all like the feel of the water over his boot-tops.

'Hooray! Come along!' Miss Sperrit's lantern, not fifty yards away, waved cheerily.

The woman threshed towards it like a panic-stricken goose, fell on her knees, was jerked up again by Midmore, and pushed on till she collapsed at Miss Sperrit's feet.

'But you won't get bronchitis if you go straight to Mr. Midmore's house,' said the unsympathetic maiden.

'O Gawd! O Gawd! I wish our 'eavenly Father 'ud forgive me my sins an' call me 'ome,' the woman sobbed. 'But I won't go to '*is* 'ouse! I won't.'

'All right, then. Stay here. Now, if we run,' Miss Sperrit whispered to Midmore, 'she'll follow us. Not too fast!'

They set off at a considerate trot, and the woman lumbered behind them, bellowing, till they met a third lantern—Rhoda holding Jimmy's hand. She had got the carpet up, she said, and was escorting Jimmy past the water that he dreaded.

'That's all right,' Miss Sperrit pronounced. 'Take Mrs. Sidney back with you, Rhoda, and put her to bed. I'll take Jimmy with me. You aren't afraid of the water now, are you, Jimmy?'

'Not afraid of anything now.' Jimmy reached for her hand. 'But get away from the water quick.'

'I'm coming with you,' Midmore interrupted.

'You most certainly are not. You're drenched. She threw you twice. Go home and change. You may have to be out again all night. It's only half-past seven now. I'm perfectly safe.' She flung herself lightly over a stile, and hurried uphill by the footpath, out of reach of all but the boasts of the flood below.

Rhoda, dead silent, herded Mrs. Sidney to the house.

'You'll find your things laid out on the bed,' she said to Midmore as he came up. 'I'll attend to—to this. *She's* got nothing to cry for.'

Midmore raced into dry kit, and raced uphill to be rewarded by the sight of the lantern just turning into the Sperrits' gate. He came back by way of Sidney's farm, where he saw the light twinkling across three acres of shining water, for the rain had ceased and the clouds were stripping overhead, though the brook was noisier than ever. Now there was only that doubtful mill-pond to look after—that and his swirling world abandoned to himself alone.

'We shall have to sit up for it,' said Rhoda after dinner. And as the drawing-room commanded the best view of the rising flood, they watched it from there for a long time, while all the clocks of the house bore them company.

''Tisn't the water, it's the mud on the skirting-board after it goes down that I mind,' Rhoda whispered. 'The last time Coxen's mill broke, I remember it came up to the second—no, third—step o' Mr. Sidney's stairs.'

'What did Sidney do about it?'

'He made a notch on the step. 'E said it was a record. Just like 'im.'

'It's up to the drive now,' said Midmore after another long wait. 'And the rain stopped before eight, you know.'

'Then Coxen's dam '*as* broke, and that's the first of the flood-water.' She stared out beside him. The water was rising in sudden pulses—an inch or two at a time, with great sweeps and lagoons and a sudden increase of the brook's proper thunder.

'You can't stand all the time. Take a chair,' Midmore said presently.

Rhoda looked back into the bare room. 'The carpet bein' up *does* make a difference. Thank you, sir, I *will* 'ave a set-down.'

'Right over the drive now,' said Midmore. He opened the window and leaned out. 'Is that wind up the valley, Rhoda?'

'No, that's *it*! But I've seen it before.'

There was not so much a roar as the purposeful drive of a tide across a jagged reef, which put down every other sound for twenty minutes. A wide sheet of water hurried up to the little terrace on which the house stood, pushed round either corner, rose again and stretched, as it were, yawning beneath the moonlight, joined other sheets waiting for them in unsuspected hollows, and lay out all in one. A puff of wind followed.

'It's right up to the wall now. I can touch it with my finger.' Midmore bent over the window-sill.

'I can 'ear it in the cellars,' said Rhoda dolefully. 'Well, we've done what we can! I think I'll 'ave a look.' She left the room and was absent half an hour or more, during which time he saw a full-grown tree hauling itself across the lawn by its naked roots. Then a hurdle knocked against the wall, caught on an iron foot-scraper just outside, and made a square-headed ripple. The cascade through the cellar-windows diminished.

'It's dropping,' Rhoda cried, as she returned. 'It's only tricklin' into my cellars now.'

'Wait a minute. I believe—I believe I can see the scraper on the edge of the drive just showing!'

In another ten minutes the drive itself roughened and became gravel again, tilting all its water towards the shrubbery.

'The pond's gone past,' Rhoda announced. 'We shall only 'ave the common flood to contend with now. You'd better go to bed.'

'I ought to go down and have another look at Sidney before daylight.'

'No need. You can see 'is light burnin' from all the upstairs windows.'

'By the way. I forgot about *her*. Where've you put her?'

'In my bed.' Rhoda's tone was ice. 'I wasn't going to undo a room for *that* stuff.'

'But it—it couldn't be helped,' said Midmore. 'She was half drowned. One mustn't be narrow-minded, Rhoda, even if her position isn't quite—er—regular.'

'Pfff! I wasn't worryin' about that.' She leaned forward to the window. 'There's the edge of the lawn showin' now. It falls as fast as it rises. Dearie'—the change of tone made Midmore jump—'didn't you know that I was 'is first? *That*'s what makes it so hard to bear.' Midmore looked at the long lizard-like back and had no words.

She went on, still talking through the black window-pane:

'Your pore dear auntie was very kind about it. She said she'd make all allowances for one, but no more. Never any more. . . . Then, you didn't know 'oo Charlie was all this time?'

'Your nephew, I always thought.'

'Well, well,' she spoke pityingly. 'Everybody's business being nobody's business, I suppose no one thought to tell you. But Charlie made 'is own way for 'imself from the beginnin'! . . . But *her* upstairs, she never produced anything. Just an 'ousekeeper, as you might say. Turned over an' went to sleep straight off. She 'ad the impudence to ask me for 'ot sherry-gruel.'

'Did you give it to her,' said Midmore.

'Me? Your sherry? No!'

The memory of Sidney's outrageous rhyme at the window, and Charlie's long nose (he thought it looked interested at the time) as he passed the copies of Mrs.

Werf's last four wills, overcame Midmore without warning.

'This damp is givin' you a cold,' said Rhoda, rising. 'There you go again! Sneezin's a sure sign of it. Better go to bed. You can't do anythin' excep''—she stood rigid, with crossed arms—'about me.'

'Well. What about you?' Midmore stuffed the handkerchief into his pocket.

'Now you know about it, what are you goin' to do—sir?'

She had the answer on her lean cheek before the sentence was finished.

'Go and see if you can get us something to eat, Rhoda. And beer.'

'I expec' the larder'll be in a swim,' she replied, 'but old bottled stuff don't take any harm from wet.' She returned with a tray, all in order, and they ate and drank together, and took observations of the falling flood till dawn opened its bleared eyes on the wreck of what had been a fair garden. Midmore, cold and annoyed, found himself humming:

> 'That flood strewed wrecks upon the grass,
> That ebb swept out the flocks to sea.

There isn't a rose left, Rhoda!

> An awesome ebb and flow it was
> To many more than mine and me.
> But each will mourn his . . .

It'll cost me a hundred.'

'Now we know the worst,' said Rhoda, 'we can go to bed. I'll lay on the kitchen sofa. His light's burnin' still.'

'And *she*?'

'Dirty old cat! You ought to 'ear 'er snore!'

At ten o'clock in the morning, after a maddening hour in his own garden on the edge of the retreating brook, Midmore went off to confront more damage at Sidney's. The first thing that met him was the pig, snowy white, for the water had washed him out of his new sty, calling on high heaven for breakfast. The front door had been forced open, and the flood had registered its own height in a brown dado on the walls. Midmore chased the pig out and called up the stairs.

'I be abed o' course. Which step 'as she rose to?' Sidney cried from above. 'The fourth? Then it's beat all records. Come up.'

'Are you ill?' Midmore asked as he entered the room. The red eyelids blinked cheerfully. Mr. Sidney, beneath a sumptuous patch-work quilt, was smoking.

'Nah! I'm only thankin' God I ain't my own landlord. Take that cheer. What's she done?'

'It hasn't gone down enough for me to make sure.'

'Them flood-gates o' yourn'll be middlin' far down the brook by now; an' your rose-garden have gone after 'em. I saved my chickens, though. You'd better get Mus' Sperrit to take the law o' Lotten an' 'is fish-pond.'

'No, thanks. I've trouble enough without that.'

'Hev ye?' Mr. Sidney grinned. 'How did ye make out with those two women o' mine last night? I lay they fought.'

'You infernal old scoundrel!' Midmore laughed.

'I be—an' then again I bain't,' was the placid answer. 'But, Rhoda, *she* wouldn't ha' left me last night. Fire or flood, she wouldn't.'

'Why didn't you ever marry her?' Midmore asked.

'Waste of good money. She was willin' without.'

There was a step on the gritty mud below, and a voice humming. Midmore rose quickly saying: 'Well, I suppose you're all right now.'

'I be. I ain't a landlord, nor I ain't young—nor anxious. Oh, Mus' Midmore! Would it make any odds about her thirty pounds comin' regular if I married her? Charlie said maybe 'twould.'

'Did he?' Midmore turned at the door. 'And what did Jimmy say about it?'

'Jimmy?' Mr. Sidney chuckled as the joke took him. 'Oh, *he's* none o' mine. He's Charlie's look-out.'

Midmore slammed the door and ran downstairs.

'Well, this is a—sweet—mess,' said Miss Sperrit in shortest skirts and heaviest riding-boots. 'I had to come down and have a look at it. "The old mayor climbed the belfry tower." Been up all night nursing your family?'

'Nearly that! Isn't it cheerful?' He pointed through the door to the stairs with small twig-drift on the last three treads.

'It's a record, though,' said she, and hummed to herself:

> 'That flood strewed wrecks upon the grass,
>   That ebb swept out the flocks to sea.'

'You're always singing that, aren't you?' Midmore said suddenly as she passed into the parlour where slimy chairs had been stranded at all angles.

'Am I? Now I come to think of it I believe I do. They say I always hum when I ride. Have you noticed it?'

'Of course I have. I notice every——'

'Oh,' she went on hurriedly. 'We had it for the village cantata last winter—"The Brides of Enderby."'

'No! "High Tide on the Coast of Lincolnshire."' For some reason Midmore spoke sharply.

'Just like that.' She pointed to the befouled walls. 'I say. . . . Let's get this furniture a little straight. . . . You know it too?'

'Every word, since you sang it, of course.'

'When?'

'The first night I ever came down. You rode past the drawing-room window in the dark singing it—"And sweeter woman——"'

'I thought the house was empty then. Your aunt always let us use that short cut. Ha-hadn't we better get this out into the passage? It'll all have to come out anyhow. You take the other side.' They began to lift a heavyish table. Their words came jerkily between gasps and their faces were as white as—a newly washed and very hungry pig.

'Look out!' Midmore shouted. His legs were whirled from under him, as the table, grunting madly, careened and knocked the girl out of sight.

The wild boar of Asia could not have cut down a couple more scientifically, but this little pig lacked his ancestor's nerve and fled shrieking over their bodies.

'Are you hurt, darling?' was Midmore's first word, and 'No—I'm only winded—dear,' was Miss Sperrit's, as he lifted her out of her corner, her hat over one eye and her right cheek a smear of mud.

They fed him a little later on some chicken-feed that they found in Sidney's quiet barn, a pail of buttermilk out of the dairy, and a quantity of onions from a shelf in the back-kitchen.

'Seed-onions, most likely,' said Connie. 'You'll hear about this.'

'What does it matter? They ought to have been gilded. We must buy him.'

'And keep him as long as he lives,' she agreed. 'But I think I ought to go home now. You see, when I came out I didn't expect . . . Did you?'

'No! Yes. . . . It had to come. . . . But if any one had told me an hour ago! . . . Sidney's unspeakable parlour—and the mud on the carpet.'

'Oh, I say! Is my cheek clean now?'

'Not quite. Lend me your hanky again a minute, darling. . . . What a purler you came!'

'You can't talk. Remember when your chin hit that table and you said "blast"! I was just going to laugh.'

'You didn't laugh when I picked you up. You were going "oo-oo-oo" like a little owl.'

'My dear child——'

'Say that again!'

'My dear child. (Do you really like it? I keep it for my best friends.) My *dee-ar* child, I thought I was going to be sick there and then. He knocked every ounce of wind out of me—the angel! But I must really go.'

They set off together, very careful not to join hands or take arms.

'Not across the fields,' said Midmore at the stile. 'Come round by—by your own place.'

She flushed indignantly.

'It will be yours in a little time,' he went on, shaken with his own audacity.

'Not so much of your little times, if you please!' She shied like a colt across the road; then instantly, like a colt, her eyes lit with new curiosity as she came in sight of the drive-gates.

'And not quite so much of your airs and graces, madam,' Midmore returned, 'or I won't let you use our drive as a short cut any more.'

'Oh, I'll be good. I'll be good.' Her voice changed suddenly. 'I swear I'll try to be good, dear. I'm not much of a thing at the best. What made *you* . . .'

'I'm worse—worse! Miles and oceans worse. But what does it matter now?'

They halted beside the gate-pillars.

'I see!' she said, looking up the sodden carriage sweep to the front door porch where Rhoda was slapping a wet mat to and fro. '*I* see. . . . Now, I really must go home. No! Don't you come. I must speak to Mother first all by myself.'

He watched her up the hill till she was out of sight.

THE GARDENER

> One grave to me was given,
>   One watch till Judgment Day;
> And God looked down from Heaven
>   And rolled the stone away.

> *One day in all the years,*
>   *One hour in that one day,*
> *His Angel saw my tears,*
>   *And rolled the stone away!*

Every one in the village knew that Helen Turrell did her duty by all her world, and by none more honourably than by her only brother's unfortunate child. The village knew, too, that George Turrell had tried his family severely since early youth, and were not surprised to be told that, after many fresh starts given and thrown away, he, an Inspector of Indian Police, had entangled himself with the daughter of a retired non-commissioned officer, and had died of a fall from a horse a few weeks before his child was born. Mercifully, George's father and mother were both dead, and though Helen, thirty-five and independent, might well have washed her hands of the whole disgraceful affair, she most nobly took charge, though she was, at the time, under threat of lung trouble which had driven her to the South of France. She arranged for the passage of the child and a nurse from Bombay, met them at Marseilles, nursed the baby through an attack of infantile dysentery due to the carelessness of the nurse, whom she had had to dismiss, and at last, thin and worn but triumphant, brought the boy late in the autumn, wholly restored, to her Hampshire home.

All these details were public property, for Helen was as open as the day, and held that scandals are only increased by hushing them up. She admitted that George had always been rather a black sheep, but things might have been much worse if the mother had insisted on her right to keep the boy. Luckily, it seemed that people of that class would do almost anything for money, and, as George had always turned to her in his scrapes, she felt herself justified—her friends agreed with her—in cutting the whole non-commissioned officer connection, and giving the child every advantage. A christening, by the Rector, under the name of Michael, was the first step. So far as she knew herself, she was not, she said, a child-lover, but, for all his faults, she had been very fond of George, and she pointed out that little Michael had his father's mouth to a line; which made something to build upon.

As a matter of fact, it was the Turrell forehead, broad, low, and well-shaped, with the widely spaced eyes beneath it, that Michael had most faithfully reproduced. His mouth was somewhat better cut than the family type. But Helen, who would concede nothing good to his mother's side, vowed he was a Turrell all over, and, there being no one to contradict, the likeness was established.

In a few years Michael took his place, as accepted as Helen had always been—fearless, philosophical, and fairly good-looking. At six, he wished to know why he could not call her 'Mummy,' as other boys called their mothers. She explained that she was only his auntie, and that aunties were not quite the same as mummies, but that, if it gave him pleasure, he might call her 'Mummy' at bedtime, for a pet-name between themselves.

Michael kept his secret most loyally, but Helen, as usual, explained the fact to her friends; which when Michael heard, he raged.

'Why did you tell? *Why* did you tell?' came at the end of the storm.

'Because it's always best to tell the truth,' Helen answered, her arm round him as he shook in his cot.

'All right, but when the troof's ugly I don't think it's nice.'

'Don't you, dear?'

'No, I don't, and'—she felt the small body stiffen—'now you've told, I won't call you "Mummy" any more—not even at bedtimes."

'But isn't that rather unkind?' said Helen softly.

'I don't care! I don't care! You've hurted me in my insides and I'll hurt you back. I'll hurt you as long as I live!'

'Don't, oh, don't talk like that, dear! You don't know what——'

'I will! And when I'm dead I'll hurt you worse!'

'Thank goodness, I shall be dead long before you, darling.'

'Huh! Emma says, "Never know your luck."' (Michael had been talking to Helen's elderly, flat-faced maid.) 'Lots of little boys die quite soon. So'll I. *Then* you'll see!'

Helen caught her breath and moved towards the door,

but the wail of 'Mummy! Mummy!' drew her back again, and the two wept together.

At ten years old, after two terms at a prep school, something or somebody gave him the idea that his civil status was not quite regular. He attacked Helen on the subject, breaking down her stammered defences with the family directness.

'Don't believe a word of it,' he said, cheerily, at the end. 'People wouldn't have talked like they did if my people had been married. But don't you bother, Auntie. I've found out all about my sort in English Hist'ry and the Shakespeare bits. There was William the Conqueror to begin with, and—oh, heaps more, and they all got on first-rate. 'Twon't make any difference to you, my being *that*—will it?'

'As if anything could——' she began.

'All right. We won't talk about it any more if it makes you cry.' He never mentioned the thing again of his own will, but when, two years later, he skilfully managed to have measles in the holidays, as his temperature went up to the appointed one hundred and four he muttered of nothing else, till Helen's voice, piercing at last his delirium, reached him with assurance that nothing on earth or beyond could make any difference between them.

The terms at his public school and the wonderful Christmas, Easter, and Summer holidays followed each other, variegated and glorious as jewels on a string; and as jewels Helen treasured them. In due time Michael developed his own interests, which ran their courses and gave way to others; but his interest in Helen was constant and increasing throughout. She repaid it with all that she had of affection or could command of counsel and money; and since Michael was no fool, the War took him just before what was like to have been a most promising career.

He was to have gone up to Oxford, with a scholarship, in October. At the end of August he was on the edge of joining the first holocaust of public-school boys who threw themselves into the Line; but the captain of his O.T.C., where he had been sergeant for nearly a year, headed him off and steered him directly to a commission in a battalion so new that half of it still wore the old Army red, and the other half was breeding meningitis through living overcrowdedly in damp tents. Helen had been shocked at the idea of direct enlistment.

'But it's in the family,' Michael laughed.

'You don't mean to tell me that you believed that old story all this time?' said Helen. (Emma, her maid, had been dead now several years.) 'I gave you my word of honour—and I give it again—that—that it's all right. It is indeed.'

'Oh, *that* doesn't worry me. It never did,' he replied valiantly. 'What I meant was, I should have got into the show earlier if I'd enlisted—like my grandfather.'

'Don't talk like that! Are you afraid of its ending so soon, then?'

'No such luck. You know what K. says.'

'Yes. But my banker told me last Monday it couldn't *possibly* last beyond Christmas—for financial reasons.'

'Hope he's right, but our Colonel—and he's a Regular—says it's going to be a long job.'

Michael's battalion was fortunate in that, by some chance which meant several 'leaves,' it was used for coast-defence among shallow trenches on the Norfolk coast; thence sent north to watch the mouth of a Scotch estuary, and, lastly, held for weeks on a baseless rumour of distant service. But, the very day that Michael was to have met Helen for four whole hours at a railway-junction up the line, it was hurled out, to help make good the wastage of Loos, and he had only just time to send her a wire of farewell.

In France luck again helped the battalion. It was put down near the Salient, where it led a meritorious and unexacting life, while the Somme was being manufactured; and enjoyed the peace of the Armentières and Laventie sectors when that battle began. Finding that it had sound views on protecting its own flanks and could dig, a prudent Commander stole it out of its own Division, under pretence of helping to lay telegraphs, and used it round Ypres at large.

A month later, and just after Michael had written Helen that there was nothing special doing and therefore no need to worry, a shell-splinter dropping out of a wet dawn killed him at once. The next shell uprooted and laid down over the body what had been the foundation of a barn wall, so neatly that none but an expert would have guessed that anything unpleasant had happened.

By this time the village was old in experience of war, and, English fashion, had evolved a ritual to meet it. When the postmistress handed her seven-year-old daughter the official telegram to take to Miss Turrell, she observed, to the Rector's gardener: 'It's Miss Helen's turn now.' He replied, thinking of his own son: 'Well, he's lasted longer than some.' The child herself came to the front door weeping aloud, because Master Michael had often given her sweets. Helen, presently, found herself pulling down the house-blinds one after one with great care, and saying earnestly to each: 'Missing *always* means dead.' Then she took her place in the dreary procession that was impelled to go through an inevitable series of unprofitable emotions. The Rector, of course, preached hope and prophesied word, very soon, from a prison camp. Several friends, too, told her perfectly truthful tales, but always about other women, to whom, after months and months of silence, their missing had been miraculously restored. Other people urged her to communicate with infallible Secretaries of organisations who could communicate with benevolent neutrals, who could extract accurate information from the most secretive of Hun prison commandants. Helen did and wrote and signed everything that was suggested or put before her.

Once, on one of Michael's leaves, he had taken her over a munition factory, where she saw the progress of a shell from blank-iron to the all but finished article. It struck her at the time that the wretched thing was never left alone for a single second; and 'I'm being manufactured into a bereaved next of kin,' she told herself, as she prepared her documents.

In due course, when all the organisations had deeply or sincerely regretted their inability to trace, etc., something gave way within her and all sensation—save of thankfulness for the release—came to an end in blessed passivity. Michael had died and her world had stood still and she had been one with the full shock of that arrest. Now she was standing still and the world was going forward, but it did not concern her—in no way or relation did it touch her. She knew this by the ease with which she could slip Michael's name into talk and incline her head to the proper angle, at the proper murmur of sympathy.

In the blessed realisation of that relief, the Armistice with all its bells broke over her and passed unheeded. At the end of another year she had overcome her physical loathing of the living and returned young, so that she could take them by the hand and almost sincerely wish them well. She had no interest in any aftermath, national or personal, of the war, but, moving at an immense distance, she sat on various relief committees and held strong views—she heard herself delivering them—about the site of the proposed village War Memorial.

Then there came to her, as next of kin, an official intimation, backed by a page of a letter to her in indelible pencil, a silver identity-disc, and a watch, to the effect that the body of Lieutenant Michael Turrell had been found, identified, and reinterred in Hagenzeele Third Military Cemetery—the letter of the row and the grave's number in that row duly given.

So Helen found herself moved on to another process of the manufacture—to a world full of exultant or broken relatives, now strong in the certainty that there was an altar upon earth where they might lay their love. These soon told her, and by means of time-tables made clear, how easy it was and how little it interfered with life's affairs to go and see one's grave.

'So different,' as the Rector's wife said, 'if he'd been killed in Mesopotamia, or even Gallipoli.'

The agony of being waked up to some sort of second life drove Helen across the Channel, where, in a new world of abbreviated titles, she learnt that Hagenzeele

Third could be comfortably reached by an afternoon train which fitted in with the morning boat, and that there was a comfortable little hotel not three kilometres from Hagenzeele itself, where one could spend quite a comfortable night and see one's grave next morning. All this she had from a Central Authority who lived in a board and tar-paper shed on the skirts of a razed city full of whirling lime-dust and blown papers.

'By the way,' said he, 'you know your grave, of course?'

'Yes, thank you,' said Helen, and showed its row and number typed on Michael's own little typewriter. The officer would have checked it, out of one of his many books; but a large Lancashire woman thrust between them and bade him tell her where she might find her son, who had been corporal in the A.S.C. His proper name, she sobbed, was Anderson, but, coming of respectable folk, he had of course enlisted under the name of Smith; and had been killed at Dickiebush, in early 'Fifteen. She had not his number nor did she know which of his two Christian names he might have used with his alias; but her Cook's tourist ticket expired at the end of Easter week, and if by then she could not find her child she should go mad. Whereupon she fell forward on Helen's breast; but the officer's wife came out quickly from a little bedroom behind the office, and the three of them lifted the woman on to the cot.

'They are often like this,' said the officer's wife, loosening the tight bonnet-strings. 'Yesterday she said he'd been killed at Hooge. Are you sure you know your grave? It makes such a difference.'

'Yes, thank you,' said Helen, and hurried out before the woman on the bed should begin to lament again.

Tea in a crowded mauve and blue striped wooden structure, with a false front, carried her still further into the nightmare. She paid her bill beside a stolid, plain-featured Englishwoman, who, hearing her inquire about the train to Hagenzeele, volunteered to come with her.

'I'm going to Hagenzeele myself,' she explained. 'Not to Hagenzeele Third; mine is Sugar Factory, but they call it La Rosière now. It's just south of Hagenzeele Three. Have you got your room at the hotel there?'

'Oh, yes, thank you. I've wired.'

'That's better. Sometimes the place is quite full, and at others there's hardly a soul. But they've put bathrooms into the old Lion d'Or—that's the hotel on the west side of Sugar Factory—and it draws off a lot of people, luckily.'

'It's all new to me. This is the first time I've been over.'

'Indeed! This is my ninth time since the Armistice. Not on my own account. *I* haven't lost any one, thank God—but, like every one else, I've a lot of friends at home who have. Coming over as often as I do, I find it helps them to have some one just look at the—the place and tell them about it afterwards. And one can take photos for them, too. I get quite a list of commissions to execute.' She laughed nervously and tapped her slung Kodak. 'There are two or three to see at Sugar Factory this time, and plenty of others in the cemeteries all about. My system is to save them up, and arrange them, you know. And when I've got enough commissions for one area to make it worth while, I pop over and execute them. It *does* comfort people.'

'I suppose so,' Helen answered, shivering as they entered the little train.

'Of course it does. (Isn't it lucky we've got window-seats?) It must do or they wouldn't ask one to do it, would they? I've a list of quite twelve or fifteen commissions here'—she tapped the Kodak again—'I must sort them out to-night. Oh, I forgot to ask you. What's yours?'

'My nephew,' said Helen. 'But I was very fond of him.'

'Ah, yes! I sometimes wonder whether *they* know after death? What do you think?'

'Oh, I don't—I haven't dared to think much about that sort of thing,' said Helen, almost lifting her hands to keep her off.

'Perhaps that's better,' the woman answered. 'The sense of loss must be enough, I expect. Well, I won't worry you any more.'

Helen was grateful, but when they reached the hotel Mrs. Scarsworth (they had exchanged names) insisted on dining at the same table with her, and after the meal, in the little, hideous salon full of low-voiced relatives, took Helen through her 'commissions' with biographies of the dead, where she happened to know them, and sketches of their next of kin. Helen endured till nearly half-past nine, ere she fled to her room.

Almost at once there was a knock at her door and Mrs. Scarsworth entered; her hands, holding the dreadful list, clasped before her.

'Yes—yes—*I* know,' she began. 'You're sick of me, but I want to tell you something. You—you aren't married, are you? Then perhaps you won't . . . But it doesn't matter. I've *got* to tell some one. I can't go on any longer like this.'

'But please——' Mrs. Scarsworth had backed against the shut door, and her mouth worked drily.

'In a minute,' she said. 'You—you know about these graves of mine I was telling you about downstairs, just now? They really *are* commissions. At least several of them are.' Her eye wandered round the room. 'What extraordinary wall-papers they have in Belgium, don't you think? . . . Yes. I swear they are commissions. But there's *one*, d'you see, and—and he was more to me than anything else in the world. Do you understand?'

Helen nodded.

'More than any one else. And, of course, he oughtn't to have been. He ought to have been nothing to me. But he *was*. He *is*. That's why I do the commissions, you see. That's all.'

'But why do you tell me?' Helen asked desperately.

'Because I'm *so* tired of lying. Tired of lying—always lying—year in and year out. When I don't tell lies I've got to act 'em and I've got to think 'em, always. *You* don't know what that means. He was everything to me that he oughtn't to have been—the one real thing—the only thing that ever happened to me in all *my* life; and I've had to pretend he wasn't. I've had to watch every word I said, and think out what lie I'd tell next, for years and years!'

'How many years?' Helen asked.

'Six years and four months before, and two and three-quarters after. I've gone to him eight times, since. To-morrow'll make the ninth, and—and I can't—I *can't* go to him again with nobody in the world knowing. I want to be honest with some one before I go. Do you understand? It doesn't matter about *me*. I was never truthful, even as a girl. But it isn't worthy of *him*. So— so I—I had to tell you. I can't keep it up any longer. Oh, I can't!'

She lifted her joined hands almost to the level of her mouth, and brought them down sharply, still joined, to full arms' length below her waist. Helen reached forward, caught them, bowed her head over them, and murmured: 'Oh, my dear! My dear!' Mrs. Scarsworth stepped back, her face all mottled.

'My God!' said she. 'Is *that* how you take it?'

Helen could not speak, and the woman went out; but it was a long while before Helen was able to sleep.

Next morning Mrs. Scarsworth left early on her round of commissions, and Helen walked alone to Hagenzeele Third. The place was still in the making, and stood some five or six feet above the metalled road, which it flanked for hundreds of yards. Culverts across a deep ditch served for entrances through the unfinished boundary wall. She climbed a few wooden-faced earthen steps and then met the entire crowded level of the thing in one held breath. She did not know that Hagenzeele Third counted twenty-one thousand dead already. All she saw was a merciless sea of black crosses, bearing little strips of stamped tin at all angles across their faces. She could distinguish no order or arrangement in their mass; nothing but a waist-high wilderness as of weeds stricken dead, rushing at her. She went forward, moved to the left and the right hope-lessly, wondering by what guidance she should ever come to her own. A great distance away there was a line of whiteness. It proved to be a block of some two or three hundred graves whose headstones had already been set, whose flowers were planted out, and whose new-sown grass showed green. Here she could see clear-cut letters at the ends of the rows, and, referring to her slip, realised that it was not here she must look.

A man knelt behind a line of headstones—evidently a gardener, for he was firming a young plant in the soft earth. She went towards him, her paper in her hand. He rose at her approach and without prelude or salutation asked: 'Who are you looking for?'

'Lieutenant Michael Turrell—my nephew,' said Helen slowly and word for word, as she had many thousands of times in her life.

The man lifted his eyes and looked at her with infinite compassion before he turned from the fresh-sown grass toward the naked black crosses.

'Come with me,' he said, 'and I will show you where your son lies.'

When Helen left the Cemetery she turned for a last look. In the distance she saw the man bending over his young plants; and she went away, supposing him to be the gardener.

jaws

Peter Benchley

the pan book
of horror stories

Selected by Herbert van Thal

not a penny more,
not a penny less

Jeffrey Archer

ten stories

Rudyard Kipling

dead simple

PAN ⬤ Peter James

last bus to woodstock

PAN ⬤ Colin Dexter

ey of the needle

PAN ⬤ Ken Follett

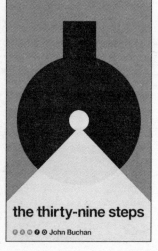

the thirty-nine steps

PAN ⬤ John Buchan

the dam busters

Paul Brickhill

born free

Joy Adamson

england,
their
england

A.G. Macdonell

it
shouldn't
happen
to a vet

James Herriot

P A N 7 0

The Hitchhiker's Guide to the Galaxy – Douglas Adams

Born Free – Joy Adamson

Not a Penny More, Not a Penny Less – Jeffrey Archer

Jaws – Peter Benchley

The Dam Busters – Paul Brickhill

The Thirty-Nine Steps – John Buchan

Childhood's End – Arthur C. Clarke

Savages – Shirley Conran

The Provincial Lady – E. M. Delafield

Last Bus to Woodstock – Colin Dexter

The Lost World – Sir Arthur Conan Doyle

Eye of the Needle – Ken Follett

It Shouldn't Happen to a Vet – James Herriot

Dead Simple – Peter James

Ten Stories – Rudyard Kipling

England, Their England – A. G. Macdonell

Gone with the Wind – Margaret Mitchell

The Time Machine – H. G. Wells

The Lady Vanishes – Ethel Lina White

The Pan Book of Horror Stories